LOST NOTES

A DEVIL'S CROSS NOVEL

EMMA RAE SULLIVAN

Emma Rae
Happily Ever Afters with a Kick
Sullivan

For Emily and Savannah.
May your imagination always transport you to only the best places, may your laughter never be stifled, and may your exuberant joy never cease lifting the spirits of all those you encounter.

You are the very best daughters, and I love you more than you will ever know. XOXO

CHAPTER 1

KATIE

> "And the danger is that in this move toward new horizons and far directions, that I may lose what I have now, and not find anything except loneliness."
>
> — SYLVIA PLATH

I closed my eyes, softly smiling at the brush of Cade's lips on my forehead. I didn't know what I would do without him, but I was forever grateful to whatever deity was responsible for having him move in across the street all those years ago. I had known the first time I laid eyes on him, that the gangly, blue-eyed boy would be important to me. I just hadn't realized how vital he would become. When Cade arrived, I not only stumbled across my best friend in the entire world, but I also found the other half of my heart.

A purr of contentment crossed my lips when he pulled me into his familiar arms. Cade nuzzled the tender skin below my ear before holding a skinny navy-blue velvet box in front of my face. "Happy anniversary, Katie-mine."

I squealed and pulled the lid off to find a gorgeous sterling silver locket. I cradled the necklace in my palm and choked up a bit when I saw the picture my mom had snapped of us just before we left on our first official date as a couple. *God, I missed her.*

I wasn't sure how I would have survived those black months after my parent's car accident without Cade, especially once my jerk of an uncle moved in. He had taken what had once been a home filled with laughter and love and morphed it into an evil place I couldn't wait to be free of. I hated it, and I hated him. None of that mattered though. In a few months I would graduate, and Cade and I had already discussed getting an apartment together. I turned the locket over, and my heart swelled at the engraving on the back.

My love for you shines brighter than any star in the sky and is sweeter than any note I could ever hope to play.

Happy 3rd. I love you, always.

— Your Cade

Throwing my arms around his broad shoulders, I gave him a long kiss. "It's amazing. You're amazing. Thank you."

Cade gave me a quick peck, ending our kiss before he pointed at the blanket he'd laid out on the floor of our club house. "Sit. I'll be right back with dinner."

"Ooh! And he plans to feed me too? Hurrah! Go forth, my hunter-gatherer! Show me the offerings you have procured."

A mischievous grin was my reply, then he blew a kiss my way before turning and walking up the stairs.

~

Cade

As soon as I was out of sight, I let my smile slip. Time was running short, and I still wasn't sure what I should do. Katie was my home. Her soul matched mine perfectly, but there was so much at stake. I'd been racking my brain, trying to figure out a way to have everything I wanted, but no matter how it all played out, something always had to give. My phone buzzed against my thigh and I pulled it out of my pocket.

Asshat: I expect you here by 4 p.m. on Tuesday. Don't be late.

Pissed, I threw my cell across the room and tugged at my hair, hoping it would spur my brain to come up with a better plan, but none came. Unshed tears burned the back of my throat as I made my way over to the table in the corner. Sheets of paper with hastily scribbled lyrics covered the surface and I grabbed the one nearest to me. When I saw the first few lines of a love song I'd been writing for Katie, I scoffed. Of course that would be the one I grabbed. Out of options, I snagged a pen, turned it over, and began writing, my heart cracking a little more with each word.

Katie-mine,

I wish I could explain, to make you understand. I cannot stay here with you. I want to, so badly, but I can't. I have to go. I'm so sorry. Please don't hate me, because no matter what I love you. Never doubt that, not for one second. I hope you'll forgive me one day. Be careful with my heart. Its always belonged to you, and I couldn't fathom leaving it with anyone else. Be happy.

Love you, for always
Your Cade

I slowly folded the note, hoping that if I took my time, somehow the letters would disappear so she would never have to read them. Never have to realize how much I'd fucked up. But like everything in my life lately, it wasn't something hope would be able fix. Sliding the letter into my pocket, I grabbed the plate of pizza rolls and two sodas, and forced a smile on my face before heading back downstairs.

I gently ran my fingers through her raven hair, memorizing the way the silky strands felt sliding across my skin. Her dark lashes stood out, a stark contrast against her fair skin, and her full lips were parted ever so slightly. She was always so animated; rarely did she ever sit still. I loved her for that, and I loved that I was the only person she ever let see her at rest. I loved her for a whole lot of things. I loved her compassion. I loved her humor. I loved how she was always ready to lend a hand, no questions asked. Heck, I even loved how stubborn she was.

Lying next to her, I committed everything to memory. From the tiny freckle above her upper lip to her soft snore, I made sure I didn't overlook even the smallest of details. I had loved her for so long I should have every inch of her memorized, down to each mole and scar, but I needed to be sure. I couldn't forget one single thing. Leaning forward, I ran my nose along her hairline, breathing in the smell of honey and peaches that was unique to her.

I closed my eyes and let the memories wash over me—every smile, every laugh, the first date, the first kiss, the first dance, the first time we said "I love you," and our fumbling first time together a few months after. I held each one close, before putting them in a box in my mind and sealing them away. I would take them out later, but I didn't have time right now. I placed a soft kiss on her lips and wrapped my arms around her, savoring the way her body fit against mine.

My phone vibrated as the alarm went off. I was out of time. Regret threatened to swallow me whole, but there was no other choice. I knew, because I had been racking my brain trying to find one for days. I carefully untangled myself from Katie and climbed out of bed, making a grab for the pile of my clothes on the floor. My heart was shattering, while my soul screamed at me to turn around and climb back in her bed. I ignored them both and instead quietly slipped on my jeans. Taking a deep breath, my eyes glided over her sleeping form one last time.

The plum sheets had slipped down, showing teasing glimpses of the little dimples at the base of her spine I'd so tenderly kissed only a few hours ago. Her long dark hair was spread across the pillowcase, tangled in a few spots from our earlier lovemaking. Things had been a bit rocky those first few times, but like everything between her and me, once we ironed out the kinks, it was beautiful.

Seeming to sense my pending departure, she began shifting in her sleep, but I couldn't let her wake up. If she gazed at me with those beautiful emerald orbs, she would know, and she would either hate me or convince me to stay. I had to leave. I refused to let her suffer because of me. She deserved more than I was able to offer her now—she deserved everything. I could stand many things in this life, but having her watch as I betrayed every promise I'd ever made to her, and seeing the devastation this would leave behind was more than I could handle. Which is why I resorted to sneaking out in the middle of the night like the reprehensible bastard I had become.

Needing to touch her one last time, I reached my hand out and cradled her cheek. Like always, she curled into my touch with a contented sigh. The corner of her lush lips quirked up in a peaceful smile as she settled into a deeper sleep, making the fist around my heart squeeze even tighter. Unable to bear another second, I pulled my hand away and placed a soft kiss on her forehead, then whispered, "I love you more than you will ever know. Be happy."

My phone vibrated once again, and I was keenly aware that my time was up. If I was going to leave, I needed to do it now. I propped the letter I had written earlier against my favorite picture of us. Emotion balled in my chest as I ran a finger over the photo. Rhys had taken it at her seventeenth birthday party last year without us knowing, but it was perfection. She was tucked under my arm, her hand lying on my chest right above my heart. Her head was thrown back in laughter, green eyes sparkling with amusement, while I gazed at her like she was the most perfect person in the entire world.

I brushed away a tear. I needed to hold it together. Taking a shuddering breath and burying my emotions down deep, I turned and strode towards the window. Katie had been my guiding star, the one thing I always relied on to pull me back to center and keep my path true. I wasn't sure what kind of man I would become without her, but I supposed I'd be finding out soon enough.

To assuage the guilt plaguing me, I kept repeating in my mind that someday she would understand and she would forgive me. Sitting on the windowsill, I grasped the branch on the old oak tree outside her window and pulled myself onto its ancient bough. My soul was roaring at me to climb back inside, to stay with the girl I loved so deeply—but I couldn't. *She'll understand. She'll come back to me. She'll forgive me.*

After a fortifying breath, I climbed down, away from everything familiar and toward the unknown. Every step I took away from her splintered my heart a little more, until blessed numbness set in. Climbing into my black 1968 Charger, I turned the engine over, taking a small amount of comfort in the purr emanating from my pride and joy, before shifting into first and taking off into the night.

CHAPTER 2

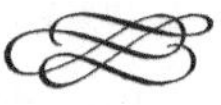

KATIE

— RICHARD III, ACT 1, SCENE 2,
PAGE 8, WILLIAM SHAKESPEARE

Four years later

Taking one last look in the mirror, I tugged the minuscule skirt one more time, hoping in vain that it would magically become several inches longer, before stepping out of the restroom into the narrow hallway. My manager, Tom—he of the beady eyes and grabby hands—paused in front of me, his gaze going wide as it slowly traveled down my body.

"My, my, my, Kit-Kat, you sure do that outfit some justice. Let me know if you need any help blowing that whistle..."

Resisting the urge to either upchuck all over his cheap blue polyester suit or kick him in the nuts, I checked my anger and took a deep breath. Looking into his black eyes, I noted how small they were for his face. Made sense—rats have beady eyes, and if the shoe fits... But then again, comparing him to a rat would be a disservice to the rodents of the world. Leaning forward ever so slightly, I pushed my ample cleavage out a hair and ran the tip of my pointer finger along the low-cut neckline of my too-tight top. Licking his lips, his eyes greedily followed the path across my chest for a few beats before he reached down and adjusted himself. *Oh yuck.* I was officially scarred for life.

Deciding I'd had about enough of this game, I waited an extra second before giving him a wide-eyed stare and, using the same finger, hooked the chain of the bright-blue whistle, holding it up to eye level. Smirking, I ran my eyes over Tom, taking in his balding head, ruddy complexion, and abundant waistline. Seeing his eyes light up in anticipation, I leaned forward and whispered, "But, Tom, how can you help me blow if you can't even find your whistle? I don't have the time nor the inclination to go on a search and rescue mission."

Eyes bugging out, he shot a hand out to grab me, but I dodged it and continued down the hallway. Dropping all pretenses, I turned my head toward him and, in a sugary sweet voice, shouted back, "Oh, and Tom? Try to proposition me again, and I will break your goddamn dick, you lech."

CHAPTER 3

KATIE

"Every experience, no matter how bad it seems, holds within it a blessing of some kind. The goal is to find it."

— GAUTAMA BUDDHA

The front door swung open, and I stepped inside. Mindful of my noise level, I quietly set my bag down and glanced at the living room. The apartment was cast in a soft glow, compliments of the lamps Mrs. Jenkins left on. Following the soft snore, I carefully stepped over the myriad of blocks and Barbies that littered the floor, before stopping in front of the teal lounge chair. Mrs. Jenkins was sound asleep, her chest slowly rising and falling with each breath. Holding in a giggle, I noticed the purple princess crown listing sideways on top of her head and the yellow crayon sticking out of her shirt pocket.

Gently, I prodded her shoulder to wake her. "Mrs. J, I'm home. Would you like to stay?"

She sat upright and blinked a few times before her kind brown eyes settled on mine. Eyes crinkling up at the corners with her smile, she whispered back, "Oh, thank you, dear, but no. You look exhausted, and I don't want to take your bed. Would you like me to make you some tea or something to eat before I go? You look a bit skinny to me."

"No, thanks, Mrs. J, I've got it. And don't you worry about me. I can find somewhere else to sleep if you'd rather stay."

Pursing her lips, she narrowed her eyes at me. "I'll worry about you if I want to, young lady. Besides, if I don't worry over you, who will?"

Well, that's the million-dollar question, isn't it? Deciding to do what I always did, I put on a brave face and held out a hand to help Mrs. J up. With a strength I didn't feel, I replied, "Oh come now, Mrs. J. I take care of myself just fine, you know that. Now, speaking of people to take care of, how was Finn?"

As I expected, the mention of my daughter made Mrs. Jenkins soften and forget about me. She chuckled and winked at me. "We had a wonderful night, dear. She had 'macreeroni and cheeses' for dinner with some 'beenanas,' then we played quite a bit, had a bath, read a few stories, and watched a bit of *Cinderella* before heading off to bed. She went down at about eight, and I haven't heard a peep since."

Walking her to the door, I gave her a quick hug goodbye. "Thanks, Mrs. J. You're the best. I don't know what we would do without you."

She affectionately patted my cheek before heading into her apartment next door. I knew she thought I was only being kind, but we really would be lost without her. Resting my palm on the closed door, I recalled the first time I encountered the force that was Mrs. J.

I slipped silently out of the bedroom, pulled the door closed behind me, and took stock of my tiny apartment. A threadbare burgundy couch I had found at a garage sale for fifteen dollars occupied most of the rear wall, facing a dented and scarred entertainment center I'd picked up from Goodwill for cheap last week. I placed the small TV and DVD player I'd won in a work raffle the previous year on top of the battered surface. Moving to the next container, I unpacked the short stack of movies a co-worker had given Finn over the last year and set them beneath the DVD player on the shelf.

Dragging over a worn end table, I positioned it next to the couch and lovingly set one of the few remaining photographs I had of my parents and me on top. Kissing my fingers, I touched each of their faces, before saying a quiet "Love you." Moving on, I began the process of unpacking the few boxes I had for the kitchen. When I broke down the last box, I spun in a circle, and fought the urge to burst into tears.

The naked white walls taunted me, reminding me of how alone I was. A lone tear rolled down my cheek when I realized my apartment was like me—lonely, worn out, and unwanted. At least I had Finn. She was my little ray of sunshine and always made everything better and brighter. I allowed myself a few more seconds of self-pity before forcing myself to stop. I had spent enough time wallowing; it was time for me to embrace our new reality and create the best life I could for us both.

My mother and father had raised me to always look forward and to do the best I could with what I had been given. I brushed the moisture from my cheek, closed my eyes and created a mental picture of a cozy, warm apartment done in creams, teals, and grays. I bit my lip and scanned my shabby furniture one more time, making a list of a few items I would need to transform the place. My budget was tight, but fabric and paint were cheap, and it wouldn't take much to transform the dreary space.

Suddenly, a 'tap, tap, tap' caught my attention. I paused and waited to hear it again. Zeroing in on the front door, I stared at it in confusion. Who on earth could that be? I had only been in town a few days and knew absolutely no one here. I cautiously turned the knob, pulling it open just wide enough to peek through.

On the other side stood a petite older woman with the kindest brown eyes I had ever seen. Her gray hair was swept into a neat bun, accentuating a lovely heart-shaped face. Smile lines and crow's feet peppered her face, making it obvious she laughed often and lived with joy. Pushing her glasses higher on her nose, she gave me a warm smile, then the adorable stranger surprised me by pushing my door open and pulling me into a hug.

Eyes wide, I stood stiffly in this random woman's arms. My brain went into overdrive trying to make sense of what was happening. Oh my God. Who just hugs a stranger without permission? Should I be concerned about this? I mean, after all I've never seen this woman in my life. I was well on my way to a panic attack, when suddenly she squeezed a bit tighter. Unbidden, a thought popped up. This wasn't an ordinary hug—this was a mom hug. One of those that envelops you in comfort and safety, where sadness and loneliness seemingly melt away. I hadn't had a hug like this *since my mom died, and up until this moment, I hadn't been aware of how badly I had needed one.*

Fighting tears, I finally pulled back, to find a soft, wrinkled hand cupping my cheek. Giving it an affectionate pat, she said in a soothing voice, "Hello, dear, my name is Mrs. Jenkins. I'm your next-door neighbor, and if I'm not mistaken you and that adorable little one I saw earlier look like you might need a grandma. All my grand babies live far away, and it has been so long since I've had someone to take care of. Would it be okay if I was here for you?"

Smiling at the memory, I locked up, then turned and walked the short distance down the hallway. Cracking open the bedroom door, I snuck inside and approached Finnley's crib. Brushing the brown curls off her forehead, I leaned down and placed a goodnight kiss on her forehead.

Grabbing the blanket she'd kicked off, I covered her back up and tucked her pink bunny back under her arm. Softly running my hand over her wayward ringlets, I whispered, "Goodnight sweet pea. I love you, and I'll see you in the morning time, okay? Sweet dreams, my little angel," before backing out of her room and heading to bed.

CHAPTER 4

CADE

> "Music expresses that which cannot be said
> and on which it is impossible to be silent."
>
> — VICTOR HUGO

Red Rocks Amphitheater, Denver, Colorado

Thunder boomed and raindrops steadily pinged against the towering rocks framing our stage. Looking out over the sea of eager faces, letting their screams and applause wash over me, made me feel invigorated and alive. I grabbed a towel, wiped the mixture of rain and sweat from my face, then tossed it out into the screaming crowd.

Giving them my trademark smirk, I shouted, "I love it when you get me all wet! Thank you, Denver! We'll catch ya later, and it's good to be home!"

The boys and I left the stage, still high off the energy from the crowd. The sound of deafening applause followed us all the way to the SUV waiting patiently in the parking lot to whisk us back to the hotel. Once inside, Zane, Trev, and Rhys began chatting quietly in the corner and Dante whipped out his phone, most likely messaging his crazy-ass girlfriend.

Ignoring them, I rubbed my temples, doing my best to push images of *her* from the forefront of my mind. I'd spent years doing my best to forget what I had lost, to overlook the fact that I had spent the last four years floating through life in a sea of gray. She'd brought color to my world, bright bursts vibrantly pulsing with love and light.

Normally, I could lock these feelings up tight, pretend they didn't exist, and play the role of the egotistical rock star I'd been assigned. Yet every time we crossed the border into Colorado, they battered my subconscious, forcing me to acknowledge they were still there. That *she* was still there.

I fought the urge to pull my cell out and dial her old number on the off-chance I could hear her voice. *God, I missed her voice.* I'd saved one of her voice mails for years, listening to it over and over every night until my battery died, but when our PR rep, Kelly, walked in and found me piss drunk, sobbing to the recorded *"Love you, see you soon!"* she told me I was too famous to be that pathetic and deleted it.

I pulled up my contacts, and my thumb hovered over her name, but at the last minute, I chickened out and slid my phone into my pocket. She wouldn't want to speak to me. I had ruined everything. I'd made my choice, and she deserved to life her life without me interfering. She was better off without me anyway. *Is she, though?* Shaking that thought from my head, I pulled the flask out of my pocket and knocked back a shot.

"Cade." The warning in Trev's gaze was loud and clear. "Be careful with that."

I glared at him before taking one more drink then putting the flask away. As much as I hated to admit it, he was right. I'd tried drowning out her face with booze before, and that was not a road we needed to travel down again. In need of a distraction, I focused on Rhys, knowing he could never be quiet for long.

His leg was bouncing with post show energy, and Rhys patted a random beat on his thighs for a few moments before announcing, "Dude, I am so stoked. I cannot *wait* to go home. I've been Face-Timing Mom, and Liv has a boyfriend I haven't had a chance to vet yet. I mean, seriously, I am sucking hardcore at this big-bro thing. I didn't even realize she was interested in anyone—or dating for that matter—until mom accidentally let it slip yesterday."

Trev, calm and collected as always, paused before turning his attention to Rhys. "It's not a big deal, Rhys. I'm sure they've barely started seeing each other. You'll have plenty of time to threaten him with bodily harm before things get serious."

"No, dude, you don't get it. They've been together nine months. *Nine months,* and I'm just finding out about it!"

Tugging at his hair in frustration, Rhys went on, "I mean, yeah, I'm not home often, but damn. You'd think it would've been worth mentioning, since my mom and I talk every day and Liv checks in *every fucking week!*"

At this announcement, all conversations ceased, and every head slowly turned to Rhys. "Are you telling me,"

Dante bit out, "Little Livvie has a serious boyfriend none of us knew about?"

Jaw clenched, Rhys crossed his arms and gave a single nod. Aw, hell. Of all Rhys's siblings, Liv had always been the most supportive one. She'd demanded to attend every single show when we were first starting out, and she'd started our very first fan club. Livvie was smart as a whip and had an amazing sense of humor, which was part of the reason we loved having her around. Anytime Liv was around, you were guaranteed to laugh.

As she grew older, though, she'd morphed from a cute, but awkward kid into a startlingly beautiful young woman. The more attractive she became, the more intensely we guarded her. So it was no surprise, really, the she's purposefully decided to keep her romantic life to herself. While part of me understood, most of me was pissed and hurt that she had kept him a secret for so long.

Zane, our bassist and generally the quietest of the bunch, made eye contact with Rhys and cracked his knuckles threateningly. "Tell the little fucker if he hurts Livvie, he is a dead man walking. Also, I need a name. There's no way in hell I'm letting that little shit continue spending time with Livvie until I've done a thorough background check."

I arched my brow at Zane's bold statement. He was the least aggressive of all of us, so threats from him were rare. He was lucky that Rhys was too oblivious to register the way Zane's eyes softened whenever the topic of Livvie came up, but if he went around beating his chest like a caveman every time a boy sniffed around Livvie, Rhys would connect the dots and Zane would get his ass kicked.

Pointedly ignoring my knowing stare and refusing to meet my gaze, Zane focused on the buildings blurring past the window. The rest of us nodded in silent agreement, and after a beat, the mood shifted back to anticipatory excitement, with everyone talking about who they wanted to visit and things they wanted to do during our short break. I was the only one not participating, which was no surprise.

Once the SUV reached the hotel, we all piled into the service elevator, waiting for it to whisk us up to the suite we were sharing on the top floor. Flinging the door open, Dante and Trev rushed to their rooms and began gathering their things, while Zane whipped out his laptop and began running searches on *"that little fucker"* with some computer program he'd created a few months ago. My pace was much slower, and much less enthusiastic as I ambled across the living room to my suite. Feeling Rhys's eyes glaring at the back of my head, I wanted nothing more than to avoid the inevitable conversation we'd had a million times before. I considered diving into my room and locking the door, but the last time I tried, the asshole had just picked the lock.

Deciding we may as well get it over with, I rolled my eyes and sighed. "Spit it out, man. Your eyes are burning a hole in my brain. Obviously, you have something on your mind, so say what you need to say."

In a voice laced with irritation, Rhys surprised me by saying, "Why? You already know. I say it every goddamn time we're within six hours of home. Seems to me, she isn't that important, or else you would've dragged your sorry ass to her door, apologized for being a complete and utter jackass, and begged her to take you back forever ago. You haven't because either you don't actually care, or you're too much of a coward. Step up or step out, man. I can't spend another year watching you alternate between sulking around looking like someone kicked your puppy and drunkenly pining for your long-lost love. It's past time to settle shit, Cade."

Enraged that he would even suggest I didn't care, I whipped around and faced him. I let loose the anger that was always simmering below the surface, and shouted, "Don't you fucking dare. You know goddamn well she is *everything to me.* I may love you like a brother, but I will not be responsible for my actions if you ever pretend otherwise again. I want to go to her."

"I've been dreaming of being with her for *years.* But look at me, Rhys. Not the rock star, not the heartthrob, not the lead singer—me. I am a shit show. What do I have to offer her? I have money, but she never cared about that. I have fame, but she hates to be in the spotlight. I had her love, and I threw it back in her face. Why would she ever want to see me?"

Since my voice was loud and hotel walls weren't known for being thick, all three doors in the suite opened and the rest of my bandmates stepped out. Trev's eyes bounced between Rhys and me a few times before his astute gaze locked on me. Then, without preamble, he delivered what felt like a punch straight to my heart. "Cade, I love you like a brother and I will always look out for you, so that is what I'm doing."

Taking a deep breath, he continued, "You had your reasons for leaving her the way you did—reasons we all think are a crock of shit, by the way—but reasons none-the-less. But it has been four years, Cade. *Four freaking years* since you left. After everything you two have been through, the least she deserves are some answers. No amount of booze or groupies is going to lessen your feelings of guilt or fill the Katie-shaped hole in your life. It's long past time to go and face her. You both need closure, and we need you to stop beating yourself up over things you can't change. Go talk to her. Please."

The possibility of seeing Katie called to me. To witness her green eyes spark with joy once again and watch a smile light up her face. To revel in how perfectly she fit in my arms. Trev was right—it had been years, and here I was, still lost without her love to guide me. Maybe they had a point. Silently turning away, I let myself into my room for some peace and quiet so I could think.

The guys were right. I didn't want to admit it out loud, but that didn't make what they'd said any less true. For four years I had been making excuses not to talk to her, terrified she had moved on. Too scared by the idea of pulling up to her house only to find her looking at some faceless man with the same adoring expression she used to bestow upon me. I'd forced myself to remain in an emotional limbo, unable to go back, yet unable to move forward.

It was well past time to deal with the fallout of that fateful day. Taking a fortifying breath, I began packing my bags. Looked like I was heading home.

CHAPTER 5

CADE

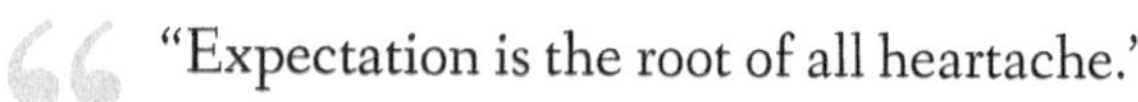

"Expectation is the root of all heartache."

— WILLIAM SHAKESPEARE

I pulled up to the gate and punched in the code, waiting for the wrought iron gates to open so I could head up the winding drive. Once I had my first royalty check, I'd tried to purchase a mansion for my parents, thinking I could buy their forgiveness. Turned out they loved me even if I broke their hearts when I left, and I was forgiven long before I'd even hit the California border.

They were never angry with me for pursuing my dream, only hurt at the way I had gone about achieving it. I doubted I would ever know for sure, but I'd always thought the reason my mother agreed to let me build them a house was because she somehow knew I needed it to assuage my own guilt. I'd had grand plans, but while she deeply cared about all of us, Mom was no pushover and had made sure that I knew she that she had zero interest in living in a massive house.

In the end, my parents found a beautiful plot of land and built their new home smack in the middle of twenty acres of rolling green hills, pine trees, and clear streams. They'd constructed a charming sage-green two-story craftsman with cream-colored pillars and a pair of red shutters on each window that my mom adored.

Now, I parked the Charger in front of one of the garage bays and meandered up the stone walkway, admiring the lush flowerbeds lining the path. The scent of roses, tiger lilies, hydrangeas, and lilacs, coupled with the sharp scent of pine made me smile because those scents always represented home. Impatient to see everyone, I took the steps onto the wraparound porch two at a time and pushed open the bright-red door.

Once I cleared the doorway, I kicked off my shoes while hollering, "Mom! Dad! Case! I'm home!"

The scent of freshly baked biscuits hit my nose, causing my stomach to rumble. I made a beeline for the kitchen, anticipating the deliciousness that awaited, only to slide through the door and crash into what I was positive was a human disguised as a brick wall. Sprawled out on the floor, I groaned and glanced up to find my little brother looking down at me and rubbing his shoulder. "Dude, Cade, I understand that sometimes road food is shit, but seriously, body checking for biscuits? That's a new low."

Casey waited until he had a solid grip on my hand before pulling me to my feet with a surprising amount of strength. I dusted myself off, and said, "Shut it, little bro. These aren't just any biscuits; they're Kay's, and I will straight take your ass out if you come between me and those biscuits."

He chuckled and nodded his head before adding, "Fair point, and same."

I greedily grabbed two biscuits in one hand and shoved another in my mouth. In between bites, I joked, "By the way, Case what the hell have you been eating? Last time I was here, you were my lovably *scrawny* little brother. Now I come back, and you look like you ate half the NFL. What gives?"

Casey shrugged and sheepishly replied, "Well, it turns out that not even being the brother of *the* Cadeon Cross will get you chicks if you're a bean pole. Especially one who's so pale that people question whether you've ever seen the sun. So, I used some of that cash you keep dropping in my savings account to start going to the gym and figured out I actually enjoyed it; so yeah..."

Casey began to rub the back of his neck, a sure sign he was uncomfortable with me knowing about his newfound fitness obsession. The last thing I wanted to do on one of my rare visits home was make my family feel awkward. Wanting to smooth things over, I threw out the first idea that popped into my head. "Hey, if you want, while I'm home we can work out together. My trainer is planning to swing by a few times, and he can be brutal, but he's outstanding."

Shocked at my offer, Casey studied my face for a moment to judge if I was being serious. Realizing I meant what I'd said his face broke out into a huge grin before he answered, "That would be awesome!"

Voices carried from the stairs, and I turned to find my

mom and dad discussing their plans for the day on their way into the kitchen. As soon as she spotted me, my mom clapped before sprinting across the living room and dragging me into an intense bear hug. Enthusiastically, she began talking a mile a minute. "My baby! I'm so glad you're home! I've missed you so much! Oh, how long are you here for? Is there anything special you'd like to do? Oh, I'm so *happy*!" Then she spontaneously burst into tears.

Baffled, I swung my gaze over to Casey, who was eyeing her like she was a rabid tiger, while slowly edging himself out of the kitchen and into the living room, intending to make a stealthy exit. Concerned and confused, I searched out my dad and mouthed, *What the hell?* Shoulders shaking with silent laughter, he silently replied, *Menopause*. Ah, crap. It seemed like rather than a relaxing visit home, I had stepped onto a one-way train heading for crazy town. Awesome.

Getting a grip on herself, my mom released me from her vice-like grip and wiped away the stray tears. She scanned my face once again, before landing on the empty space where Casey had been. Her eyes narrowed a moment before she called out, "Casey Nathaniel Cross, your brother just got here, and we are having breakfast as a family, young man. You better haul your butt back in here and sit down at this table. NOW."

Less than a minute later, Casey returned, pausing to give her a half-hug before taking a seat at the table. Not wanting to prod the bear any more than necessary, Dad and I hastily followed suit. My mother—who was now the picture of serenity—slid into the chair beside mine and began passing around eggs, French toast, and Kay's fresh biscuits with butter and honey. Focused on loading up my plate, I missed a question that had been directed at me.

"Earth to Cade." My dad good-naturedly nudged me to get my attention, before repeating, "Mom and I were wondering if there is anything in particular you'd like to do this visit."

I picked up my fork and poked at my breakfast. Deciding now was as good a time as any, I nonchalantly said, "Oh, yeah. I, um, wanted to swing over to the Troyer's and say hey."

I shoveled some bites of egg in my mouth, chewed, and continued, "I thought it might be nice to check on Katie. Make sure she's been all right."

Uncomfortable with their scrutiny, I stared at my food. Fully expecting some affectionate teasing to commence any minute, I was surprised when I was met with silence. My gaze roamed around the table, and I found myself suddenly unsure about my plan to visit Katie. The confidence I'd had upon my arrival was rapidly dissipating. No one would meet my eyes, and for the first time since we'd reconciled, I realized I was out of the loop. The feeling was foreign and decidedly unpleasant, particularly because up until now, my family had never made it seem as if I was the odd man out.

I made myself wait another minute before my nerves got to me and I couldn't take the awkward silence anymore. Focusing my attention on the occupied seat next to mine, I asked, "Mom?"

"Baby." Her voice was gentle, yet laced with sadness.

"We haven't seen Katie in years."

The idea of Katie having left Colorado seemed wrong, but that was only because, as far as I could remember, Creede and Katie were synonymous with one another. I wasn't sure why I assumed she would still be around instead of off doing bigger and brighter things. It was terrible that she and my parents hadn't kept in touch, but I knew the responsibility for their falling out sat squarely on my shoulders. I felt like shit, completely aware that I had ruined another relationship with my selfishness. I mumbled a litany of curse words under my breath.

My mom's chastising glare made me flush with embarrassment. "Sorry, Mom. I get that I'm probably the reason she didn't keep in touch. I screwed up pretty badly, leaving the way I did, and left a lot of hurt behind. Can you at least tell me where she is? I'd like to try to make amends if I can."

Casey was fidgeting on my left, and my dad was looking anywhere but at me, causing my anxiety level to ratchet up another notch. They were holding something back, I was sure of it. Tired of the evasiveness and running short on options, I gave Casey a pleading look. His gaze bounced between my mom and me before his jaw set. I had given up hope that he would tell me anything, when he set his elbows on the table and dropped his head into his hands. "She's gone, Cade. Like, *poof*—gone. No one can figure out where the hell she is."

Unable to process this new information and afraid to examine what that might mean, I turned to my dad. He had always been the most straightforward of us, and I needed answers. Now. I pointed at him and said, "Explain, please."

Rapidly tapping his finger on his leg, he opened and

closed his mouth a few times, like he couldn't decide how to tell me whatever it was he wanted to say. He paused once more before clearing his throat.

"She's in the wind, son. The last time we spotted her was about three months after you left. No one knows what the hell happened. One day she was living—albeit miserably—with that asshole uncle of hers, and the next day she was MIA. The uncle had some story about them arguing because her behavior was 'shameful' and 'unacceptable,' which resulted in Katie departing for places unknown."

"I called bullshit, but by that point, she was gone and hadn't left any clues behind. I tried to report her as a missing person, but she was so close to being eighteen, the sheriff recommended I let it lie, so I did. I regret that decision every time I think about that girl."

I couldn't breathe. Panic overrode all my senses. My lungs were in a vice grip, and no matter how hard I fought, I couldn't draw a breath. Black dots danced across my vision. *Missing.* I had been touring the country drowning in women and booze, and the other half of my heart was lost and all alone God knew where. Did she have somewhere to go? Had she been hungry? Had she been afraid? I was going to either be sick or pass out, whichever came first.

Moments later, a paper sack was shoved in front of my face, and a large hand was patting my back. "Breathe, bro. Breathe! You gotta calm down. It's gonna be okay. We aren't sure where she is, but we *do* know she is okay. Every six months or so, she sends a random postcard telling us she's all right."

The grip on my lungs relaxed, and I greedily inhaled some much-needed air. Even with that information, fear was still clawing at me, so I took advantage of the paper sack to help regulate my breathing and slow my heart rate down. Once I could breathe easily again and my emotions had returned to solid ground, I ran a hand through my hair and looked at Casey.

"Let's lead with that next time, yeah?"

I took another deep breath and centered myself before addressing Casey again. "That's all you're going to give me? That she says 'she's fine?' Can I have a little more detail?"

Casey gave me a small grin and lightly punched my bicep before he said, "I wish, but no can do. It's literally what they all say. Every single one has a slight variation of *'Wanted to let you know I'm still doing good. Don't worry. XOXO'* and a signature."

Grasping for straws, I threw out, "Postmark?"

"Never the same," my mom answered.

Frustrated, I dropped my napkin onto my half-eaten plate. "Well, damn. Guess I'm gonna be putting some of the money I've been ignoring toward hiring a PI to find Katie."

I grabbed my phone from my pocket, pulled up my contacts, scrolled down to Zane's name and shot off a text asking him to start digging and to do some research on a reputable PI service. Sometimes it paid to have a kickass bassist who also happened to be a closeted computer genius.

CHAPTER 6

> "Everything flows and nothing abides, everything gives way and nothing stays fixed."
>
> — HERACLITUS

Greenville, North Carolina

"So help me, Jesus," Layla panted, flapping her hands in a sad attempt to fan herself," Ryan better hurry his ass up. I am too damn fine to pull an Olaf and melt all over the damned sidewalk."

I pulled my purple Metallica T-shirt away from my sticky skin and nodded in agreement. "God, I hate how humid it is here. No matter how much I try to tame my hair, as soon as I set food outside... BAM! I become a yeti."

Suddenly, fingers grasped my shoulder and the world was a blur. Seconds later, another hand popped out and jerked me to a stop. After taking a moment to steady myself,

I glanced up at Ryan, arching my brow in mock irritation. Ryan stepped back and gave me a once-over while stroking his chin. "Yes! You look like yeti...but a pretty yeti. Make all the boy yetis go WAAAAAHHHHHH!"

I made a strange sound somewhere between a snort and a laugh, then playfully punched his arm. "Come on, you goof. Let's grab Layla and get into the AC before we all die from heat exhaustion."

I looked around, realizing Layla was no longer next to me, and wondered where she had wandered off to. My eyes scanned the crowd for a beat before I spotted her telltale hot-pink locks across the courtyard. I waved my arms above my head to catch her attention, but whatever she was staring at had her sole focus.

After a few more exaggerated flails, I gave up on the silent approach and hollered, "Lay! Layla! EARTH TO LAYLA!"

Unsure of whether she legitimately couldn't hear me, or if she was ignoring me on purpose, I strode over to her. Brows pinched in concentration, Layla was scrutinizing a banner as it rippled in the breeze. I nudged her and asked, "Whatcha doin', Lay?"

Still staring intently at the image, she absentmindedly answered, "Devil's Cross is playing here in a few weeks."

Oh God. No. No,no,no. Feigning indifference, I examined my fingernails and replied, "Oh, yeah? That's cool."

Layla shifted that laser-like focus to me, and I swear I could feel her arctic-blue eyes reading my mind. Suspicion was rolling off her in waves when she said, "Yeah. It is. They're amazing. Funny thing, though, I never noticed their lead singer looks a lot like our little bug. Same big old dimples, same aquamarine eyes...the lead singer is originally from Colorado too, right?"

Shit. Shit, shit, SHIT. Okay, Troyer, you can do this. I braced myself for the inevitable pang in the vicinity of my heart before regarding the advertisement, fully aware of what I would see. Saying Finn looked a lot like Cade was a massive understatement. If you took Cade, slapped curly brown hair on him, and shrunk him down until he was three feet tall, he would be Finn's doppelgänger.

Eyes scrolling across his perfect form, I felt a sharp kick in my chest. Over the years, I had perfected the art of avoiding Cade in every possible way. Stumble across an interview on TV? I changed the channel. Spot a billboard or poster with Cade's face on it? Glance the other way until I'd passed. This habit hadn't been born of bitterness, or anger, for that matter, but of pain.

Looking up at his visage in full Technicolor, I could feel the memories nipping at my heels like rabid dogs, making me want to break down and cry. I tried so hard to keep memories of us locked away. Each one was beautiful and wonderful in its own way, but they hurt. Even now, years later, any time I gave in and allowed myself to drag my memories of Cade into the light, I was left feeling raw and bruised for days.

Unexpectedly, a conversation from long ago broke through my barriers and danced across my mind, as if to taunt me with could-have-beens.

Cade tucked a strand of hair behind my ear before gently cradling my face in his strong hands. Resting his forehead against mine, he gifted me with one of the lopsided smiles I adored so much. His azure gaze was filled to the brim with love and affection as it roamed over my face.

"I love you, Katie-mine. One day, I'm gonna marry you and buy you a beautiful house to fill with our beautiful babies. They'll have your laugh and your smile, and be stubborn just like you—and I will adore them, almost as much as I adore you. You're my forever, Katie."

Heart so full I was afraid it might burst, I asked, "For always?"

He snuggled closer, rubbing the tips of our noses together. "For always."

I planted a soft kiss on his lips and whispered, "I love you, Cadeon Cross, and I plan to keep you. You're my forever, too."

Shaking my head to clear away the memory, I forced my mind back into the present and mentally slammed the door leading down memory lane. Keeping my tone neutral, I said, "Yep, he's from Creede."

Layla's "hmmm" let me know she wasn't buying a word I was saying. She crossed her arms in what I had dubbed her "lawyer pose" and turned to analyzed me even further before she asked, "Who did you say Miss Finn's daddy was again?"

Short on patience and ready to be done with this mini interrogation, I bit out, "I didn't."

Narrowing her eyes at my tone, Layla popped back with "Are you gonna divulge that bit of information any time soon? Or are you embarrassed because it's a 'Maury'-type situation? 'Cause, girl, you know I don't judge. I'll help pass out *all* the DNA test kits, don't you worry yourself. I'm hella good at whodunit's...Or, in this case, a who-tapped-it."

At that point, I swore if I rolled my eyes any harder, I'd see my brain. "I know who he is, Lay. And no, before you ask, I'm not telling. Besides, it's not like it matters. Knowing who he is won't change anything. He still won't be here, and I still wouldn't *want* him here."

Done with this conversation, I grabbed her arm and started to drag her back toward the restaurant. "Now come on! We better go get some food before either my stomach eats itself or Ryan sees something shiny and wanders off. You know how short his attention span is, and it's already been, like, five minutes."

CHAPTER 7

> "The truth is rarely pure and never simple."
>
> — THE IMPORTANCE OF BEING
> EARNEST, OSCAR WILDE

Two weeks later, Knoxville, Tennessee

Rolling down the window, we gazed at the imposing Victorian-style home. The exterior was a deep navy blue, the shutters a crisp white, and the gingerbread trim a bright cherry red. The grounds were flawlessly manicured, ensuring each shrub was evenly spaced and pruned within an inch of its life to create a path of perfect identical spheres on either side of the walk. The walkway was level and scrupulously maintained—not even a single blade of grass or bit of dirt dared to mar the path. The grounds radiated an air of coldness and rigidity—there was no doubt in my mind the owner would not be the welcoming sort.

Leaning forward between the two front seats, Rhys whistled and asked, "Dude, are you sure this is the right house? 'Cause I'm definitely getting some hella creepy Stepford vibes right now."

Double-checking the GPS one more time, Dante stared at the imposing house and answered, "Unless Cade's PI sent us the wrong address, GPS says this is it. But I've got to agree that this house gives me the creeps. It's like that Hansel and Gretel shit. Looks all perfect from the outside, but then you go inside, and WHAM! Someone's trying to go all people-eating witch on you and toss your ass into an oven."

Taking one last look at the intimidating house from the safety of the car, I reminded myself of the reason we were there and took a bracing breath before opening the door. I climbed out, and turned around, ducking my head back into the open car door and gaving them each a level gaze. "If I'm not back out in fifteen, someone call D and send him in for a rescue."

Trev glanced at his phone and cringed before looking up at me. "Speaking of D, I think he's a *mite* pissed we ditched him and the rest of the security team for this adventure. Especially because he just said he is going to, and I quote, 'Kick our pale lily-white asses as soon as he figures out where the fuck we are.' I believe it would be in all our best interests to make this a quick stop."

Cringing at the thought of the pissed off three-hundred-and-fifty-pound former Navy SEAL, I enthusiastically bobbed my head up and down once before saying, "Agreed."

I closed the car door and took a moment to straighten

my clothes and smooth down my hair. Deciding I was as presentable as I was going to get, I made my way toward the porch, getting more and more nervous the closer I got to the front door. *What if she's here? Will she be excited to see me? Angry? Oh man, calm down, dude. You got this.*

I stared at the imposing door one more second before taking a deep breath and ringing the doorbell. After a small eternity, the large door creaked halfway open, revealing a tall, lean man with graying hair. The sharp planes of his cheeks jutted out, giving him a gaunt appearance. His mouth was turned down into a permanent frown, stretching his almost nonexistent lips into a thin line, and his faded blue eyes narrowed as he scanned me from top to toe. Based on the irritated expression he wore, he had judged me and found me lacking.

Letting out an aggravated huff, he crossed his arms, and positioned himself in the narrow opening, preventing me from getting a good look inside. "Whatever you are selling," he spat out, his nasally voice laced with irritation, "I don't want any. I also am not planning on donating any money to anything, so don't bother to ask. I cannot believe they're letting hoodlums like you into this neighborhood. I suggest you leave before I call the police and report you for trespassing!"

Taken aback by the unwarranted vehemence in his tone, I almost missed the fact that he had stepped back and was already beginning to close the door. Holding up my hands in a nonthreatening manner, I called out, "Wait! Wait! I'm not selling anything, I swear! I don't want any money—I just need some information on Katerina Troyer and was told you might be able to help me."

He paused, and his eyes narrowed with suspicion. *So, this is how things would be playing out? Alrighty, then.* Leaning forward, he glared down his beak-like nose, until his eyebrows shot up and recognition lit his face. He whipped an accusatory finger in my direction and screeched, "It's *you.* I knew back then that you would turn out to be a good-for-nothing bum. I told that idiot niece of mine you were bad news."

Sneering, he pulled himself up to his full height and stepped halfway onto the porch before addressing me further. "Young man, I make it a habit not to waste my time with people who are beneath me. And my sister was not worth giving the time of day *before* she married the pathetic waste of space she met in college and decided to spawn with him. All her death did was inconvenience me and force me to save face by caring for a child I had hoped never to see."

It took everything in me not to punch this man in the face. How dare he? How dare he speak so poorly of such wonderful people? Anne had never spoken about her family, and after they passed, I could count on one hand the number of times I recalled even seeing Katie's uncle. In fact, thinking back on it, I didn't believe we'd ever actually spoken to one another until this moment.

Katie had always come over to my house, constantly making excuses about why spending time at her home wasn't an option. Now I understood why Anne and Max had never discussed their relatives. If I were faced with pretending I had no one or dealing with people like this, I would have chosen option A in a heartbeat too. Reigning in my temper and being polite was almost impossible, but

Mom had always told me something about catching more flies with honey or some shit. As much as being nice to this asshole pained me, I needed his help.

I moderated my tone to disguise the anger and disgust coursing through my body, and said, "Well, sir. That is why I'm here. I'm looking for the Troyer's daughter, Katerina. If you would tell me where I can find her, I can promise neither of us will ever bother you again."

Hearing her name aloud once again unmasked the rage he'd been trying to hide throughout our short conversation. His entire being vibrated with barely controlled fury before he snapped, letting his temper run wild.

"Katie?"

Spittle flew from his cracked lips and rage mottled his features, making him seem like a fairytale monster come to life."How dare you assume I know where she would be! I am an upstanding citizen, and I DO NOT ABIDE WHORES IN MY HOUSE!"

Seeming crazed, he advanced on me, continuing to spew venom-laced words. "Her mother may have been a blight on the family name, but at least she managed to keep her legs closed until she married that sorry excuse for a man. Katerina? I do not know where the vile creature is, nor do I care. That disgusting creation hasn't darkened my doorstep in years, and I am lucky that fate saddled me with her only a short time before revealing to me what an unconscionable harlot she was!"

He paused with his face a few scant inches from my own, and his thin lips pulled into a twisted smile. "I threw her out, and thankfully the little tart was smart enough to stay away. If fate had any amount of kindness, that trollop would be dead in a ditch somewhere so no one else ever has to be inconvenienced with her care!"

A bony hand slammed into my chest, causing me to stumble back a few steps. I regained my balance just in time to witness Katie's uncle stomping into the house and forcefully slamming the door, still cursing Katie and her parents with every step he took.

A red haze covered my vision, and before I fully registered the potential repercussions of my actions, I began blindly grabbing anything within reach. The sounds of ripping and snapping echoed around me for several minutes before a blaring car horn pulled me back from my blind rage.

Looking at the debris littering the ground, I ran a hand through my hair before turning to head back to the car, making sure to repeatedly kick each of the meticulously manicured bushes on the way. Since her uncle was so keen on destroying beautiful things, I felt it was only fair that at least a small amount of destruction made its way to his doorstep as well.

Once I reached the car, I gripped the door handle, jerked the door open, and slipped inside. Looking at me like I was unhinged, Rhys jostled my shoulder and said, "Dude, what the hell? All I saw was some crazy old dude getting up in your face, then you going all Hulk on the outdoor furniture and shrubberies. Did you find out anything, or...?"

Pulling myself back to the present, I looked at Rhys and said, "Not really. Apparently, he and Katie's mom had been estranged for a long time before she passed. He never met Katie before they died, and only took on the role of guardian to 'save face.' Then, from what I was able to glean in between the impressive number of insults aimed at both Katie and her parents, a few months after I left Creede, he kicked Katie out and hasn't heard from her since."

Not knowing what else to do, I looked to Zane, the unofficial problem solver of our little quintet. Face scrunched in concentration, he absently spun his ring around his thumb for a few moments before speaking. "Okay, guys. So, from what I'm understanding, the uncle threw Katie out and has no clue where she is, which means we are essentially back at square one. We need to regroup and come up with a plan B."

He cracked his knuckles, and then began to dole out instructions. "Cade, you are going to contact your PI and see if he has anything else we can use. Trev, you need contact Bryce and Kelly and tell them to hop on this as well."

At Trev's low groan, Zane shrugged and went on. "Sorry, man. None of the rest of us have the patience to deal with either of them without losing our shit. Tell them this is interfering with our focus. If we are distracted with our concern for Katie, it might affect our performances on the rest of the tour, which in turn could potentially cause a direct hit to their wallets. I'll dig a little deeper and see if I can get any hits on her info once we're back at the suite."

I watched the scenery as it passed, too lost in my own thoughts to pay much attention to what the guys were joking about in the car. I still could not believe Katie's uncle had been that horrible, and the knowledge that my actions had likely prevented her from coming to my family for help settled on my shoulders like a weight. I could feel the guilt dragging me down. I needed something to pull me out of my head, to keep me from slipping below the surface and help me stay on track. Pulling out my phone for a distraction, I smiled when I saw a new text from my mom.

Mom: Cade, tell your father I do too need a new puppy.

Me: Mom, why do you need a puppy?

Mom: All my babies left me. My house is lonely. Also, your dad is a terrible cuddler. It's like cuddling with an octopus. Arms and legs everywhere! Plus, he snores.

Me: What are you talking about, all your babies left? Casey still lives there, Mom. Also, how do you know the puppy won't snore?

Mom: Don't you try and thwart me with your logic! Casey is never home, and I won't care if the puppy snores. It will be too cute for it to bother me. Also, unlike your father, a puppy cannot get into my snack drawer and eat the last Twix in my emergency candy stash.

Me: ...I am Switzerland. I'm not telling dad anything.

Mom: Well, you know what? I've already decided I'm getting the puppy. I don't need to ask your father's permission anyway. Plus, he ate my last Twix. You never take a menopausal woman's chocolate! He owes me. I'll send pics. Stay safe, love you!

Full-on grinning at my mom's antics, I typed "Love you, too!" and hit send, before pulling up my dad's number and hitting the call button. His booming "Hey there, Cadester! What can I do ya for?" instantly made my sour mood lift.

"Hey, Dad! You talk to Mom today?"

My dad paused for a beat before saying, "Oh, hell. She asked you about that damn dog, didn't she?"

I laughed and replied, "Yeah. I figured I'd give you a heads-up that she may come home with a new family member."

My dad sighed, but I could picture him smiling on the other end of the line. In a voice laden with affection, he told me, "Cade, let me tell you something. One of the reasons your mama and I have been together so long and are so happy is that we learned early on to pick our battles."

"Do I want a puppy? No. To me, a puppy is just one big adorable mess. But, will getting a puppy hurt me in any way? No. It may inconvenience me on occasion, but that's about it. I knew the minute your mama mentioned that puppy that we would be getting it one way or another, and I love her enough that I'm okay dealing with chewed up shoes and messes for a bit because I know in the long-run it will make her happy."

Baffled at his nonchalance about the whole thing, I couldn't help but argue. "But she said you told her no! I'm so confused."

In between laughs he said, "Of course I did! Gotta give the woman a little grief, otherwise she'd walk all over me."

Finally understanding, I chuckled and was just getting ready to tell him I had to go, when he said, "And by the way, you remember that when you find your Katie. It's all about give-and-take, son. You treat her with love and respect, and you'll do just fine."

"How did you...?"

I could picture his eyes sparkling with mirth when he

answered, "How could I not? I knew the minute you said you wanted to talk to Katie what you were all about. I'm old, son, not blind. You two may have been young, but it was obvious to anyone who bothered to look that you two were it for each other. It's about damned time you went looking for that girl, and this time, don't screw it up. Now, it seems I might need to make a trip to the pet store, so I'm gonna let you go for now. You give your mama and me a call when you find her, you hear?"

Nodding my head, I told him, "Yes, sir. Talk to you soon, Dad," and hung up.

The cloud that had been hanging over my head had dissipated, and for the first time in days, I felt like I could breathe. Talking to my family had always centered me, which was something I hadn't realized until they weren't there for me to lean on. For the most part, I remembered that, but sometimes I still waited too long in between calls. The confidence my dad had that I would find Katie was a balm to a festering wound, and I doubled down my resolve. I was going to find Katie, one way or another.

CHAPTER 8

> "We are all faced with a series of great opportunities brilliantly disguised as impossible situations."
>
> — CHARLES R. SWINDOLL

Greenville, North Carolina

I stood in front of the mirror and gave my ponytail one final adjustment before deciding I looked passable. Getting ready for work was usually a breeze, but tonight it had proved to be a daunting task. It was the night. Devil's Cross was playing down at the amphitheater, and I couldn't shake the dread that had been plaguing me since this morning. I didn't understand why I was freaking out.

To my knowledge, Devil's Cross had played at the Thompson—Boling Arena in Knoxville at least twice during the short period Finn and I had lived there, and we never ran into one another. Granted, Greenville was a lot smaller than Knoxville, but not small enough that I should be so concerned.

In fact, just like I always did when they performed anywhere nearby, I'd hunkered down with Finn and hidden us away in the apartment all day. I'd appeased her with a dance party and princess stickers, and had allowed her to make me watch *Olaf's Frozen Adventure*. Twice. Unfortunately, unlike the previous close-calls, tonight I had to leave the safety of my hidey-hole to go to work. I had tried to call off, but was informed by Senior Douche that "We're expecting multiple VIP clients tonight, and I need all my best waitresses on staff. So get your ass here or don't come back in at all."

Which is why I was now standing in the shitty women's locker room at a testosterone-filled sports bar dressed in a cheerleading outfit that would garner the Hugh Hefner stamp of approval. The black metal door creaked as it was pulled open, and I glanced over my shoulder to see Layla strut in. She paused next to me, adjusting her top before pulling her fuchsia-pink hair into two pigtails. I elbowed her, and teased, "Pigtails, really, Lay?"

"You know it. Apparently, we're cheerleaders turned porn stars today. I say, rah-rah, bitches!"

I grimaced at the amount of skin on display and gave my top a half-hearted tug before giving up. "Not gonna lie, Lay. This is the worst outfit yet. I swear to God they keep getting smaller. I'm afraid if I lift a tray, my nipples are gonna pop out and say howdy-do. Plus, I can feel the breeze on my ass cheeks. There is no reason on God's green earth the man couldn't give me a skirt long enough to cover my ass cheeks."

Layla looked me up and down, then shrugged. "Well, sister, we got bills to pay, you've got a baby to feed, and as much as I hate this shithole, on nights like tonight, we do make bank. So suck it up, buttercup, put on your perky face, pretend like you don't have a functioning brain in that gorgeous head, and let's hop to it."

With that, she flipped a pigtail over her shoulder and sauntered out the door. Knowing she was right, I decided to give myself a pep talk before heading out. "Okay, Troyer, you got this. You may look like a hooker, but I'll be damned if you can't be a classy hooker. You have nothing to worry about. Nothing at all. Go in, grab tips, go home."

"Troyer, Johnson, Brown, in my office now!" Tom barked, making sure his order was heard over the din of the bar.

I rolled my eyes, dropped a round of drinks off at a rowdy table of frat boys—making sure to include a flirtatious wink for good measure—and made my way to the back of the house. Layla, Amberleigh, and I all stood outside of Tom's office waiting to hear why he'd dragged us back here. Losing patience, Amberleigh narrowed her eyes and waved her hand in a *come-on* gesture. "Tom, you're costing me tips. You have thirty seconds to tell me why you called us in here before I say, 'Screw it,' and go back out."

Tom's beady little eyes roamed from the tops of our ponytails to the tips of our shoes, and he licked his lips before giving us a salacious grin. Layla, still carrying the paring knife she'd been using to cut lemons for the bar, arched a brow and glared at Tom's crotch while holding the small blade at eye level. Thankfully, his smile dropped, and he steepled his fingers before addressing us all.

"Ladies, we have three VIP clients that are expected to arrive within the next half hour. Each of these are high profile, and if they have an enjoyable experience, we have an enjoyable experience. I picked you three because you're my most attractive waitresses, and you don't suck at your jobs. I want to see the drinks flowing and smiles on everyone's faces."

"Layla, you and Amberleigh can decide who wants to work the Dugout and who wants the Penalty Box. Katie, you were requested by name and will be in the Batter's Box. I'm entrusting you three with my reputation here, so either they leave happy, or you leave permanently. Do we have an understanding?"

With a chorus of scoffs, nods, and eye rolls, the three of us left his office and headed toward the locker room for a quick round of touch-ups. Layla broke the silence when she quipped, "Special request, huh? Well, well, well now, it seems someone has the hots for my Katie-did. Lord knows if I swung that way, I would too, 'cause Katie, my Katie, yo' ass is *fine*."

Bouncing on the balls of her feet while clapping, Amberleigh chimed in with a "Oh, Katie, you so fine, you so fine you blow my mind! Hey, Katie, I'd do you, Katie!"

When she gave one high-kick in a final flourish, I doubled over laughing. "You just couldn't help yourself, could you, Ambs."

Amberleigh grinned at me and gestured at her ensemble with one hand. "No, I really couldn't. I was *inspired*."

I wiped tears of laughter from the corners of my eyes,

and we finished getting ready, then went out to prep our VIP areas. While Amberleigh and Layla may not have known who they would be serving, I did. There was only one person who requested me personally, and sadly he was someone I would have preferred to avoid at all costs.

Antonio Vicari was the twenty-four-year-old wayward son of Italian oil tycoon Lorenzo Vicari and his supermodel wife, Serena Rossi. Since Antonio was the product of "busy people" who happened to have billions of dollars, he was your typical rudderless, spoiled playboy whose parents had early on replaced love with presents. Because of this, Antonio had built his life around two ideals: one, if I want it, I deserve it because Vicari's get what Vicari's want, and two, everything has a price.

Regrettably, I served Antonio not long after I'd started working at The Field House and immediately was put on his radar as something he wanted. I had little romantic interest in him then. Now,after a year and several more encounters with him, I could officially say that hell could freeze over and I still would not hop on that crazy train—no matter how hot the conductor might be. Alas, that was not something that Antonio understood.

Over the last twelve months, what started as occasional random visits had morphed into some sort of unhealthy pattern. Every month he came in, I was specifically requested, and he spent the evening lavishly spending money in an attempt to impress his friends, while I did my very best to minimize the number of ass grabs I was forced to endure throughout my shift. As the night waned, Antonio would make some grand gesture, trying to buy his way into my good graces before asking me out.

As per the norm, I would refuse—generally more than once—and try to make myself scarce until I could go home and scrub the stench of desperation off myself. He would make one more depressing attempt to woo me around last call, and then proceed to storm off fake-crying and ranting in Italian to anyone that would listen about his poor broken heart. Yet, he kept coming back every month to do it all over again. *Wash, rinse, repeat—it is a great time, let me tell ya.*

Looking around, I made sure everything was set up to reflect his preferences and stepped over to the curtain to see who was assigned to me for the night. After my third encounter with Antonio's "friends," I'd learned it was in my best interest to find out which bouncer would be guarding the VIP entrance, so I was aware in advance if my bouncer was friend or foe. I pulled back the red material, closed my eyes, and said a silent prayer. *Please be Ross or Tyler.* When I opened them and found myself face-to-face with Paul, I realized tonight was going to suck. Hard.

Moments later, a green light came to life, telling me my VIP guest was here. I stepped back from the entrance, nervously shook my hands out, and girded my loins. *Please be a small group tonight.* A heartbeat later, the Batter's Box was packed. It was obvious Antonio was celebrating something, because he didn't just bring a group of friends—he had a full-blown entourage. An all-male entourage. Already feeing the stirrings of a migraine, I gritted my teeth and plastered a fake smile on my face.

Weaving my way through the bodies over to Antonio proved to be a challenge, but if I wanted nice tips, I needed to follow protocol and rule number one was to always greet the guest of honor first. As he turned toward me, his eyes heated with desire and he greedily scanned me from head to toe.

His large hands engulfed my shoulders when he leaned forward to plant a kiss on each of my cheeks before he announced, "Friends! *Miei amici!* Let me introduce you to my Katie. She is *bellissima*, no? She keeps playing hard to get with Antonio, but we all know how the ladies like to pretend, yes? Come, my Katie, we are here to celebrate. Take good care of my friends, *si?*"

Dear sweet baby Jesus, will this night never end? It had been well over three hours and exhaustion was nipping at my heels. Antonio's group was proving to be every server's least favorite things combined—high-maintenance, rude, and rowdy. Between sprinting up and down the stairs fetching drinks and dodging wayward hands, I was about ready to drop.

I tapped on the bar top impatiently while I sat, waiting for my latest order. The bartender was skillfully pouring drinks at a rapid clip, and I knew he was doing his best, but my good mood had dissipated hours ago. Losing what little patience remained, I moved to stand directly in front of him. "Zac, you know I love you, but if I could have those drinks sometime this century, that would be *great.*"

Zac playfully smacked his hand across his chest, and dramatically cried out, "Katie, you wound me! Here I am, slaving away at your behest, and it is still not enough for you. However will I survive in the face of your disappointment?"

Knowing I was being a bitch, I dropped my head onto my arms. "Sorry, I'm having a long one. I'm hoping, based on their current levels of inebriation, this will be the final round. The lord and master informed me that once they head out, I can go home."

He nodded in understanding and began to quickly fill my tray, before gesturing behind my shoulder with a single digit. Eyes tracking his movement, I noticed a frazzled and pissed off Amberleigh. She gave Zac a tired smile, then said, "Zac, hold up on her drinks for a sec."

Amberleigh grabbed my hand and dragged me around the corner. Eyes hopeful, she pleaded, "I need you to do me a solid. I've had groupie whores shoving at me all night, but on my way down here, one of them crossed the line and dumped a cosmo down my back. I need to go clean up and change into a new uniform. Can you please drop off my drinks for me? I peeked in your room, and they are too drunk to notice if it takes a few extra minutes. Plus, they all seem super happy."

Seeing my indecision, she gave me puppy dog eyes and begged, "*Please?*"

I knew how much it sucked to have drinks dumped on you, so I gave her a comforting pat and relented. "I got you. Just don't take too long, 'kay? I'm thinking Vicari is one shot shy of his security detail deciding it's time to pour him into his limo whether he's ready to go or not, and I am *so* ready for all their asses to go."

Amberleigh gave me a thumbs-up, then turned around and hustled through the black doors behind the bar. Having overheard our conversation, Zac swapped my tray for one filled with mostly Patrón, Jack Daniels Black Label, and some Grey Goose along with a hefty number of shot glasses. Grunting at the weight, I hauled it up onto my shoulder, headed for the stairs, and began to dodge and weave my way through the masses of half-naked girls draped all over the stairwell leading to the Penalty Box. *Jesus, and I thought my uniform was lacking in coverage.*

The closer to the curtain I got, the more aggressive the women became, jostling and elbowing one another in an attempt to try and maneuver themselves closer to the entrance. Tyler and two other heavily muscled gentleman who may as well have had "Security" scrawled across their foreheads in neon Sharpie were forcefully blocking the area behind the velvet rope. Unable to keep my curiosity at bay, I wondered which guest was important enough to warrant a bouncer plus two security guards? *Who the hell is in there? Why do I even care?*

Tyler locked eyes with me, leaned over to the giant next to him, and mumbled something. Seconds later, a hand the size of a dinner plate attached to an arm the size of a tree trunk sporting whorls of ink and some writing I wasn't able to decipher pulled open the curtain covering the doorway and permitted me entrance with a curt nod. The quicker I could drop off the drinks and get out, the happier I would be, so I made a beeline for the circular marble table set in the center of the room.

No longer interested in who happened to be occupying the black leather couches and lounge chairs this evening, I wasted no time unloading the heavy bottles. I rolled my shoulders to release some of the tension from carrying over-loaded trays all night, before expediently arranging the bottles and shot glasses on the table to make them easily accessible from all sides. Once that task was completed, I loaded up the dirty dishes and empty bottles on the tray and hefted it onto my shoulder once again. Hurriedly making my way towards the exit, I mentally high-fived myself for a job well done.

Halfway to freedom, my escape was stalled when a deep, yet playful voice purred, "Well, sugar, I'm not sure how you got in here, but if the front of you looks half as good as the back I'm not gonna complain. How about you sit down and stay awhile?"

I scrunched up my nose in disgust, shifted the heavy tray, and, without looking back, snapped, "Yeah, that'd be a no from me. In fact, let's just preemptively upgrade that to all the no's and throw in a *bless your heart.*"

Completely done with today, I walked to the exit and waited for Thing One and Thing Two to move so I could leave. After giving me a once-over, Thing One surprised me when his lip quirked up ever so slightly and a quiet chuckle met my ears. Raucous laughter erupted behind us, filling the intimate space, and a voice that sounded like it had been created from long nights chewing gravel and drinking booze teased, "Dude, she shot your ass straight down. You do realize 'bless your heart' in that tone is Southern belle for 'fuck you,' right?"

"Fuck you, Dante! Chicks love me! It's not my fault she has a stick up her ass. I bet the front isn't that nice anyway."

I fought the urge to flip them the bird, but took the high road, silently exiting once Thing Two cleared the path. I had just started to move toward the steps when Tyler popped his head out and called me back. Not bothering to hide my exasperation, I stomped over to him. "What?"

Concerned, but wanting to be discreet, Tyler loudly whispered, "Katie, you doing okay? Danny keeping an eye on you over there?"

I felt awful for being so waspish, so I offered him an apologetic smile. "Danny? I don't have Danny, Ty. I got Paul. It's cool though, I'm doing okay."

Brow crinkling with a mix of confusion and irritation, he asked, "What do you mean, you got Paul? I intentionally assigned Danny to you as soon as I saw Antonio's name on tonight's roster. For some reason, when it comes to you, Paul is complete shit at his job, and I wanted someone who'd keep an eye on you."

The voices behind us were quieting down, and I needed to finish this conversation before we drew their attention again. I wasn't sure I could be hit on one more time without losing my temper and likely my job. Plus, if our chat disrupted the guests, or they felt like our attention was divided, they might complain. Tom did not handle complaints well, and I was not in the mood for his version of a talking-to. Add to that the uncomfortable sense I was being watched, and all I wanted was to exit stage left pronto.

I laid my palm on Ty's arm to soothe his concern. "I'm fine, I swear. Paul is Paul. He's hated me ever since he asked me out the third week I worked here, and I shot him down. He may not watch me like a hawk, but he keeps everyone relatively in check."

I broadened my smile and added, "Plus, you knew damn well as soon as Danny realized Layla was the other VIP waitress, he'd be on her like white on rice. That boy thinks the sun shines out of her ass, even if she is oblivious.

Let him be. I've got one more round to drop off for Antonio and I'm pretty sure his crew is heading home, which means I'll be able to go home too."

Ty's cornflower-blue eyes scanned my face to gauge my level of honesty, before he gave me a wink and stepped back into the lounge. Not wanting any more delays, I rapidly descended the stairs, making a pit stop at the bar to drop off Amberleigh's tray and trade it for my own, before heading back up to Antonio. *Almost done, thank God.*

CHAPTER 9

CADE

> "Beware of missing chances; otherwise it may be altogether too late someday."
>
> — FRANZ LISZT

I turned my head away from the set of very fake, yet very perky tits that had been thrust in my face and leaned forward, considering the bevy of liquor and empty glasses littering the table. *Fuck me, I don't want to be here. I may as well drink another shot to help pass the time.* The bottle of Jack was closest, so I snagged it and poured a large portion into a shot glass. The all-too-familiar tingle in my fingertips made me smile as I took the shot and hoped the impending buzz would make this seemingly unending night more enjoyable. It had been quite some time since I last let myself get a good buzz going.

When she realized she no longer held my attention, Tits began rubbing herself all over my bicep. I rolled the empty glass between my palms, pointedly ignoring her, hoping she would turn her attention elsewhere. Unfortunately, she decided my lack of attention meant she needed to put forth more of an effort.

She pouted for a moment, before seductively biting her lip and sliding one foot along the length of my calf while letting her finger trail across the waistband of my jeans. Surprised, I arched a brow at her boldness, my eyes looking down and following the path of her hand for a moment, before deciding I wasn't up for groupies tonight. Gently, I stilled her hand. "Sorry, sugar, I'm not feeling it tonight."

For some damn reason, that didn't dissuade Tits. Instead, she decided to take it as a challenge and straddled my lap, resting both of her arms over my shoulders so her ample cleavage hovered just beneath my chin. Whoever raised this girl to believe "not interested" equated "try harder" needed a swift punch to the junk. Her injection-filled lips brushed against my neck as she nibbled her way up the column of my throat. The sting of teeth biting into my earlobe made me flinch.

Still trying to be sexy, she purred, "You sure, handsome? 'Cause I'm a gymnast and I'm *real* flexible. I guarantee you will have a good time."

I paused a beat to consider her offer one last time, but as attractive as she was, I wasn't in the mood for desperation tonight. Not keen on having her interpret a second rejection as a suggestion to double up her efforts, I grabbed her wandering hand to ensure I had her full attention. "I believe I said I'm not feeling it. Thanks for the offer, but not gonna happen."

Disappointment and a hint of hurt flashed across her

face, making me feel like a dick. Guilt drove me to do her a solid, and since she was intent on going home with somebody, I added, "But Zane over there is a sucker for bendy blondes, and I think he'd be real welcoming if you wanted to go say hi."

Almost instantly she perked up, twisting to locate Zane. Once she locked eyes on him, she gave me a grateful smile before sliding off my lap and sauntering over to him. The flirtatious smile she'd worn earlier had been replaced with a determined smirk, and I could tell she'd decided to go big or go home.

Foregoing all niceties, she straddled Zane's lap and began biting and kissing along his jawline. Once he wrapped his arms around her waist, she gave me a triumphant grin over her shoulder before leaning forward and whispering in his ear. I knew the minute she mentioned her various "talents" because Zane's eyes widened and a sly smile split his face before he gave me a nod of gratitude.

I checked the time on my phone and bit back a curse. It was just after midnight, which meant we still had a few hours to go before the guys would be ready to head back to the hotel. The cushion next to me dipped, and I looked over to find an exasperated Rhys stretched out next to me, giving me an impressive glare.

"Come on, man. Chill out. Relax. The whole point of making you come out was to distract you from the whole Katie thing and have some much-needed fun, but how are we supposed to do that when you're sitting over here looking like you're bored out of your skull? I mean seriously,"—he gestured around the room— "do you not see the options we have on the menu tonight? Pick one, and if none of these fine specimens are doing it for you, glance over the railing and choose someone new."

My shit mood was screwing up his night, and I hated it. The guys were trying to pull me out of the funk I'd been in since my run-in with Katie's uncle, and they all needed a night off as much as I did. I ran my hand through my hair and sighed in defeat. High-pitched giggles and deep voices bounced around the room, and it took all my concentration to block them out and focus on Rhys.

"I'm sorry, man. I know I've been off lately. Thanks for dragging me out. I'll try to be better company for the rest of the night, okay? Just, don't send anymore girls my way, yeah? I'm not in the mood for them tonight."

Rhys considered me a moment before enthusiastically nodding. "Deal! Now, come have some more shots while I find out if that chick's face is as spectacular as her ass."

Curious to know who had caught Rhys's eye, I let my gaze travel through the crowd, noting that Zane and Tits were absent, as were Trev and the redhead he'd had draped all over his lap earlier this evening. *Damn, I must have zoned out for a while.* Eventually, I spotted the backside Rhys was referring to. *Hot damn, maybe I shouldn't have given tonight a pass.* I wasn't able to catch a glimpse of her face, but what I could see was mouthwatering.

Long tan legs led up to a black skirt that scarcely covered a perfect heart-shaped ass. Her figure was lithe, yet she was still packing some impressive curves. Slender fingers repositioned a tray laden with empty bottles and glasses, and once it was balanced, she tossed a long dark ponytail over her shoulder.

Raven locks swayed back and forth across the middle of

her back, dancing across a sea of sun-kissed skin as she sauntered away. Hell, I hadn't even seen her front, and I was hard as a rock. Pissed that I'd let Rhys call dibs, I slumped down in my seat and grumpily sipped the whiskey Rhys had slid into my hand.

Knowing she wouldn't be coming home with me should have been enough for me to turn my attention elsewhere, but her movements were mesmerizing, and I couldn't make myself look away. There was something about her that was so terribly familiar. The longer I watched her, the more I felt like I should be doing *something*, but the question was what?

The closer she got to the exit, the more unsettled I felt. My fingers stretched out of their own accord, reaching for her, but I caught myself and jerked my hand back. I must have cruised right past buzzed and gone straight to drunk. Concerned with my lack of control, I was considering calling it a night when Rhys made his play.

"Well, sugar, I'm not sure how you got in here, but if the front of you looks half as good as the back, I'm not complaining. How about you sit down and stay awhile?"

A surge of protectiveness for this nameless woman consumed me, and I had to force myself not to punch Rhys in the face—which, seeing as he was acting perfectly normal, was a huge problem. *What the hell is wrong with me?* I was so engrossed in my own mental gymnastics that I almost missed the slight stiffening of her shoulders. Almost, but not quite.

Not impressed with his offer, then? Anticipation thrummed in my veins, as I waited for her to turn and answer him. I wasn't sure why, but somewhere in the last ten minutes, my primary goal for the night had changed from hanging out and having some drinks to getting a good look at her face. Yet, like everything else recently, fate had once again decided I was not going to have my way.

Without bothering to even spare us a glance, she kept moving, and in a sugary sweet voice called out, "Yeah, that'd be a no from me. In fact, let's just preemptively upgrade that to all the no's and throw in a *bless your heart*."

Dante busted out laughing. "Dude, she shot your ass straight down. You do realize 'bless your heart' in that tone is Southern belle for 'fuck you,' right?"

I snorted and swung my head to the side so I could catch Rhys's reaction. His face was flushed, and even the tips of his ears were red from embarrassment. Yet even that paled in comparison to seeing Rhys's jaw hang open in shock. I knew I should throw him a bone and be sympathetic, but it had been so long since he was flat-out rejected, I couldn't.

I doubled over, laughing so hard that tears were streaming down my face. Rhys, who undoubtedly was one of the most beloved members of our group, was not used to being told no, and seeing a grown-ass man pouting on the couch like a five-year-old made the situation even funnier. Once my laughter died down, I wiped the tears from my eyes and zeroed in on the exit. The bouncer the club had provided was leaning out of the doorway animatedly speaking to someone. I spotted a flash of midnight-colored hair in the gap and assumed it was the sassy waitress, which piqued my curiosity.

Still unable to see her face because of the angle of my seat, I quietly stood and made my way toward the door as unobtrusively as possible. No matter how I shifted, there wasn't a clear view of her.

Compelled to learn more about her, I set my sights on the bouncer to see if I could glean any information from him. Though his expression remained impassive, I noted a few small tells that made him an easy read, which was a huge benefit to me. At one point in their conversation, his relaxed features tightened, and his mouth turned down at the corners.

I couldn't hear what he was saying, but he was definitely upset about something. Placating murmurs met my ears, and after a long, considering look, his face relaxed and his eyes softened once again before he let the curtain drop, signaling the end of their conversation.

Still burning with a desire to know who she was, I grumbled in frustration that I hadn't learned anything at all. It had been far too long since anything—or anyone—had caught my eye, and I wasn't about to miss my shot. I strode over to Rhys, unsurprised to find him soothing the sting of rejection with the two brunettes currently occupying his lap.

One was busying herself attempting to unbutton his jeans, while the other seemed to be intent on familiarizing herself with his tonsils. On a good day, Rhys had the attention span of a Jack Russell terrier on a coffee high, so I knew better than to waste my breath telling him I was heading out.

I maneuvered around the scant number of people left, and noted that Trev hadn't returned, which meant red must be killer in bed. Trev liked to get in and out—no muss, no fuss—so it was rare that he actually kept someone around longer than a few hours, though he always made sure his bed partners left with smiles on their faces and presents in their hands.

I asked him about it once, and he told me if he ever treated a woman disrespectfully, his mom would beat his ass, and that by making sure his women were treated right, there was less of a chance they would blab to the press out of spite. Zane was still gone as well, which was pretty typical. Zane tended to pick one keep them for the night, make them breakfast, then send them on their way.

The only ones left were Dante, Rhys, and me. I caught Dante's attention, gesturing to him that I was heading out, before setting my empty glass on the table. Still mulling over the best way to approach the hot waitress once I found her—because I would be finding her—I was caught off-guard when a deep voice with a heavy twang said the one thing guaranteed to stop me dead in my tracks.

I frantically looked around to determine who had spoken, when I realized it was the same bouncer who I had been watching before. I all but sprinted toward him, ignoring the stares I was attracting, and slid to a stop. Not wanting to be rude, I impatiently bounced on the balls of my feet, waiting for him to finish speaking into his earpiece so we could have a chat.

Unaware of my close proximity, he mashed down a button on his earpiece before saying with barely leashed fury, "I don't care if you are tired, and I don't give two shits if your shift is supposed to be over. You will walk Layla to her car, then you will park your ass outside the girls' locker room and walk Katie to her car as penance for disobeying my orders and leaving her with fucking Paul all goddamned night. Then, and only then, can you go home. Do I make myself clear?"

I hadn't heard wrong. He had said "Katie." I was aware that there were hundreds of thousands of Katie's in the world, and that I was more than a little drunk, but my mind clamped down on that name and I couldn't let it go unless I knew. I cleared my throat, but the quiet sound couldn't penetrate the pounding bass pumping through the speakers.In too big of a rush to waste any more time, I tapped his arm. He jerked and glanced at me over his shoulder. He held my gaze for a moment, then jostled D with his elbow and cocked his head in my direction.

Irritated that he didn't seem to grasp that I needed to speak to *him*, I grabbed his bicep and jerked on his arm. His brows shot up, and he gave me a pointed glare before glancing at the hand still resting on his bicep then back at my face. Based on the blatant irritation in his expression, I was seconds away from being thrown out, which would not do.

I quickly let him go and held my hands up in surrender. "Sorry, sorry!"

I needed to check myself, otherwise there was a real possibility that my inability to control my impulses was going to bite me in the ass. Urgency nipped at my heels, but I forced myself to remain calm. "Katie? You said the name Katie, right?"

His cornflower-blue eyes were filled with suspicion when he drawled, "Yes."

I let go of the hope that I would win this guy over and decided to stop playing nice and just be blunt. "The waitress who was here earlier, was that her?"

He looked me over, most likely trying to decide how much trouble I was going to be, before he offered me a single nod. Done with me, he turned toward the two members of the security team we'd brought along and hooked his thumb in my direction. "I think y'all might want to take him home. He seems to be well past sober, and I don't care who he is or how sizeable his bank account may be. If he harasses any waitresses under my watch, we're gonna have a problem."

Pissed that Deliverance's hick ass was being a judgmental prick, I threw my arms up in frustration and bit out, "I may be buzzed, but I am not drunk, and I'm not intending to harass anyone. I just need to speak to Katie. Can you tell me where she is? Please? It's really important."

The bouncer stood up straighter in an attempt to intimidate me. When that got no response, he crossed his arms, clearly doing his damnedest to assert his dominance. Not willing to give an inch, I hung out with a bored expression on my face until he relented.

"Well, *sir*, with all due respect, every gentleman who meets Katie needs to "speak" with her. I'm gonna tell you the same thing that I tell them. If Miss Katie wanted anything to do with you, you'd already know where she is. I don't know what business you think you have with her, but I strongly suggest you leave her be."

Motherfucker! Done dealing with this oversized gorilla, I pushed past him and jogged down the steps into the area for general patrons. D's irritation was impossible to miss as he signaled for Chris to maintain his post and silently followed behind me. Unconcerned with the bodies writhing on the dance floor, I shoved them out of my way, intent on getting to the bar. I leaned my forearms on the silver bar top, frantically searching for the bartender. When none was found, I loudly rapped my knuckles on the surface.

A minute later, a blond head popped up, and his expression told me he was less than pleased with how I'd gone about paging him. Part of me felt guilty for perpetuating the rude rock star stereotype, but I was in too big of a hurry to bother apologizing. Not wanting to waste any more time than necessary, I held up a hundred-dollar bill and slid it across the shiny surface. Not taking his eyes off the cash, he set down the glass he'd been cleaning and asked, "What can I make ya?"

"Nothing. I'm not here to order a drink. I'm here about Katie. I want to talk to her, but I'm not sure where she is. Point me in her direction, please."

His hazel eyes bounced between me, D, and the cash sitting on the bar a few times before he exhaled in resignation. With a pained expression on his face, he slowly pushed the cash back toward me. "Judging by your expression, and the fact that you have a human tank watching your every move, I'm guessing I may regret this decision later. That being said, as much as I could use an extra hundred bucks, my answer is no. I will not tell you where she is, nor will I point you in her direction. I know she's gorgeous, man, I get it, but she's untouchable. Trust me. Leave her be."

I was seconds away from slamming my fist into the bar out of frustration, when a nasally voice called out from the shadows. "Zac, Mr. Cross is one of our VIP clients. I don't care if it offends your delicate sensibilities. If he wants to visit with our Katie, he gets to. Are we clear?"

Glaring at the paunchy man who was obviously in

charge, Zac proved to have more balls than I would have assumed. In a voice filled with resentment, he snapped, "Fuck you. I don't give a shit who he is. She doesn't deserve to be bothered, and even though your uniforms may lead men to think otherwise, this isn't a brothel and she isn't for sale. You want to let him talk to her so bad, take him yourself. I want no part in this," then he turned on his heel and stormed into the back.

Moments later, a balding, overweight man in a gray polyester suit who looked like he had been scraped off the asphalt of a skeezy used car lot slid in front of me. "Sorry about that. I'll deal with him later. So hard to find good help."

He adjusted a worn gold name tag that read "TOM MONKHOUSE, GENERAL MANAGER." Tom rubbed his hands together and offered me a lecherous smile. "So, you caught sight of Katie, huh? Man, she's a beaut. Too bad she's got one hell of an attitude on her. Guess that makes her more fun though, right? Follow me, Mr. Cross. I'll take you up to the Batter's Box. She's taking care of Mr. Antonio Vicari's group this evening, but I'm sure Mr. Vicari wouldn't mind the interruption, since it is you."

I pasted a bland smile on my face, then let it fall as soon as he turned away, rolling my eyes at his pathetic attempt to name-drop. Not having another option, I followed the slimy bastard across the dance floor and up a set of stairs opposite from where our lounge sat. His movements were slow, intentionally prolonging the trip, likely hoping someone snapped a picture of us together so he could pretend I'd voluntarily spent time with his skeevy ass.

Finally, after what seemed like the longest hike known

to man, we reached the entrance to another room with the words "Batter's Box" emblazoned across the top in neon-green lights. A meathead-looking bouncer with no neck glanced at the owner, then at myself before offering a lazy shrug and opening the curtains. Seconds later, I spotted the sexy waitress from before, just as she was dodging a hand that had shot out, desperately trying to grab her jaw-dropping ass. Huffing in annoyance, she spun around, and I was lost in a familiar field of green. *Katie.*

CHAPTER 10

KATIE

> "Ever has it been that love knows not its own depth until the hour of separation."
>
> — KAHLIL GIBRAN

Dodging the same pervy guy's hand *again*, I whirled around, intent on giving him a verbal bitch slap and telling him exactly where this beer bottle would be going if he tried touching me one more time, when movement at the entrance to the lounge caught my eye. I glanced over to find a smug-looking Tom leering at me, which immediately put me on edge.

Unsure of why he was bothering me, I gave him a *what gives?* gesture and he subtly nodded toward some dark-haired guy standing on his right. Irritated beyond belief at having another person demanding my attention, I crossed my arms in exasperation and turned my focus toward the new addition.

When the painfully familiar aqua eyes that had been

haunting my dreams for the last four years met mine, my stomach dropped. I snapped my eyes closed, hoping that when I opened them again, he would merely be a figment of my imagination. Yet, when I looked over once again, he was still standing there, staring at me. The blood drained from my face, and I battled the urge to hide under the table and army crawl my way out the door. *This can't be happening.*

Like most girls, I had envisioned multiple scenarios of how things would go and what I would say if I ever crossed paths with Cadeon Cross again. However, in none of my imaginings was I wearing a microscopic cheerleader uniform six hours into the shift from hell, smelling like rank beer compliments of Signor Grabby Hands. I also had never envisioned that I'd look like I was trying out for the lead role in *Zombie Hooker Cheerleaders Volume 5* thanks to the fact that my makeup had given up and slid off my face two hours ago.

Honestly, this was the cherry on top of the shit sundae this night had become, and I really wanted to flip fate the bird. I wasn't sure what the hell she was so damn salty about, but at this point, I had more than paid whatever karmic debt she thought I owed.

Thankfully, he didn't say anything, choosing instead to stand there and stare at me, which wasn't awkward *at all.* He looked as shocked to see me as I was him, which was oddly comforting, all things considered. Though it would have been nice if he wasn't standing over there looking frus-tratingly perfect in a fitted black tee and dark-wash jeans, while I was over here looking like the Joker's brunette sister.

A small eternity passed before Cade took a few tenta-tive steps forward and gave me that damn lopsided smile I used to love so much. Seeing it once again caused my traitorous brain to flood me with bittersweet memories. *I love you, Katie-mine. I'll never leave you. I'm gonna marry you one day. You're my always, Katie.*

As soon as the memories cropped up, so did the desire to smack that damned crooked smile right off his pretty face. My emotions were all over the map, rapidly shifting between happiness that he was here, sadness over what we had lost, and long-forgotten anger over being deceived.

Did I want to stand here like an idiot and study his flawless face? That'd be a yes. Did I want to wander over and let my fingers explore all those new and improved dips and ridges I knew I would find underneath the black T-shirt he was wearing so well? Also, yes. Did I want to deal with the fallout once this all blew up in my face again? That would be a hell no.

Needing a reminder as to why Cadeon Cross was my persona non grata, I allowed myself to recall how I'd felt when I'd woken up alone after a beautiful night together. To remember the sting of betrayal I'd felt as I'd found myself cold and lonely with only a hastily scribbled letter as company in the harsh morning light, the boy I loved nowhere in sight.

Centered once again, I ruthlessly shoved the memories back down. This was not the time or the place to fall apart, and I'd be damned if I let him know how much seeing him was throwing me. Fool me once, shame on you, and all that. Not willing to go down that path again, I steeled myself against any lingering feelings that seeing him envoked, and went into default mode. Cade might have spent the last several years winning people's hearts, but I had spent just as much time building an impenetrable wall around mine.

Life, I had found, sometimes taught unexpected lessons in surprising ways. A perfect example of this came in the form of my uncle. I loathed that man with a burning passion, and for the most part, I ignored anything and everything the evil man spewed from his hateful mouth. But there were two things I'd learned while living with him that had turned out to be helpful in the long run. The first was that relying on others will only set you up for a life filled with disappointment and heartache. The second was that I didn't need to share every emotion I was experiencing.

My parents had been very open and loved to express themselves, as had Cade, so I had never become adept at keeping things to myself. However, after hearing my uncle continually scream '*Fix your face, Katerina! No one wants to be forced to witness your pathetic feelings!*' for days on end after Cade left, I figured out how to school my features pretty quickly. Since then, I had become a pro at controlling my expressions and compartmentalizing most of my emotions until I was in a place where I was able to safely unpack and process them.

This was not the time nor the place for a breakdown, so I placed every wayward thought I had into a box, locked it up tight, and released the breath I had been holding. Without bothering to acknowledge either Tom or Cade, I turned and got back to work, biding my time until I could make my escape.

Cade

My feet were rooted to the floor, and all I could to do was stare. The minuscule uniform left little to the imagination, giving me ample opportunity to compare grown-up Katie to the girl I had known so intimately before.

Her long black hair was pulled back, accentuating her heart-shaped face and pert nose. Thick black lashes framed her striking emerald eyes. Soft pink gloss coated her full lips, making them appear infinitely kissable. The tiny outfit hugged her lithe figure, the deep V of her top flashing tantalizing glimpses of ample cleavage before drawing my gaze down to her flat, toned stomach. The skirt barely covered the award-winning ass I'd familiarized myself with earlier, before exposing her mile-long legs that ended in a sexy pair of black Converse wedges.

My eyes gradually worked their way back up before once again settling on her face. I couldn't help the mixed emotions coursing through me now that we were face-to-face. Everything about her was so familiar, so right, yet at the same time completely different. Not sure how warm my welcome would be, I scanned her features, searching for any hints as to how she was feeling. Once upon a time, I used to always tease her, telling her that I never needed to ask what she was thinking because it was always written all over her face. Yet now, no matter how hard I focused, I couldn't read her at all.

My confused gaze swung up to hers in a silent question.

Katie paused for a moment before closing her eyes and releasing a slow, deep breath. Gradually, her lashes lifted, and her green gaze hardened before a mask of indifference effortlessly slid over her features.

A heartbeat later, she disregarded me entirely, giving me her back as she busied herself pouring shots for the other patrons in the lounge. Katie had never taken anyone's shit, but she'd also never been intentionally rude. Seemed more had changed than I thought.

~

Katie

I sensed him. It was as if we were still connected by some invisible tether. No matter where in the room I went, I could pinpoint precisely where he was, which pissed me off to no end. It didn't help that his eyes followed my every motion, silently begging for my attention. Too bad that wasn't going to happen though. I might have my game face on, but his presence was wreaking havoc with my emotions, making me feel off-center and vulnerable.

I knew ignoring him was hurtful, and knowing Cade, was also likely pissing him off, but I really didn't give a shit. I couldn't control the fact that he chose to walk out of my life, but I would damn well control his ability to waltz back into it. Cade hadn't seemed to care one way or the other what the consequences of his actions were back then, so I figured I wasn't obligated to take into account how my behavior was affecting him now.

Moving opposite of where Cade was casually lounging against the wall, I picked up a few errant glasses left on the side tables, before turning around to scan the space one more time. Antonio's massive group had begun to trickle out of the bar, leaving Antonio, Cade, and about seven other hangers-on who were dead set on sticking with Antonio until he decided he was ready to depart.

Noticing Antonio had finished downing the last shot I could shake out of Patrón bottle number nine, I mentally high-fived, myself knowing he was about to leave. Only one final step remained in our awkward monthly dance. And Cade would get to watch. *Fan-fucking-tastic.*

Drunkenly stumbling over to where I was wiping down one of the tables, Antonio flung a well-muscled arm over my shoulder and pulled me into his side, loudly bellowing, "*Cara mia!* My lovely Katie, no more playing this game of cat and mouse, yes? The Antonio, he likes the chase, but he thinks we have played long enough, eh? Now be a good girl and go tell your boss we are leaving together."

I looked at the ceiling, praying for patience, before I slapped on a placating smile. Opting to ignore Antonio's hand, which had abandoned my shoulder and was making its way to the small of my back, I gently pivoted out of his hold and faced him. Usually I flirted and giggled a bit before giving him a gentle let down, but I didn't have it in me tonight. I snapped my fingers in front of his face, forcing him to focus, and waited for his semi-vacant gaze to meet mine. *Goddamn drunk people. Attention span of a friggin' goldfish, I swear.*

"Antonio." My voice was firm, yet polite. "We have this conversation every single time you come in. While I am extremely flattered to have caught your eye and would love to experience your...charms...I am, unfortunately, unavailable. And will remain so for the foreseeable future."

To soften the sting of my rejection, and avoid running off one of the best tipping customers I'd ever had, I gave him a peck on the cheek and stepped back. True to form, Antonio doubled over laughing. "Ah, *cara mia*, how I love it when you tease."

He stood and dramatically placed his hand over his heart before continuing, "You think to wound me, but I know better. You think Antonio does not know that though you say no, you secretly mean yes? Do not worry, *farfallina*. I will not abandon you. Antonio cannot be long without his *tesoro*, even if she pretends she does not wish to be caught in my net."

Antonio offered what I assumed was meant to be a seductive wink, but instead looked as if his eyelid were having a seizure. If that wasn't unfortunate enough, he then pursed his lips, leaned in, and did his damnedest to deliver a sloppy, drunken kiss. Thinking on my feet, I dropped a cocktail napkin. "Oh dear, better pick that up before someone trips!"

I ducked down just in time to dodge his seeking lips and was careful to put some space between us when I stood back up. Done with his shenanigans, I grabbed my tray full of empties and gave him a small wave before bowing out of the room and heading down the stairs to the main club, completely forgetting Cade was still here.

CHAPTER 11

KATIE

> "Wise men speak because they have something to say; fools because they have to say something."
>
> — PLATO

Successfully making it to the bar, I dropped my tray off and hustled toward the black doors representing the end of my shift and freedom from this hellish night. *Almost there.* I extended my hand to shove open the door, when a broad chest clad in black blocked my path. *Seriously, fate? Come on! Can't you cut a girl a little slack? Just once?*

Frustrated beyond belief, I dropped my head in defeat, and rested my hands on my hips. Cade lifted my chin with a finger, and I found myself confronted with a whole lot of fury. His jaw was clenched, and his blue eyes blazed with anger.

Without speaking, his hand wrapped around my upper arm, and he started to guide me to a nearby table. I wasn't sure who the hell he thought he was, but *no one* touched me without my permission—him included. I planted my feet, jerking us to a stop. Once I had his full attention, I pointed to the offending appendage still clinging to my bicep. "I suggest you remove that. Now."

He hastily dropped my arm and held up his hands apologetically. "Katie, I just want to talk."

Not in the mood to take a stroll down memory lane, I replied, "That's nice. Too bad I don't. Now, if you'll excuse me, it's been a long night, and I have things to do."

Cade pivoted in front of me, and when I attempted to maneuver around him, he blocked me yet again. So frustrated I could scream, I clenched my fists and imagined punching him in his stupidly perfect nose. Irritation skittered across his face just before he said, "I understand what I did was a shit thing, but come on. It has been *years*."

At my limit, I threw my hands up in frustration and asked the heavens, "Goddamn it! What is it, International Asshole Day?"

Losing the paltry grip I'd had on my temper, I snapped, "You know what, Cade? You seem to be under the misapprehension that I'm one of your minions you get to order around. I realize you're used to people bending over backward trying to kiss your ass, but I've already worshipped at that altar and found it lacking. You want to talk? Well, good for you."

"I, however, have zero interest in hearing what you have to say. In fact, since your entitled ass seems to have forgotten how to read basic body language, let me spell it out for you. *Go. Fuck. Yourself.*" With that, I shoved him out of my personal space and barreled through the black doors.

I stormed past a panicked-looking Danny, threw the changing room door open, and stomped over to my locker. After three failed attempts, I got it open and pulled out my street clothes. Still furious, I slammed the door of my locker a few times to release some steam before jerking the ridiculous cheerleader uniform off and chucking it into the laundry bin. Mumbling under my breath about assholes and douches, I stabbed my feet into my ripped black skinny jeans and pulled on my gray Foo Fighters T-shirt.

Taking a seat on the bench, I groaned in relief when I pulled my Converse wedges off and set them aside. I flexed my toes a few times to relieve the ache before setting them inside my locker and slipping on my well-worn Converse All Stars. Still fuming, I angrily marched out the door, bypassing Danny without even bothering to say goodbye, intent on reaching the metal exit door leading to the staff parking lot so I could officially end the shit show that was my night.

"Katie, wait!" Danny's voice echoed down the hallway, and I could hear his heavy steps as he jogged toward me.

In my periphery I saw him reaching out to snag my elbow, but before he made contact, I spun on my heel and glared at him. No longer caring about moderating my noise level, I shouted, "Danny, I swear to God, if you touch me, you will LOSE YOUR DAMNED HAND!"

Danny looked at me like I had kicked his favorite puppy and slowly shuffled back a few feet. His big brown eyes regarded me for a second, then he began making calming motions with his hands and rambling about thinking zen thoughts. I had no clue why all the men I had encountered today felt the need to treat me like a feral animal on the verge of an attack. I was pissed off, yes, but I wasn't some rabid raccoon set to star in an episode of *When Animals Attack!*.

"I'm sorry, Katie. I won't try to touch you again, I swear. I just wanted to apologize for not staying at my assigned post and swapping with Paul. It was a crummy thing to do, and considering I've never heard you raise your voice to anyone, I can only guess how awful your night must have been. Will you please at least let me walk you to your car?"

Of course I would choose to end the world's worst night by acting like giant a-hole and raging at an overgrown Boy Scout. Feeling like a jerk, and beyond ready to block out the world for a little while, I shrugged and looked up at Danny's towering frame. "I'm sorry too. Tonight wasn't the best, and I took my temper out on you, which isn't fair. My bad night wasn't your fault, so please don't feel guilty for anything. I would, however, love it if you'd walk me out."

A giant grin lit up his face, and Danny bounded over to me, hooking my arm into his before pushing open the heavy exterior door. Exaggerating his drawl, he tipped an imaginary hat before playfully saying, "Well, ma'am, if you weren't aware, we southern boys specialize in all things gentleman like, particularly escorting pretty ladies to their car."

Appreciative that Danny had found a way to brighten an otherwise crap day, I gave him a grateful smile. I channeled my inner Scarlett O'Hara, placing my free hand on my chest and batting my eyelashes to achieve the full effect. Then replied, "Well, I do declare! That was by far the most fabulous escortin' I done ever did see! You, sir, are one fine gentleman."

Danny chuckled and pulled me in for a side hug. He affectionately patted my head before opening the door of my beat-up gray Volvo and helping me inside. Once I was settled, he ducked down into my line of vision. "Drive safe, Katie. And get some sleep, okay?"

I nodded, pulled my door shut, turned the key in the ignition, and *finally* headed home.

CHAPTER 12

CADE

> "Failure is the key to success; each mistake teaches us something."
>
> — MORIHEI UESHIBA

I stood frozen in the same spot long after she'd left. The Katie I'd encountered tonight and the one I had left behind were like two completely different people. Try as I might, my brain couldn't seem to grasp how much she had changed. When she'd been mine, she was full of jokes and smiles. Always quick to laugh and slow to anger.

My Katie had rarely raised her voice and always did her best to temper honesty with sweetness. She'd worn her emotions on her sleeve, her expressive face always open and easy to read.

For some reason, even after everything, I had this expectation that once I found Katie, she would be the same as she was before. I couldn't count the number of times I had lain awake at night, imagining how amazing it would be when I saw Katie again. How her face would light up when I walked in.

Logically, I had always acknowledged the possibility that she would still be hurt or upset. I had even and had subconsciously expected it when I went chasing after her tonight, but in my mind, she was always willing to listen. In every fantasy I had ever concocted, she would let me explain what happened and why I left, then she'd understand and forgive me. There would be a few tears, since she'd always been a bit of a crier, but we would kiss, make up, and my world would once again be perfect, just like before.

I had not anticipated finding myself faced with a sassy, sexy woman with unreadable eyes who had zero problems giving me a verbal bitch slap. I was also unprepared for the possibility that she wouldn't even be willing to hear me out. The entire interaction kept repeating over and over in my mind, playing on an unending loop, and the more I thought about it, the more determined I became.

Even with how poorly things had gone, for the first time since I left, I felt alive. Lyrics were bouncing around in my head, and the hollow place in my heart was a little less empty. I had been too long without the other half of my soul, so no matter how long it took or how painful it was, I *would* be winning her back. In need of a little support, I pulled out my phone and sent off a text to Casey.

Me: Found her.

Casey: No way! How is she? How did it go?

Me: She seems fine and...not good.

Casey: On a level of one to Paris is burning, how bad

are we talking?

Me: Paris is ash, the villagers are seeking asylum, and a plague has ravished the land.

Casey: Damn, bro. Can we rebuild?

Me: Working on it.

Casey: Let me know if you need supplies. We are plentiful in trees and motivational speeches. Now go kick some ass!

I chuckled and slid my phone into my back pocket. Busy thinking of then discarding various plans, I distractedly followed D out to the car so we could head home. Not wanting to disturb the guys, I quietly slipped into the room and was surprised to find everyone hanging out in front of the TV playing video games.

Trev set a can of soda on the table in front of an empty cushion on the couch. I took the hint, sat down, and picked up the can, taking a long drink. When I set it back down, the TV had been turned off, and I looked around to find four faces studying me intently. I stretched out my legs and waited. Soon enough, Dante's gravelly baritone cut through the silence. "What happened?"

The last thing I wanted to do was discuss the night, but considering how epically I had failed on my own, help would not be a bad thing. Plus, these guys were family, and I had learned the hard way that keeping secrets from family is a bad plan. "I found Katie."

Rhys let loose a "Whoop!" and Trev's enthusiastic "Hells yeah!" made me smile, but it quickly fell. Moments later, all four guys started talking at once, firing off questions left and right. Then a shrill whistle sounded, and everyone stopped talking. Zane pulled his fingers away from his mouth and shifted his focus my way. "Two questions. One, how? And two, where?"

Grateful I was being asked one question at a time and actually given the chance to *answer*, I replied, "At The Field House. You remember the hot waitress who shot Rhys down?"

The man in question flipped me the bird and murmured, "Yeah. Thanks for bringing that up again. Dick."

I ignored his outburst and continued, "Yeah. Apparently, that was Katie."

Rhys's jaw dropped, and he wordlessly flopped back into the cushions. Zane stared at the far wall like he was trying to solve some impossible equation. Trev shrugged and said, "Well, that was unexpected, but also awesome," before heading to the mini bar for another beer.

Dante summed up the situation when he announced, "Well, fuck me sideways and call me Suzie. I didn't see that one coming. Also, I vaguely recall her being cute, but *damn* if she didn't grow up nice. I was not adequately prepared for that level of hotness."

Dryly chuckling, Rhys looked over at Dante. "You forget dude, out of all of us, I'm the one who was around Katie the most. I'm kind of embarrassed I didn't recognize her. I mean, she was bangin' back then, but it was more of a girl-next-door type of cuteness. I'm not sure what she's been up to since we saw her last, but she's like Victoria's Secret hot now."

Realizing pointing that out was a dick move, Rhys

grimaced at me. "Sorry, dude. Can't help speaking the truth."

"I'm not mad, Rhys. I didn't realize it was her at first either. I mean, I think in the back of my mind I did, but I didn't, ya know?"

Rhys gave me a nod of understanding, and Dante redirected us back to the matter at hand. "Okay, so crazy-hot waitress was Katie. Surprising, but whatever. Is that why you flew out of the VIP area like your ass was on fire?"

There was an unpleasant pang in the vicinity of my heart when I thought about how indifferent Katie had been to my presence, and I grimaced when I recalled the vehemence in her tone when we'd spoken. Offering the CliffsNotes version, I gave my bandmates a quick rundown of everything that happened from the time I left the VIP lounge to when I caught up with her, before finishing with, "And then she told me to go fuck myself."

Trev let loose a low whistle and said, "Well, damn. I think this may be the first time in my recollection that someone mentioned you and 'fuck' in the same sentence and meant it in that particular way. Sexy as hell and resistant to your charms? I think I may be in love."

A surge of jealousy coursed through me at the thought of Katie with someone other than me, taking me by surprise. I was aware when I left that there would never be anyone else for me. Katie was my One, no question about it. She had been the love of my life before, and she was the love of my life now, but I had never had cause to be jealous. She had been mine and I had been hers—there had been no reason for me to worry. Now, though, I definitely had cause for concern.

I took a few calming breaths, reminding myself now was not the time to untangle the web of emotions I was currently stuck in. Trev was only joking, and I needed to hold myself together for the time being. Feeling antsy, I paced back and forth, waiting for either a barrage of questions or some unsolicited advice that would likely do nothing but get me into trouble. When none came, I let my eyes roam around the room to find all of them hunched over silently laughing. Not in the mood for their childish bullshit, I snapped, "What?"

Zane looked me over, realizing I was not in a teasing mood. "So, when it comes to Katie, we do still have some legit feelings?"

Uncomfortable with being put on the spot and still unsure of how to answer, since I hadn't had any time alone to sort out my emotions, I shrugged and gave him the most honest answer I could. "I dunno. It's just...it's Katie. I see her and everything inside me lights up. I'm still just figuring it all out, I guess."

Zane nodded before staring at the wall for a bit, rhythmically drumming his fingers on the table. Once, not long after we met, I asked Zane why he stared off into space so much. He told me that computers ran slower when too many programs were running at the same time and it made it harder to process new information. Back then, I thought he was nuts. Now, I still thought he was nuts, but I also got that this was just his default when he was working through a problem.

After a few minutes, he blinked and rapped his knuckles on the end table to get our attention. "Okay, here's what I'm thinking. This was the last stop on this leg of our

American tour, and we have a couple of months before we have to go over to Europe, right?"

Not knowing where he was going with this, I shrugged and said, "Yeah."

"I know we all had plans for our break, but what do you guys think of staying here instead? I realize Cade can stay behind alone, but based on his progress so far, he's going to need help. Plus, no offense, dude, but you're much more fun when you're with Katie. Solo, you're all whiny and boring. It's depressing."

My first reaction was to shout out *'Hell yeah!'* but I didn't want to influence anyone's decision. We had been touring regularly for the last four years, so time off was a precious commodity. I would fully support whatever my band members chose to do, regardless of if it was what I wanted or not. I held my breath and anxiously awaited their answers.

After a drawn-out pause, Rhys loudly said, "Fuck yeah!"

Dante cracked his knuckles and said, "I'm in."

Trev smiled at me and added, "I can dig spending a few months enjoying some of these Southern belles. So far, I'm loving their specific brand of *hospitality*."

"Grateful" didn't even begin to describe how I was feeling. I had gotten a lot of things wrong in my life, but one thing I'd never regretted was striking up friendships with every member of this band. "Thanks, guys. You all kick ass."

Zane gave me a mischievous grin before clapping and announcing, "Let Operation Fix Cade's Monstrous Fuck-up begin!"

CHAPTER 13

KATIE

"Difficulties are but dares of fate, obstacles but hurdles to try his skill, troubles but bitter tonics to give him strength; and he rises higher and looms greater after each encounter with adversity."

— ELLA WHEELER WILCOX

Three days had passed since my unfortunate run-in with Cade, but for once, I was somewhat confident things were going to go my way. The likelihood of the band still being in town was slim, which meant Finn and I could go back to our regularly scheduled programming. But there was a troublesome twitch in the region of my heart at the idea of never seeing Cade again, and no matter how much I tried to ignore it, it kept coming back.

What are you thinking? You know what kind of devastation that man can rain down. Redoubling my efforts to pull myself out of the funk I'd been in since our "chat," I hummed my go-to happy song, "Wouldn't It be Loverly" from *My Fair Lady*, while making lunch for Finn and myself.

I finished the last verse and smiled to myself. *My Fair Lady* was my mom's and my visual version of comfort food. Anytime one of us had had a bad day, or were feeling crummy, she and I would snuggle up on the couch and laugh at Miss Eliza Doolittle's antics, while we shoved my mom's amazing snicker doodle cookies into our mouths. Even now, anytime something went awry in life, the answer was always baked goods and Eliza Doolittle. *My Fair Lady* hadn't left my DVD player in three days, and I had made so many snicker-doodles I'd run out of flour. More than once.

Cade's sudden appearance had blasted the lid off of my box of memories, and now they were scampering through my subconscious day and night, taunting me with long-forgotten dreams and buried desires. During the day, I could keep myself busy enough to ignore their presence, but at night, when the world was peaceful and quiet, they haunted me. No matter how tired I was, or how much I prayed I would fall into a dreamless sleep, every time I shut my eyes, a montage filled with my best memories of Cade and me danced across my mind. Beating them back into submission was proving to be a much bigger challenge than I had anticipated.

The night of my encounter with Cade, I had been so wound up I hadn't slept at all. The next morning, while chugging coffee, I'd come to terms with the fact that Cadeon Cross was and always would be my Achilles' heel.

The question then became how to deal with him, while not only preserving my sanity but also protecting my traitorous heart, as well as Finn's. So, I made the very adult decision to avoid Cade at all costs, and for the first time in the two years I had been employed at The Field House, I actually called in sick and refused to come in, even in the face of Tom's fury. Twice.

I'd tried for a third time this morning, but Tom had lovingly informed me that "he didn't give a shit if I was on my death bed, I better have my ass there and ready to work by eight p.m. or find a new job." Which was why I was sitting here in the middle of the afternoon contemplating whether or not I *really* needed my job. Too bad I already knew the answer.

Since my unsuccessful call to Tom this morning, I had been feeling on edge. The closer it got to the start of my shift, the heavier the feeling of dread became. I'd managed to make it through one encounter with Cade relatively unscathed, but what if he hadn't left town like I thought? What if he showed up again? Would I be able to keep my distance, or would I crumble? I supposed I would be finding out soon enough.

I wasn't thrilled that the potential possibility of seeing Cade had outweighed my desire to keep building up my savings account, but the knowledge that I had quite a tidy nest egg saved up softened the financial blow. I was proud of the fact that at twenty-two I almost had enough stored away for a down payment on a house in one account and enough to cover tuition for the upcoming semester and then some in a second account.

Layla made fun of my penny-pinching ways, but providing Finn with a home of our own had become a priority for me the moment a pink plus sign popped up on that pregnancy test. The old adage about not knowing how precious something was until it was gone most definitely rang true for me—I hadn't registered how much I'd relied on walking in my door and being enveloped in the feeling of home until I had no home to go to.

When Cade left, I was a complete emotional wreck, and a positive pregnancy test could have completely derailed my life. Instead, it had saved me. The knowledge that I had someone precious who needed me gave me the focus I had lost. I'd spent days pouring over family photos and albums, reminding myself of how amazing and wonderful my parents had been and doing my best to remember all the lessons they had taught me before they died. As I went along, I wrote down memories or things they used to tell me so I could pass them on to Finn as she grew up.

One of my most treasured recollections was the day I had found out that not only did I *not* get into the art program I'd applied for, but that Cade had begun dating the bane of my high school existence. At the time, I thought my world was ending and had come home crying.

My mom had pulled me into her arms and held me until my tears had dried, then she'd cradled my face in her palms and told me, "My precious Katerina, you will find more often than not that life has a tendency to kick you when you're down. But, my beautiful girl, don't ever let it keep you down. Never forget that no matter how dire a situation may seem, you are the brightest of lights and can always find your way."My mother had been a force to be reckoned with, always forging her own path, and had raised me to fearlessly pursue my dreams.

Fueled by my desire to take charge of my life and build something beautiful for Finn and me, I had created a list of goals. The first thing on my list was graduating high school. Thanks to my desire to avoid being anywhere in the vicinity of my uncle, I had completed several required courses in summer school—plus a correspondence course or two—putting me on track to graduate when the semester ended a few weeks later.

College was an absolute must for me, so after a ton of research, I had chosen a school far from Colorado where I could start fresh. The university not only had an amazing reputation, but also happened to offer an affordable child-care program. Selecting my major had been a bit difficult, because rather than going with my passion for art, I forced myself to choose from career options that would be financially sound enough to support Finn and myself. When Finn looked back on our lives when she was older, I wanted her to have me and my mom as examples that just because life threw twists and turns your way, it didn't mean you couldn't still accomplish amazing things.

Thus far, I was on track with every goal I'd put down on my sheet. Unfortunately, I wanted to stay on track, I did, sadly, need to keep my job. So, my three days of refuge with Finn would be ending in a few short hours when I went in for my evening shift. For now, at least I had a little more time to squeeze in some last-minute snuggles before I headed back into the lion's den.

The *ding* of the timer drew my attention, and I pulled the sheet tray from the oven, then put Finn in her highchair. Once I slid the tray on, I went about setting bite-size pieces of grilled chicken, green beans and applesauce on her favorite pink unicorn plate before placing it in front of her. Finn scrunched up her face in displeasure at the offerings and pushed her food around a few times before proudly stating, "I full Mama. Now, I hab ice creen?"

I crossed my arms and looked down at her still full plate, then at her angelic face. "No, ma'am. No ice cream until you finish your lunch."

Finn stuck her lip out and began frantically blinking, trying to draw out some fake tears in hopes that I would give in. Alas, this was not my first rodeo, so before she got too worked up, I pointed at her plate and said, "Finn can either eat her lunch like a big girl and get ice cream, or she can go have a timeout then come eat her lunch with no ice cream. Pick one."

Her intense blue eyes stared at me, judging my level of flexibility on the matter. Finding no wiggle room, she gave me an irritated huff before shoving a few green beans in her mouth. Thirty minutes later, I finished wiping the melted ice cream off her face before picking her up and carrying her toward her room.

"Okay, pretty girl," I cooed. "It's time to lie down, princess. Mommy has to go to work, so she won't be here when you get up, but Mrs. J will be here. Okay?"

Finn sleepily looked up at me and nodded before curling her arm around my neck and tucking her head into my shoulder. I hummed quietly, swaying back and forth until I felt her tiny body begin to relax, and then kissed her on top of her chocolate curls one last time before laying her in her crib. An hour or so later, I grabbed my bag and gave Mrs. J a hug before heading out the door.

I opened my locker and snagged a couple of ibuprofen to help stave off the headache that had been brewing all day. Deciding I might as well make the best use of my impromptu break, I also picked up my makeup bag for a quick touch-up.

I had just finished adding a bit more powder to my forehead, when Layla dramatically announced, "Praise Jesus! Believe in the Lord, for He hath delivered fresh from her deathbed a Miss Katerina Troyer. He hath blessed her with health and happiness so she could join us from the grave and live again!"

Snorting at her ridiculousness, I glanced over to find her standing next to me with her eyes closed, holding her arms above her head, slowly waving them back and forth while she mumbled nonsense about "raining down the Holy Spirit."

"Lay, you are ridiculous. God, I missed your weird ass."

Her face split into a broad grin, and she rushed over to give me a hug. "I missed you too, girlfriend. Though, just to check, you weren't really dying, were you? 'Cause that was a legit concern, and if you ever did die, then I would feel obligated to do myself in so I could haunt your ass and make you miserable for all eternity for crossing over without my permission."

I set my mascara down and looked at Layla like she was nuts. "That...that doesn't even make any sense. Like, at all. But I suppose I feel flattered? Also, no, I wasn't dying; I just felt like I needed some zen."

Layla's neon-purple nails glittered in the fluorescent

lights as they moved back and forth in a slow clap. "Thank you! Ry and I have only been telling you for the last year to take a break. 'Cause damn girl, you hardly ever go out or anything. You're either working your ass off here, home with my little lady love, or studying your ass off. Hell, at this point, with all the studying and working you do, it's a miracle you even have an ass."

She pulled me into a quick side hug and went on. "Honestly, you are the most grandma-like twenty-two-year-old I've ever met, and seeing as how we encounter several hundred college students every day, that's saying something. For reals, though, I'm glad you took some time to yourself. You deserved it."

Personal time wasn't high on my list of priorities, but even I realized it was necessary on occasion. As for the rest, I just shrugged and said, "I know the way I do things isn't typical for someone my age, or particularly fun for that matter, but my situation isn't the norm either. For most college students, their biggest worry is getting an invite to the end-of-year bash the frat's throw or if they are going to pass their classes. I have to make sure to stay on track so I can guarantee Finn has the life and stability she needs and deserves."

"I know I don't take a lot of time for myself, but what would I do with more free time anyway? I have zero interest in dating anyone, and most college guys aren't equipped to handle a three-year-old. My life may be boring, but I like it, Lay. I've got money in the bank, I'm one year away from graduating, and I have you, Ryan, Finn, and Mrs. J. I'm good."

Layla's ice-blue eyes warmed with affection, and she

pulled me into a bear hug. When she released me, she gave me a lopsided smile. "You know I like to tease, but you are one badass mama. If our positions were reversed, I'm not sure I could have handled it the way you did. When I grow up, I want to be you."

I gave her a wink, then flipped my ponytail over my shoulder and said, "I promise, you would have handled it just fine—you never give yourself enough credit. Now, move your fine ass out of my way. This mama needs to go fetch some tips!"

~

Cade

One of the large, black doors began to swing open, and I jumped off the barstool so fast I almost knocked it over in my haste to get closer. *Come on, come on...there!* With a glorious smile on her face, Katie confidently strode into the main area of the floor and paused to talk to the bouncer who'd threatened me earlier. I wasn't sure what they were discussing, but whatever he said made her smile instantly vanish. Not even a second later, her furious green gaze clashed with mine.

I had assumed she would avoid me like last time, so I was taken aback when Katie stormed across the bar and stopped directly in front of me. Not wanting to miss the first window of opportunity I'd had for days, I began rapidly speaking. "Katie! I know you're mad, but I need to explain. I—"

Before I could finish my sentence, two palms connected with my chest with surprising strength and shoved me back into the bar. Eyes blazing, Katie bit out, "No."

A rebuttal hung on my lips, and I opened my mouth, prepared to argue my point, but she cut me off. "I said, no! You seem to be under the impression that you have the right to barge into my life whenever it suits you and tell me what to do. Well, I have some news for you, you raging asshole."

She sucked in a breath and jabbed me in the chest with her finger before going on. "I don't owe you shit. Do you understand me? I may have thought you hung the moon before, but I am a far cry from the naive little girl you abandoned in her bed. And you, sir, and whatever pathetic excuse or explanation you think you have, are not worth my time."

Her icy expression took me aback, and I was scrambling, trying to think of a way to gain some ground, but she wouldn't give an inch. Her eyes narrowed, and she took a few steps forward, trapping me between her rage and the hard surface of the bar top.

"As far as I am concerned, you and your big-ass bodyguard..." Her frosty gaze whipped over to D, and she rolled her eyes in response to whatever expression he was wearing. "Yes, I mean you. You're not exactly freaking stealthy back there, Jolly Green."

She paused a beat before continuing, "Can take a flying leap. Get the fuck out of my bar and out of my life. As far as I'm concerned, you can straight-up kiss my ass, and I sincerely hope karma gives you a wave and guarantees that whatever woman's snatch you decide to crawl into this evening gifts you with the sensation of violent burning every time you need to pee."

The word "burning" in combination with anything involving my nether regions made me wince. Katie gave me a satisfied smirk before shoving past me up to the bar. After a moment of silent communication, the bartender filled a shot glass with tequila and wordlessly slid it across the bar top.

Katie looked around to check for prying eyes and must have decided she was in the clear because seconds later, she'd downed the shot like a champ. Her eyes closed, and she inhaled deeply before gradually exhaling.

Upon opening her eyes, the expression of animosity she'd been wearing was gone, replaced by a cheery smile that didn't reach her eyes. She tightened her ponytail and tugged her shirt down before moving past me and heading out into the crowd.

Sensing his significant presence next to me, I mumbled, "What's up, D?"

His dark-brown eyes were full of pity as he placed a hand the size of a Volkswagen Beetle on my shoulder and gave me a comforting pat. "Well, Mr. Cross"—the deep bass of his voice vibrated inside my skull—"normally, I keep my opinions to myself, but I'm gonna go out on a limb here 'cause it seems like you need some advice. Boy, when you piss off a woman so badly she sincerely wishes you'd procure a case of the clap, it may be time to take a breather and re-evaluate your game plan."

Sighing, I ran a hand through my hair, tugging at the strands. I knew I fucked up, leaving the way I did. It had been a dick move from a frightened, naive boy who had backed himself into a corner because he was too stupid to consider the potential repercussions of his actions.

I had known there was a massive chance Katie would think I was a piece of shit, but goddamn did it sting like a motherfucker to hear it. The worst part was, I couldn't disagree. She didn't owe me. Self-preservation demanded I do as she asked and leave her be. But sitting here, watching her, I just...couldn't. *Which made me an even bigger asshole. Awesome.*

"I don't have a game plan, D. Trying to talk to her again *was* my game plan. I don't suppose you happen to have any ideas for a plan B, do you? You did graduate from that fancy-ass smart-people school after all, right?"

D gave me an arch stare, informing me that he was done talking. Tonight was a bust. "Let's head back, and we'll see if the guys have any ideas."

CHAPTER 14

> "You gave me the key to your heart, my love,
> then why did you make me knock?"
>
> — GEORGE GORDON BYRON

I looked down at the paper clinched in my hand one last time and glanced at the numbers on the door, confirming I was at the right place, before slipping it into my pocket. After taking a deep breath, I braced myself for the worst, raised my hand, and knocked.

The sound of footsteps greeted my ears seconds before the door was pulled open, and I was met with the sight of a sexy, relaxed Katie. Her mass of raven hair was pulled up a messy bun with a few strands hanging loose, framing her heart-shaped face. Her sun-kissed skin was scrubbed clean of any makeup, making her appear younger and more vulnerable than the woman I'd encountered at the bar.

The lack of makeup in combination with her adorable black cat-eye-style glasses made her seem much softer and more touchable than the sexy siren at The Field House. This Kat I was familiar with, and for the first time in days, I was standing on solid ground. She was the girl I knew and loved so dearly, and seeing her again sent relief and longing coursing through my veins.

Seeing her here, stripped-down, lounging in black cotton shorts and an over-sized *Doctor Who* T-shirt, was like walking through a door to the past and into the life I had before. This Kat was the girl who'd told me silly stories every time I was nervous, the one who'd helped me TP Mr. Kenner's yard after he got me grounded for two weeks in junior high, who'd held my hand while getting my cast put on when I broke my arm in sixth grade.

This Kat was my first meaningful kiss, my first intimate touch, my first love. She was all the best parts of my soul reflected in another person, and sitting here facing her again was as agonizing as it was exhilarating.

Her eyes were wary when she popped a hand on her hip. She let out an exasperated sigh and asked, "What do you want, Cade?"

Not wanting to miss the only opening I was likely to have, particularly because she was being civil for the first time in recent memory, I quickly replied, "To talk. That's it. I just want to talk to you. Please."

She studied me for another moment or two, and the indecision in those emerald orbs killed me. Physically seeing her war between the desire to slam the door in my face and the desire to sate her curiosity and talk to me was painful— especially since I wasn't sure which way she would swing. Relief swamped me when she stepped back, pulled the door open wide, and said, "Come in, Cade," before turning and walking away.

My eyes followed her retreating form as I stepped into her small apartment and quietly shut the door behind me. After a beat, she tossed over her shoulder, "Have a seat, but don't get too comfortable, because you will not be staying long. I'll be out in a second—I have a feeling this conversation is going to require some liquid patience on my part."

"I suggest while I'm preoccupied that you figure out the least creepy way to explain to me how in the hell you found out where I live. Then you can follow that up with the CliffsNotes version of whatever is so damned important that you resorted to stalker-like behavior to tell me about it. I have shit to do, and your time is limited."

With that warning hanging in the air, she strode over to the kitchen counter and busied herself with making coffee, leaving me alone in her living room. Closing my eyes, I reviewed the list the guys and I had made last night.

Step 1: Gain access to the castle grounds—Check.

Step 2: Learn as much about the princess as possible; inside information is invaluable.

Step 3: Use the aforementioned information to infiltrate the princess's tower.

This was the perfect opportunity to enact the beginnings of Step 2, so I surveyed the space.

The apartment wasn't large, but everywhere I looked, there were touches of Katie. The sofa, while seeming to be well-worn, was covered with a pale-gray slipcover. Teal accent pillows and a velvety teal blanket laying across the back added pops of color. Twin end tables flanked the sofa, each one painted a soft white with a teal drawer, perfectly matching a small entertainment center positioned in the center of the wall across from the couch.

An older TV took up most of the space on top, with a worn DVD player and neatly stacked DVDs beneath it. I pondered taking a step closer to peruse the movie titles to see what she liked now, but decided against it. The last thing I needed was for her to come out and find me snooping. Adjacent to the sofa sat a teal armchair with a fuzzy gray blanket tossed over the back. Katie's place was warm, cozy, and peaceful—just like I'd always imagined our house would have been.

The sputtering of the coffee pot pulled my attention toward the kitchen. Two dark-gray bar stools were lined up underneath a short breakfast bar, and a small white dining table sat in the tiny dining room to my left. A bright-pink high chair sitting next to the table caught my gaze, and I stared at it but couldn't figure out why Katie would have a highchair at her place.

Katie had always been a sucker for kids, so maybe she babysat a lot? Or maybe she had a roommate with a kid? Zane hadn't said anything about a roomie when he'd slipped me the note with her address on it, but I supposed she could have someone staying here who wasn't on the lease.

I was still staring at the out-of-place pink chair when the sound of a throat clearing made me jump. Nervous, I shoved my hands in my pockets and shifted my gaze to find Katie leaning against the counter, cradling a steaming cup of coffee in her delicate hands. It did not go unnoticed by me that she hadn't offered to make me a cup, further reinforcing that she was dead serious when she'd told me I would not be staying. Too bad for her I intended to be here as long as possible.

She raised the cup to her lips and took a sip, before setting it on the counter and glancing at the clock hanging on her kitchen wall then back at me. Her arms crossed protectively around her middle, creating a barrier between us. "You're running on borrowed time here, Cade. I suggest that if you have something to say, you say it."

I had to tread carefully. I wiped my suddenly sweaty palms on my jeans, taking one last second to bolster my courage before I began. "Kit-Kat, first off, I am so sorry."

She shifted, and her full lips parted. Guessing she was getting ready to interrupt, I held out a hand. "Wait! Just let me say what I need to say, then you can have your turn, okay?"

Her eyes narrowed as she scrutinized me. Finally, she nodded, and I let out the breath I'd been been holding.

"I'm sorry for giving off stalker vibes—I swear that wasn't my intention. I really needed to talk to you, and since you kept avoiding me or shutting me down, I had to think outside of the box. I'm not proud of it, but I bribed Zane to dig up your address with twelve boxes of Gushers, two liters of Mountain Dew, and a promise that if you forgave me you would paint him a portrait of his dog. I know it's creepy as hell, but no one at your work would tell me where to find you, and I was desperate."

The irritated expression on her face did not instill any confidence in me that this was working, but I powered on. "Second, leaving you that way was a dick move. I didn't want to leave like that. Honestly, I didn't want to leave at all, but I didn't have a choice. You know some of the story, but I never told you the whole thing. After all we've been through, if there is one thing I owe you more than anything else, it's the truth about what was going on and why I left without a word."

I paused, needing a moment to organize my thoughts. I was only going to get one shot at telling her everything. I had to get it right. "Do you remember when I flew out to meet Rhys and the guys in San Diego a couple of months before I left?"

"Yes. And?"

She waved impatiently, trying to hurry me along, so I casually slid my hands into my back pockets and rocked back on my heels. I knew I shouldn't bait her, especially since I was here to see if I could earn my way back into her good graces, but I couldn't help needling her just a little.

"Well, what I didn't tell you is that while we were there to chill and hang out on the beach, the main purpose of the trip was to weasel our way into a meeting with Soundscapes International. We had been sending out demos left and right—which I know you remember because you spent hours helping me address and mail them—but we weren't getting any bites."

"The band and I decided we needed to figure out who we wanted to sign with and make them listen to us, so once we had our sights set on Soundscapes, we coordinated work schedules and bought plane tickets. I didn't bother to say anything to you, because I figured our likelihood of success was slim to none. I thought if I told you, it would make it more real and the sting of rejection and failure would be worse when they said no."

Nervous about how she would take the next part, I

began to pace. Up until then, the story was merely a telling of the beginning of Devil's Cross, but the easy part was coming to an end, and it was time to actually discuss what had happened in the weeks just before I left and why I'd felt I had no choice but to go.

Bracing myself, I said, "Well, we did manage to make it in and play for them, and while they took our info, we didn't hear anything else. Assuming they didn't want to sign us, I came home and more or less forgot about the whole thing. A few weeks later, we got a call from the label. They told us that after reviewing our demo one more time, they were interested in signing us."

"The guys and I talked and accepted, then everything spun out of control. We didn't have a manager, and the timeline was tight, so we—being young and dumb—let the label refer us to one. They gave us over to Bryce Windsor, who, while a genius at making bands huge, was also a controlling ass. Within days of signing contracts with them both, we had pages and pages of rules we had to abide by, and since each item had been stealthily worked into the contract through some crazy tiny fine print, we weren't able to refuse anything."

The rapid tapping of her toe against the laminate floors echoed around the apartment, and Katie set her empty mug down before turning to face me again. "Well, as entertaining as your story was, if I wanted a play-by-play of how you got signed, I could have asked Google. None of that explains why you're here. In my house. Uninvited. So, I suggest you get to the damn point."

I'd hoped her letting me in had been an olive branch, but she was still as prickly as ever, and talking to her was like swimming upstream—no matter how hard I tried, I was getting nowhere. It didn't help that my desire to explain myself was warring with a deeply embedded need to embrace Katie and make the distance between us disappear.

I wanted to pull her into my arms and remind her of how perfect we were together. To make her remember when we had lain next to each other under the velvety night sky, whispering about our hopes and dreams; to recall all the promises we had made. I had ruined that, though, and the reminder that I was the one who broke us apart cooled my growing ire. I closed my eyes and counted to five before exhaling and letting the last bits of my frustration go.

"Like I said before, we were young and dumb. None of us had anyone read over the contract before we signed. We never thought the label would essentially make us their bitches, and we certainly weren't prepared for the level of control they had over not only our music, but also us individually. We should have dedicated as much time to researching the process of being signed and what it would mean for us and our band as we did to creating music, but we were too focused on the ultimate goal to look at the pitfalls. There was a clause in the contract enabling Soundscapes and Bryce to have extensive control over our public images."

"Bryce informed us that attractive—and more importantly single—guys sold albums. Whether we liked it or not, as far as the public was concerned, for the foreseeable future, we all had to consider ourselves unattached. I was the only one of us in a long-term relationship, so the only one his decree directly affected was me. Not knowing what else to do, I talked to my dad about it, and he told me to do what my heart said was right."

The next part of the story was going to be the "make it or break it" part, and the possibility that Katie might decide what I had done was unforgivable was terrifying. Anxiety roiled in my gut at the knowledge that I could lose her for good if I handled this poorly.

If everything went sideways, this would be the very last time she even allowed me anywhere near her, and I would be damned if I spent what might be my last few minutes in her presence across the room. Not wanting her to feel cornered, I gingerly approached Katie and paused for a beat before cautiously reaching out to grasp her hands.

I had been fighting a burning need to touch her since I'd set foot in this apartment, but as soon as the scent of honey and peaches hit my nose, the battle was lost. The moment our fingertips touched, a zing of painfully familiar electricity shot up my arm. Amazed that it hadn't seemed to dull over time, I held her hands tighter, letting the tingles of awareness dance across my skin. Her soft gasp and startled expression let me know she still felt it too. *Thank God.*

Katie immediately began to pull away. Not ready to let the moment end, I squeezed her hands and silently pleaded for her to give me just a little longer. She bit her lip and canted her head to the side but relented and twined her fingers with mine. Her skin was still velvety soft, but there were small callouses that were new, and I noticed a few thin white scars that also hadn't been there before and wondered where they had come from.

Katie's hands felt the same in mine, but the girl attached to them was not. I knew so very little about this adult version of her. I wasn't sure how she'd learned to school her expressions so well, or when she'd morphed from a shy wallflower into a fearsome temptress. If asked, I would not be able to share the story of how she'd gotten the tiny scar below her left eye, or explain why I didn't see a single piece of her artwork adorning the walls. There was so much I didn't know, but I did know I would sacrifice everything I had and everything I was to learn it all.

Any other person in my shoes would be grateful she was letting him touch her at all, and I was, but I was also a selfish bastard. I wanted more. Hell, I wanted it all, but I had a long road to travel before I got there. For now, though, I wanted a taste of those full lips. Trying for a kiss was a risky endeavor, but in the past, every time Katie was being difficult or I had screwed up, she always softened whenever her lips touched mine. Plus, if this didn't go according to plan, I wasn't sure if I would ever have another opportunity to steal a kiss.

Heart pounding, I released one of her hands so I could cup her cheek. Her eyes widened a fraction, but she didn't move to stop me, so I slowly raised the hand still wrapped in my own, placed a kiss on top of it, and laid it over my racing heart.

Her brow scrunched in confusion, so I paused, letting her decide if she would let it remain there. When she didn't pull away, I stepped close enough to feel the heat from her body penetrate my own, but my progress was stopped when she asked, "Why did you stop? With the story, I mean."

A litany of curses sounded in my head, but she was right —I did need to keep going. Voice soft, I said, "I knew what was right, and what he was asking me to do? To pretend like you weren't my world? I couldn't do that. Not to you. So, I called him and told him no. I told him I would pretend in public, but you were my girl. Period. If he thought I would let you go, he was insane. He didn't take being told no well, and the conversation swiftly regressed into screams and curses on both our parts."

Gingerly, she placed her hands on my waist, and her body softened ever so slightly. Her faraway expression made me think that maybe she was lost in the sea of our memories too. Having her so near without touching her the way I wanted to was wreaking havoc with my self-control, particularly because until now, I hadn't needed to worry about keeping myself in check when Katie and I were together.

My eyes locked onto her mouth, and I was doing my best to force my gaze away from temptation, when her tongue darted out and she licked her bottom lip. *Oh, hell.* Giving up on keeping my distance, I sent up a silent prayer that I would leave with my balls intact, before pulling her close and running my thumb across her full lower lip.

Her breath hitched, and her emerald gaze darkened to a deep forest green. I paused a moment, enjoying the anticipation shining in the clear depths of her eyes before I gave up the fight. Her full lips were beckoning, calling to me like a siren song I was helpless to resist. Lost to the moment and the memories, and plagued with soul-deep longing, I closed the distance, softly brushing her lips with my own.

Katie stiffened for a moment, making me rethink this decision, before relaxing and opening her lips on a sigh. Not one to miss an opportunity, I deepened the kiss, giving her tongue languid laps with my own.

All too quickly, my innocent kiss took on a life of its own. Years of pent-up feelings rose to the surface, and soon our bodies were plastered together, as I nipped and licked up the column of her slender neck. If her quiet pants and my growing erection were any indication, things were shifting from a tender kiss to something more at a rapid clip. As much as I wanted to spend the night buried between her thighs—and I *really* wanted to spend the night buried between her thighs—that was not part of today's plan.

My ultimate goal was to make amends and convince her to rekindle old feelings, not to tumble into her bed at the first opportunity and then have it be written off as a mistake. Kicking myself in the ass in advance for this monumentally shitty decision, I groaned and pulled my lips away from hers, giving her one final peck before dropping my hands and stepping back.

Still panting and battling the hard-on from hell, I felt a kick of masculine pride when I took in her flushed face and swollen mouth. Kat's eyes lazily roamed down my body, pausing an extra second when she reached the visible tent in my pants. She arched her brow and gave me a sassy smirk before leaning against the counter and crossing her arms. All too soon, her smile slipped, and our magic moment faded away. "That was a mistake, Cade. We can't do that again. It was amazing, don't get me wrong, but we can't."

Irritated that she was able to dismiss me so quickly, and bristling at the idea of anything involving the two of us being labeled a mistake, I bit back the retort sitting on the tip of my tongue. I had things that needed to be said, and lashing out because something didn't go my way wouldn't do me any favors.

Needing some distance between us, I wandered over to the window and watched people milling about for a moment before I started talking again. "Finally, he snapped. He told me that regardless of what my unsupportive family thought, I had contractual obligations I'd agreed to uphold."

Life was made up of choices, and when it came to this, I had made the wrong one. Even if one day Katie did forgive me and we worked everything out, this conversation and the choices I'd made thereafter would always haunt me. Katie needed to grasp how hard leaving her was for me, and that it was the only option I thought I had at the time.

"Bryce then proceeded to tell me that romance and rockstars didn't mix, and that he would be damned if some high school crush ruined his aspirations of managing this generation's 'it' band. In the coldest tone I'd ever heard, he told me I was the lead singer of the label's newest cash cow, and I would do as I was told. I was to leave everyone in Creede behind; otherwise, he would use his extensive resources to destroy everyone I ever cared about, starting with you."

"I was terrified. I didn't see a way out, and I couldn't risk calling his bluff, not with people who were so dear to me. I tried so hard to think of something, *anything* to get out of it, but our contract was airtight, and Bryce was not known for his kindness. I'd signed my soul over to the devil without even realizing it, and I would be damned if my poor choices caused you harm. So, I left."

CHAPTER 15

CADE

— ALFRED LORD TENNYSON

The clock showed it had been a solid five minutes since I'd finished my explanation and Katie hadn't uttered a single word or bothered to look in my direction. The silence was agonizing, and the longer it went on, the more the tiny spark of hope I had dimmed. Seconds stretched by as she avoided my gaze, and my heart was pounding against my ribs so hard, I was surprised she couldn't hear it even all the way across the room.

Breathing became harder and harder, and I was convinced I was about to experience my very first panic attack if something didn't break the tension soon. My fingers tapped against my thigh, and I did my best to focus on taking deep breaths while impatiently waiting for her to decide whether she would ask me to stay or tell me to go. I prayed she would go with the first option and give me the opening I desperately needed to try and repair what I had broken, but my window of opportunity was rapidly closing.

Finally, she quit pacing and stopped to face me. Her hands settled on her hips, and anger burned in her gaze. My anxiety gave way to fear. Before, whenever Katie had gotten angry enough to whip out the fury, she always put her hands on her hips. I'd jokingly dubbed it her "power pose," but now, when I was the target of her rage, the pose was decidedly less amusing.

"So, let me get this straight." The sarcasm in her voice did not bode well for me. "You, without bothering to discuss it with the person you planned to "marry and make babies with," decided to make a life-altering decision and sign a legally binding contract. A contract that you *did not bother to fucking read*. Then, rather than owning up to the situation and discussing it with your parents and me, you decided the appropriate action was to leave a shitty letter that didn't tell me a damn thing, save for the fact that you were "sorry" and then slip off into the night."

Each statement, and the vehemence with which they were delivered, hit like a physical blow. My choices had stemmed from being young and inexperienced, and I had hoped she would be able to look at things from the perspective of a terrified nineteen-year-old.

Looking back, I realized I had made all the wrong choices, and I was aware that if the same situation arose now, I would handle everything completely differently. People always say hindsight was twenty-twenty, yet, after having Katie tell me to my face what an immature douche I had been, I decided hindsight was also a spiteful bitch.

Katie had always gotten her point across, but she used to pull her punches when I'd upset or angered her. She sure as hell wasn't now. I'd take it though; I'd stand here and take whatever she needed.

If she felt the need to give me more verbal beatdowns? Fine. Scream, yell, curse my name? No problem. Hell, I'd let her get a punch or two in if necessary. As long as she was still there when the dust settled, I could take anything she wanted to dish out.

Realization dawned that I was losing whatever paltry ground I had gained earlier, so I started grasping at straws. Pathetically, all I could come up with was "No. You didn't miss anything. But remember, I was a nineteen-year-old kid who made a terrible choice. At the time, I thought that was the only thing I could do to protect you. Looking back now, I know I did have options, and I didn't pick the right one. I get that it was shitty. What I did was a complete dick move, but I'm here now, and I'm trying. Please, let that count for something."

She hugged her torso and scoffed at me. "Cade, I would have forgiven everything if you had shown up and apologized six months after you left. Hell, I would have welcomed you with open arms had you popped up on my doorstep a year later. I wouldn't have cared if I got an explanation—I would have been happy that you came back. But you *didn't*."

"Instead, you changed your phone number and your email to make sure you couldn't be bothered. You performed, you drank, you partied, and you forgot about me. Truthfully, I'm not quite sure why you're here now. You wanted to explain why you left? Mission accomplished. Now I think it's time for you to leave."

I wasn't ready to admit defeat, and I sure as hell wasn't ready to let her go. One of the only things Katie had ever asked of me was complete honesty. I had always struggled with the ability to be vulnerable, and as I had developed the thicker skin needed to live life in the spotlight, that struggle became even harder, but for Katie I would try.

Laying myself bare at her feet, I said, "Every decision I made that first year was horrible. I had been trying to protect everyone by leaving, but instead all that did was cause everyone I loved pain. In my immature brain, I thought a clean break would be best for you, the whole 'out of sight, out of mind' thing. I figured not hearing from me and being unable to reach me would somehow help you move on. I didn't want you to derail your life because of me; you were meant for so much more than I could give you then."

Her gaze traveled all over the room, looking anywhere but at me, but I could tell by the way that she cocked her head that she was listening.

I took a tentative step in her direction and continued, "It took me twelve months before I felt it was safe enough to contact my family, and another six months before I'd mended my broken relationship with them. But even then, I couldn't go to you. I was ashamed of my actions and so damned afraid of what Bryce would do."

"Every time I thought of home or heard my mom's voice or texted Casey, I thought about you, always wondering about you, hoping that you were okay and happy. Thinking about you, about what we'd had, and what I'd lost, hurt so damned bad. Whenever your image popped into my mind, I ached. Missing you was a gaping, festering wound, and every time I prodded at those feelings, blood would start spilling everywhere."

Recalling those dark days filled me with shame, but Katie had earned the right to know all the unpleasant details of my lowest moments, so I went on. "Without you, all the color had been sucked out of the world, and I was floating in a sea of gray. I couldn't handle the pain of missing such a vital part of my soul. I was so damned depressed mourning for what I had lost. All I wanted was to drink the emptiness away. So, I did."

Katie's eyes shimmered with unshed tears as she looked at me with pity before saying, "Oh, Cade."

I crossed my arms protectively around my core, hoping to ease the feeling of being emotionally exposed. I might perform for arenas filled with thousands of fans, but to them, I was not a vulnerable man. I was a confident rock god who could strut across the stage and win the hearts of thousands with nothing more than a smirk. I was untouchable, standing there under the blazing lights, which was how they wanted to see me.

None of them cared about the man underneath the swagger, so I had stopped taking off that mask a long time ago. What Kat hadn't yet grasped, was that she was the only person I was willing to expose my tender underbelly to, and it was up to me to show her that.

Wrung out from the emotional roller coaster the last few days had been, I leaned against the kitchen table, suddenly weary. Part of me wanted to stop talking, not wanting to admit how bad things had gotten, but the rest of me understood I would not win back her trust with half-truths.

"After some time passed, I realized I was cruising down the road toward addiction at light speed. I started my day with a bottle of Jack and ended it wherever I blacked out. I sang shows I don't remember, and woke up most days not knowing where I was or who I was with. When I passed out and missed a radio appearance and then was too drunk to perform when we were recording, the guys sat me down and told me I needed to get my shit together before I surpassed their ability to help me."

"They were right. I needed to stop. So, I decided to pretend that what we had wasn't real. Convinced myself that ours was simply a fleeting first love, and that one day we would each meet our *real* forever people and laugh together over the absurdity of our youth. I shoved us in a box, locked it up tight, and buried it in the deep recesses of my mind, too afraid of the possible repercussions to take it out and dust it off."

"The thing is, though, you were my light, and even under layers of dirt and grime, you still shone through the cracks. Each year that light got brighter and brighter, pulling me in, reminding me of who I used to be. Eventually, it got to the point where I couldn't lie to myself anymore, and I had to find you. I had to reach you, to explain, and to beg your forgiveness. Because now, all these years later, after everything, I still look at you and see *home.*"

Stripped bare, I let my chin drop to my chest, hoping with everything I had that my confession had been enough. Katie's arms wrapped around my shoulders, and the panic clawing at me eased. She gave me a gentle squeeze, settled in next to me, and rested her head on my shoulder.

She stared off into the distance, unraveling all I had told her before quietly saying, "Cade, I'm not saying I don't understand, and I'm not saying your apology isn't genuine, but there's so much hurt. One apology, no matter how sincere, isn't going to undo all the pain. You *left* me, Cade. You left me naked and alone with no rhyme or reason *on our anniversary*. I wasn't even important enough to warrant an actual explanation—all I got was a note that set fire to my world and didn't explain why you had to light the match. The only thing that was clear to me was that the person who made my world go 'round had abandoned me like last week's trash."

She tucked a stray hair behind her ear and began to pace. "Cade, when you left, not only did you shatter my heart, you stole my safety net. The future I'd clung so tightly to while living with that unstable man was gone. I was left alone in that goddamned house, all but forgotten by the *one person* I'd trusted to love and protect me. I was too hurt and too ashamed to allow myself to consider calling your family, so I sat there lonely and depressed, wondering where it had gone wrong. I see you, and my heart screams *mine*, and I want to believe it so bad, but I don't know if I can."

I'd thought I had understood being broken before, but nothing had prepared me for seeing the pain and devastation written all over Katie's face as she told me how alone she had been. I had failed her in more ways than I'd even realized, and in the process, I had forever altered the person I'd left to protect.

I had no right to ask her right now, but so help me God, one day she would trust me enough to tell me what happened to her when she was living with her uncle after I'd left—no matter how painful it was for me to hear. The need to comfort her was instinctual, and I released a relieved sigh when she let me put my arm around her shoulders and tuck her into my side.

My throat burned, and my heart ached with the knowledge that I had damaged someone so precious to me. "I'm sorry, Katie. I failed you in every single way that counted, but I loved you. God, I loved you so much. You can doubt me, but please never doubt how much I cared about you. Then, or now."

She squeezed my bicep to let me know she heard me, then mumbled, almost as an afterthought, "I don't want you to think things were all bad, like I withered without you. It took a little time, but I learned I could be okay alone. I was okay. You taught me a valuable lesson about not relying on other people to be my savior. A person should be able to save themselves, because inevitably other people will let them down anyway."

Her shoulders rose as she shrugged, then she glanced up at me, and her lips tilted into a small smile. "I suppose, in the grand scheme of things, you did me a favor. I was naive before, looking at the world with rose-colored glasses. At least now I see things for what they are, rather than how I wish they would be. Thank you, I guess?"

My heart cracked. One of my favorite things about Katie had been her unfailing optimism. No matter how bad things were, she always found the bright side. My mom had nicknamed her Pollyanna when we were children after Casey had broken my mom's favorite vase and Katie had informed her, *"But it's better this way! Now you can remake it any way you want, and it will be prettier than before!"*.

Katie was the person who always looked forward, who found the best in everyone and everything. Now, my optimist had been replaced with a realist. Her rosy view was now jaded, and the only person I had to blame was myself. I'd never felt more like a pathetic, unworthy human being in my life.

Hollow and numb, I absently rubbed the vacant spot in my chest where my heart used to live. I couldn't keep the utter defeat from my voice when I said, "I never meant to take away your optimism, Katie. I was trying to do the right thing, and instead I screwed everything up. I understand how messed up it was for me to show up now and think an apology was going to fix everything, and I get why you would be hesitant to give me a second chance. I won't bother you again, I swear. I'll just...I'll just go."

I let my eyes travel down her perfect face one last time, the same way I had so long ago. This time was different though—she wasn't peacefully sleeping, dreaming about our future together. No, now she was standing here, fully aware of what this moment meant, doing nothing to stop me from walking out of her front door and her life forever.

When I'd climbed out her window, the hope that our story wasn't finished had dulled the pain. Now, the agony was almost debilitating, but the blame sat squarely on my shoulders. The least I could do was minimize Katie's guilt and keep my shit together until I left the building. Turning to go, I sucked in a fortifying breath and focused on placing one foot in front of the other, hoping I could hold myself together until I got to the parking lot.

CHAPTER 16

KATIE

> "The only way to make sense out of change is to plunge into it, move with it, and join the dance."
>
> — ALAN WATTS

I felt awful. My intention was to ease the sting of my words, to somehow absolve him of some of the guilt he'd been toting around. His explanation was by no means perfect—nor entirely sufficient, all things considered—but I had an unyielding need to soothe him.

Yet all my statement had done was make it worse. I blamed that kiss. I had forgotten how scrambled my brain became as soon as his lips touched mine, and it irritated me to no end that he still affected me on such a visceral level.

Even now, the ghost of his lips moving across my own haunted me, making gathering my thoughts almost impossible. The harder I tried to focus, the more my brain kept circling back to how good it had been to have his lips on mine and how soothing it was to be in his arms again. Thinking of his embrace made it damned hard to recall why he and I were a bad bet, but now was not the time to let myself melt—this conversation was too important.

This discussion had been a long time coming, and though it was terrible that my frankness upset Cade, I was not going to apologize for my feelings. Some words I'd meant to hurt, wanting to wound him the way he had wounded me. Others I had hoped would soften the sting of the truth. I had to admit, though, seeing his expression shift from repentant yet hopeful to looking like I'd broken into his house and made him watch as I set every instrument he owned on fire made me want to cry.

"Cade." I playfully nudged him hoping to lighten the mood. "It isn't a bad thing, I swear. Turns out, I'm super awesome at the whole solo thing. Plus, I've made some great friends here and there, so I'm not *alone* alone."

His smile lacked his usual level of enthusiasm when Cade pulled me into a hug. The comforting scent of leather and pine filled my nostrils. I'd always assumed Cade smelled like the forest because we'd lived in Colorado, but discovering that he seemed to carry the scent of the mountains with him everywhere he went was somehow fitting.

Too weak to resist, I burrowed my face into his solid chest and inhaled that oh-so-familiar fragrance. No matter where I went in life, his smell would always be associated with home because even now, as hurt as I was, I was aware down to my bones that home was wherever Cade happened to be.

It was a pity that I had figured out that version of home was no longer something I needed. A soft kiss brushed the top of my head before Cade gently placed his hands on my shoulders and stepped back.

Ducking down until he was eye-level with me, his azure gaze trapped mine as he pleaded, "Katie, I have a lot to make up for. I've failed you over and over, and I realize you have absolutely no reason to believe me anymore, but I'd like to earn both your trust and your forgiveness back if you'll let me. Please. *Please*, let me."

Warmth blossomed in my chest, and I mentally groaned. Giving him a second chance was a terrible idea. A monumentally stupid idea. Yet the possibility of seeing Cade more made my heart rate kick into high gear. I cursed my empathetic nature, unable to believe I was even entertaining the idea of reigniting a friendship with Cade. As a firm believer in the power of mental pro-con lists when making life-changing decisions, I could only hope my list didn't fail me now.

Pro: Being friendly could go a long way in helping to decide how to handle Finn.

Con: Unless he leaves us. Again.

Pro: He was exceptionally caring and trustworthy.

Con: Keyword there is "was." Especially because the last three times I needed him, he was nowhere to be found.

Pro: God, he's pretty. So. Many. Muscles.

Con: God, he's pretty. It's been long enough I'm convinced that cobwebs live in there now. For heaven's sake, the man's been here for less than an hour, and I've already pondered getting him naked at least six times. Am I seriously going to subject myself to this kind of torture on a regular basis? Note to self: find a date. Stat.

The chime of my phone pulled my attention from my silent debate. I picked it up and chuckled.

Ryan: Having the best time ever kicking Finn's booty at hopscotch! SO THE WINNER!

Me: She literally learned how to hop on one foot a week ago. Cut the kid some slack, jerk-face!

Ryan: Fine, just this once. See you soon!

Looking at the clock, I realized Cade and I had been talking way longer than I had anticipated, and it was almost lunchtime. He needed to get gone, and quick, but he was too stubborn to leave without an answer. Not seeing another option, and too short on time to further examine the pros and cons, I went with my gut instinct. "Okay." *Wait, okay? What the hell, brain?*

Cade's eyed widened in disbelief before he let loose a loud "Whoop!" Excitement lit up his face and his dimples were on full display when he asked, "Really?"

I shook my head at his ridiculousness, and answered his smile with one of my own. "Yeah, really. But I've got things to do today, so you're gonna need to scoot. We'll play the rest by ear, okay?"

Nodding, he grabbed my phone and added his number to my contacts list under "Sexypants" before I had time to change my mind. With a blinding smile, he passed it to me and gave me a friendly peck on the cheek. "Okay. See you soon."

With that, he started toward the door, and I gave myself

a mental high five at my quick maneuvering. Alas, it seemed like I must be fate's bitch today, because while admiring the way his ass looked in those jeans as he walked away, I also witnessed my front door swinging open, causing my past and my present to collide.

～

Cade

Unable to wipe the grin off my face, I all but skipped toward the door. She was giving me a chance—a small chance, but a chance nonetheless. Little did Katie know this was not a mission I planned on failing. She'd opened the door, both literally and figuratively, and I was going to bust in like the Kool-Aid man and make myself at home. Earning back Katie's trust was paramount.

Our entire relationship had been built on a foundation of friendship and honesty, and my leaving so abruptly had put some significant cracks in it. For the foreseeable future, I intended to dedicate my time and effort to finding and filling each and every one.

My mind was so preoccupied listing out all the ways I could begin to work myself back into her good graces that I almost missed the look of panic on her face as her front door swung open. Almost.

My protective instincts rushed to the fore, and I scanned the room, searching for the cause of her distress. A set of broad shoulders slowly filled the doorway, pushing her door open wider as they made their way inside. Their owner, too preoccupied with greeting Katie to notice me, grinned in her direction. My need to protect Katie morphed into burgeoning jealousy when this man began making his around the apartment with unmistakable familiarity.

Bypassing me without a glance, he swung Katie up into

a bear hug and gave her an enthusiastic "Hey, Mama! Did you have a relaxing morning?"

Eye twitching with annoyance, I found myself in the uncomfortable position of awaiting an introduction. I had no idea who this man was, but seeing his arms around Katie made me want to rearrange his face. Since that wasn't an option, I forced myself to school my features into what I hoped was a pleasant expression just as their faces swung in my direction. The moment he spotted me, his gray eyes widened in surprise before he turned to Kat. "Katie-did...is there a specific reason there's a rock star in your living room?"

Curious as to what her reply might be, I, too, turned my attention toward Kat. Her gaze volleyed between the two of us a few times before she focused on the ground and shuffled her feet, seeming conflicted about something. Finally, after the world's most awkward pause, she had a silent conversation with the mystery dude, filled with enough squints and head jerks that I was concerned she was giving herself whiplash.

After letting out a frustrated sigh, Kat nodded toward the front door with her head, then indicated me a few times. I was still confused as to what they were trying to convey with the world's most ridiculous "silent" discussion, when the guy who I'd dubbed "the Behemoth" let out a quiet "*Oh! No shit?*"

My confusion was beginning to veer toward anger. I was keenly aware that I was the topic of whatever the hell kind of conversation they were having. I was also confident that my presence was the cause of the newfound tension that I was all but choking on. The question I had was *why*. I let my irritation at the current situation bleed into my features and eyed Katie's companion.

As soon as he noticed, his face fell, and in a regret-filled whisper, he said, "Sorry, Katie-did. I didn't know you had company."

She smiled up at him and hugged mystery man's torso. "Don't worry about it. No biggie, Ry."

Her attention shifted to me, and she gave me a warning glare before pointing to the stranger. "Cade, this is my very good friend, Ryan."

Hooking her thumb in my direction, she continued, "Ryan, this is Cade. Please, for the love of all that is holy, save the fangirling for another time."

I clenched my fist, resisting the urge to pull her aside and find out exactly what she meant when she said "very good friend," and instead focused on Ryan, offering him a semi-friendly wave. Eyes wide, Ryan looked at me in amazement for a few seconds, before awkwardly waving back. Katie smacked him on his shoulder, redirecting his attention. "Ry,"— concern was written all over her face—"where is she?"

She? "She" must be a roommate, though I don't recall any of my friends normally being that concerned about an absent roomie. Luckily, Ryan answered my silent question when he said, "Oh! She saw Mrs. J in the hall and wanted to tell her all about our day. She'll be back in just a sec."

I could visibly see the calm take over Kat's body, but then her gaze swung to mine, and her posture became rigid. Hearing footsteps, I turned toward the open door, ready to greet Kat's roommate, when, in an instant, the world tilted. My mind was screaming a thousand things at once, but two stood out among the cacophony: *the "she'"in question was most definitely not a roommate,* rapidly followed by, "Dear God, what have I missed?"

CHAPTER 17

CADE

"The secret of change is to focus all of your energy, not on fighting the old, but on building the new."

— SOCRATES

The first thing I noticed were her eyes. Their vivid aqua hue, identical to my own, glowed with curiosity as they scanned me from head to toe. Her hair, like mine, was a deep chocolate brown, but while my hair was straight, hers tumbled across her petite shoulders in unruly corkscrew curls.

Still unsure of who I was or why I was here, she absent-mindedly tugged on a coil of hair and glanced over to Katie for reassurance of some sort. *Maybe she belongs to the guy? Please let her belong to the guy.*

Unsure of what was happening, but feeling like an explanation was in order, I sought out Katie. All the color had drained from her face, and the alarmed expression she'd worn when Ryan first opened her door had returned. Honestly, Katie appeared to be seconds away from passing out, which kicked my apprehension up another notch.

Ryan hadn't said a word, but his eyes kept ping-ponging between the little girl, Katie, and me like he was watching the world's greatest tennis match. He wore an expression similar to the one my grandma had worn the time she'd sat on our porch watching the neighbor kick out her cheating husband. All he was missing was a giant glass of Coke, a bowl of popcorn, and someone down the street calling out, *"Whoo, it's getting good, Lottie!"*

More disconcerting was the realization that Ryan's expression was no longer confused. In fact, judging by the knowing look on his face, he had figured out all the pieces of whatever puzzle Katie had been trying to help him solve when he arrived. My hopes that she belonged to someone else were swiftly dashed when moments later, this adorable, tiny creature maneuvered around me and skipped over to Katie. Tugging on her shirt, she glanced up at her with adoration in her eyes, and with a voice clear as a bell, she said, "Mama, who dat?"

Mama. Katie was a mother. How? *Oh my God, how old is she?* Not realizing I'd asked that out loud, I was taken aback when a male voice replied, "Three-ish, I think? She's, like, toddler age, right Katie-did?"

Glaring at Ryan, I bit out, " I didn't ask you. I asked *her.*"

Ryan cocked a brow at me before making a zipping motion across his lips and sliding over to where the little girl was clinging to Katie's leg. Squatting down, he whispered something in her tiny ear, then held out a massive paw. She scrunched up her face in dismay, and she regarded me for a long minute before placing her dainty hand in his. Katie gave him a grateful smile, as he guided the little girl down the hallway and into a bedroom, leaving Katie and me alone once more.

Panic clawed at me, as I rubbed my chest and rasped out, "How. Old. Is. She?"

"What does it matter?"

Frustrated that she wouldn't say the words, yet terrified of the answer, I approached Katie. Mindful of the child in the house, I took care to moderate my volume, but kept my tone firm. "Katie, I need to know how old she is. Please."

Fingers tapping a nervous beat on her thigh, Katie focused on something over my shoulder, refusing to meet my eyes. Finally, she replied, "Three. She is three."

CHAPTER 18

KATIE

"Everything you have ever wanted is on the other side of fear."

— GEORGE ADDAIR

Fear. Of all the myriad of emotions flashing through me, fear was at the forefront, followed closely by panic. Terror had punched me square in the face as soon as Ryan had opened my door. I had been aware that at some point, I would have to tell Finn who her father was, but I'd foolishly thought I had time. In my mind, I'd planned how the whole discussion would go. I'd assumed we would have a calm, rational discussion about Cade, complete with pictures and stories about our childhood when she was old enough to ask about him. I should have realized it wouldn't play out that way; nothing with Cade ever went as planned.

I should have known better than to let him stay. I should have told him to meet me elsewhere to talk. My list of should-haves was rapidly growing the longer Cade stared at me, wearing a bomb-blasted expression on his face. Now, he without a doubt knew. I might not have officially said one way or the other Finn was his out loud, but while Cade was many things, stupid was not one of them. Hell, I was relatively sure that even without the prior heads-up, as soon as Finn set foot inside the house and Ryan saw her next to Cade, even Ryan would have been able to put two and two together and come up with baby—and he was by far least observant person I knew.

As soon as I confirmed her age, Cade's skin paled. Emotions flew across his face too fast for me to interpret them, leaving me on shaky ground, unsure of how to move forward. I had been working with people long enough that I was good at reading faces, but Cade was giving me nothing. He had begun frantically rubbing his chest, and I was legitimately worried he was either having a heart attack or a panic attack. Even though I would rather run naked through a nest of angry bees than have this conversation, I also did not want to be responsible for the accidental demise one of the world's favorite bad boys. Taking the initiative, I shook his shoulder, pulling him out of his stupor.

"Cade. Cadeon!" I grabbed his hand and led him to the couch. "Sit. I'm getting us both some tea."

Cade woodenly sat, silently staring at the closet as if someone was going to jump out and tell him he was being Punk'd. Oh, well. Fate was apparently intent on kicking me when I was already down, so I might as well put on my big girl panties and get this over with. I set the glasses of sweet tea on an end table, and I pulled up a chair and positioned myself directly across from Cade.

Needing to push pause for a moment and gather my

courage, I picked up my sweet tea and took several large gulps. If there was ever a time for prolonged procrastination, this was it, so I drained my glass and got up for a refill. When I took a seat again, I let my gaze roam, pointedly ignoring the elephant in the room. Eventually, I concluded one of us needed to be the grown-up and start this conversation, and it looked like it was going to have to be me.

I took a bracing breath and asked, "I'm assuming you have questions?"

He wrinkled his brow in concentration, moving his lips soundlessly as he went over the mental math one last time. Coming to the same conclusion I'd watched him repeatedly reach over the last few minutes, he ran a shaking hand down his face. Since both of us needed to remain calm if we were going to get through this relatively unscathed, I nudged the glass at him. "Take a drink. You look like you're gonna pass out. The sugar should help some."

Exhausted from the emotional twists and turns the day had brought so far, I was in no mood to drag this out any longer than necessary. Part of me wanted to answer all the questions I assumed he had right off the bat, but the logical side of me argued we still needed to protect ourselves. Plus, I still did not trust him. Therefore, my best course of action would be to only answer what he asked. When he *still* didn't say anything, I repeated myself. "Cade, I'm sure you have questions. Ask them."

He rolled the icy glass between his hands ,and his eyes followed a drop of condensation as it slid down the smooth surface. "You're right. I do have questions. Hundreds of them, but let's start with the most important one." Cade looked up, and his turbulent gaze caught mine, "What's her name?"

I offered him a small smile and said, "Her name is Finnley Cadence Troyer," then waited to see if he would remember.

I could tell the name rang a bell, but it was obvious by his baffled expression that he was having difficulty placing why. I knew it didn't make any sense to expect him to remember every random conversation we'd ever had, but this one I had always held close. Even now, after all this time, I could recall that day with perfect clarity. The crisp blue of the summer sky, the musical chirping of the birds singing, and the feeling of the long grass tickling my fingers as it blew in the breeze came to life in my mind.

I settled my head into the crook of his arm and nestled deeper into Cade's embrace. His fingers lazily traced patterns on my bare shoulder, leaving tingles in their wake as they shifted from one place to the next. Turning, he nudged me, and his hand flew out, pointing at the fluffy clouds overhead before animatedly announcing, "That one! Totally a wizard."

I giggled, angling a hand across my face to block the sun. "Agreed. Though I'm thinking it looks more like Gandalf than Dumbledore."

After giving me a firm nod of agreement, Cade laid his head back on the blanket, eyes still combing the clouds, waiting to spot another shape. "Hey, Katie-mine, I've been thinking..."

I set my hand on his stomach while still scanning the sky, and absently replied, "Oh, yeah?"

"Yeah. I've decided that one day, when we're all grown

up and married, we'll have to show our kids this spot. We can hang out and watch clouds while they play."

Elbowing him in the side, I teased, "Kids as in more than one?"

Cade propped himself up on his elbow and gazed down at my face, grinning. "Heck yes, more than one! You look too good naked for us to plan on only having one. Also, I've decided that one of them is going to be a smart, sassy girl. And smart, sassy girls need awesome names, like... hmmm...Finnley!"

I could tell the minute he dug the memory up from the trenches, because his dark brows shot up and he loudly sucked in a breath. Voice a bit ragged, he repeated, "Finnley?"

The corner of his lips quirked up, and he looked at me in amazement. "Is she smart and sassy?"

"Yes. But Layla has informed me that it's not sass, it's 'future leadership potential.'"

Cade let out a bark of laughter and pumped a triumphant fist in the air before announcing, "Called it! Also, I have no clue who Layla is, but she is obviously a genius."

He grinned at me, then pondered for a moment before asking, "But why Cadence? I would have thought you'd have gone with Anne, for your mom?"

I shook my head at his apparent inability to grasp the obvious and gave him an exasperated look. Playfully rolling my eyes, I reminded him, "You know as well as I do, if my mom were here, she would have verbally chastised me if I'd gone with something as traditional as Anne. The woman had more color in our house than you would find in the entire Pantone color collection, for Chrissake. Plus, I felt like it was important to give her something that was all you, and since there isn't a female equivalent of Cadeon, I went with Cadence, since you've always been Cade to me."

His smile broadened at that statement, and the knot of anxiety that had begun forming in my chest the moment Ryan had opened my door started to unravel. Noticing that I was starting to relax some, Cade took my lead and followed suit, allowing himself to stretch his long arm along the back of the couch. He grabbed his tea and took a few small sips before his eyes focused on me. "Tell me about her? Please?"

Not going to lie, all things considered, his desire to learn about Finn was throwing me. I had not planned on them ever coming into contact, and if they ever did run into one another, I figured Cade would want as little involvement as possible. Unsettled by his easy acceptance, I couldn't focus on anything specific, so I just started rambling, hoping not to be too surprised by what flew out of my mouth.

"Umm...well, her birthday was a few weeks ago. Her favorite colors are hot pink, purple, and glitter—and yes, before you ask, glitter is most definitely a color. She's mostly easy when it comes to food, but if given a choice, she will always pick banana pancakes. She enjoys anything art-related, loves having dance parties, and loves to be read to."

It seemed the rambling was doing the trick, because the more random tidbits I threw out, the more excited he became. He reached out, gently brushing my shoulder, and quietly told me, "Her name is wonderful. She is wonderful. Thank you."

I let out a breath, relieved at how well the discussion had gone so far. I should have known better than to let my guard down though. Life had taught me well how lowering your defenses left you wide open for an attack. The realization that I had made a grave error in judgment came when Cade's smile abruptly dropped, and he leaned forward and braced his elbows on his knees. I wasn't sure what Cade would ask next, but I had a sneaking suspicion I was not going to like it.

His expression was serious, and his crooked smile was now nowhere to be found. Azure eyes void of any warmth or affection scrutinized me, making me squirm. He opened and closed his mouth a few times, seeming unable to decide how to approach the topic, when he finally settled on "Katie...Why?"

Unsure what he was asking, I held my hands out in a *what* gesture. "Why...?"

He shoved his hands into his hair and tugged at the strands before elaborating. "Why? Why didn't you tell me? Were you so mad at me you would intentionally keep my daughter from me? Was not telling me some weird-ass punishment? I mean, I fucked up, no question, but *Jesus*."

I'm generally not a violent person, but reigning in the impulse to slap the dimples off his perfect face was surprisingly hard. All the warm, fuzzy feelings I'd had when this conversation began had now been replaced with a DEFCON level of fury. Too pissed to even attempt to moderate my volume I shouted, "Are you *fucking* kidding me?"

Grasping how badly he had misstepped, Cade stood and began to make a time-out signal with his hands, but I was having none of it. He didn't have the right to waltz into my house and accuse me of using my child as a punishment. Cade might have forgotten that I was all grown up now, but he was about to get one hell of a reminder.

I abruptly stood up and stalked toward him, fuming. When just a few feet separated us, I whipped my finger toward the door. "Get. Out."

Eyes widening in panic, Cade stuttered, "Kat...Katie... that came out wrong! I—"

"No! You, sir, are done talking. Do you hear me? *Done.* I'm sorry your ego is so inflated that you assumed I could not possibly go on without you. I am sorry you are so used to people crawling up your ass to tell you how special you are that the only explanation your pea brain can come up with for being out of the loop is some elaborate years-long revenge plot."

I was so furious that I was shaking, and the tears I refused to let loose were making my throat burn, but so help me I was not going to let him witness a single one fall. "How *dare* you think I would stoop so low as to rob my child of her father for some petty-ass revenge? However, your over-inflated ego is not my problem. As far as I am concerned, this conversation is over, we are done, and you can see yourself out."

I clenched my fists so hard my knuckles turned white so I wouldn't punch him in his stupid, gorgeous face. "Let me make something crystal *fucking* clear for you. I am no longer a lovesick seventeen-year-old girl. I left that girl behind a *long* time ago. At this moment, in the grand scheme of my life, you are so unimportant that you don't even rate."

I stormed across the room, jerked the door open, and glared at Cade so hard I was surprised he didn't burst into flames. It was times like this I wished I could go full-on Firestarter on people.

"No, I did not keep Finn from you so I could inflict 'some weird-ass punishment.' I didn't keep her from you at all. *You* are the one who chose not to be here, so don't lay that shit on my doorstep. Now, I do believe I already asked you to leave. So, I'm gonna say it a little slower in case all those screaming girls have made you hard of hearing: GET. OUT."

Cade

Numbly, I stood and made my way over to the door. I couldn't fathom how everything had gone so terribly wrong. I was a father. *A father*. I had made a person. A beautiful, captivating tiny person who had no idea who I was. How had I screwed up so monumentally that I had a child *I wasn't aware of* floating around in the world.

If that wasn't enough of a revelation by itself, I was also keenly aware that whatever ground I had gained with her mother went up in flames as soon as that accusation left my mouth. I knew as soon as the last syllable passed my lips that I'd royally messed up, but I had been utterly unprepared to withstand a verbal smackdown, compliments of adult Katie. Every coldly delivered word flying from her perfect lips was like a knife, slicing me open and laying me bare.

Before I left, though, there was one more thing I had to know. "Katie?" Hating how shaky and unsure my voice was, I cleared it and tried again. "What did you mean when you said I didn't want to be here? That you didn't keep her from me?"

She uttered a few curses beneath her breath before releasing a tired sigh. Weariness tinged her features, and she slumped against the wall.

"You know what, Cade? I don't want to talk to you anymore right now. I really don't. Once I learned I was pregnant, I got ahold of Kelly. She said she'd tell you, but unless I intended to prove paternity after the baby was born, she doubted you would be interested. I didn't have any other way to reach you, so I just had to hope she'd give you the message. When I didn't get so much as a text from you, I called a few more times and was blown off each time. After Finn was born, I called one last time and sent a picture in a letter. When you didn't reach out, I figured no answer *was* my answer, so life went on. Now, I'm all talked out, and I do believe I asked you to go. Repeatedly."

Seconds later, she pushed off the wall, and I watched her back as she retreated down the hall and into the bedroom where Ryan and Finn were. I knew for a fact my time was up when Ryan came strolling down the hallway and stopped next to the open door. His voice was unyielding when he said, "I believe you've been excused. So, I suggest you get to it, before I decide to give you a hand."

Katie

Needing comfort, I sat down in Finn's room. She glanced up, took in my frown, and launched herself into my arms. One of the most beautiful things about children was their innate ability to grasp emotions. Assumptions or expectations did not color their views. They didn't need to be told the whats or the whys. To them, every feeling was black and white. Happy or sad. Smiling or crying. Angry or calm. In-betweens and gray areas did not exist.

Finn had no idea what had just happened. She didn't understand that there was a very good possibility our lives had just been forever altered. She didn't realize that while my mind was in a frenzy, creating lists and contingencies to protect us, my heart longed for Cade and the family we could have had. To her, all those things were inconsequential. All she understood was that I was upset and when someone was upset, you hugged them.

Once I mustered up an appropriate amount of calm, I kissed Finn on her forehead and released her so she could continue playing. I walked out in search of Ryan and found him sprawled across the couch, draining the remaining drops of what was once my sweet tea.

His gray eyes were stormy, their usually clear depths clouded with concern. He waved a hand, beckoning me over, and patted the empty seat next to his on the couch. He stretched his arm across the back of the couch and kicked his legs out, looking like relaxation personified, but his expression was mischievous when he asked, "So, Cadeon Cross?"

Too tired for life at this point, I defaulted into direct-ness. "Yep."

"So, that's Finn's...?"

"Yep."

"Welp." He gave me an affectionate squeeze. "Gotta say, did not see that one coming. Anyone else know?"

"Nope."

Digesting this tidbit for a moment, he asked, "Wanna talk about it?"

"Also nope."

I was all talked out, so I was thankful when he gave me an affectionate kiss on the top of my head and said, "Kay."

He gently pushed my head forward, massaging my neck and shoulders until my body slowly became Jell-O and melted into the couch. Then, suddenly, he clapped his hands together, causing me to jump. Annoyed, I looked over to find his eyes bright with excitement. "So, pizza?"

CHAPTER 19

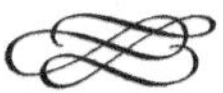

CADE

> "We crucify ourselves between two thieves: regret for yesterday and fear of tomorrow."
>
> — FULTON OURSLER

Pissed that this asshat had the right to kick me out of the place where my daughter and my girl lived, I tossed up my middle fingers, hauled the door to the stairwell open, and stormed down the steps and into the alley where D had a car waiting.

Unable to control my temper anymore, I slammed my fist into the brick exterior, relishing the scrape and burn across my knuckles. Frustration, anger, and disappointment flooded me, and I punched the facade a few more times, desperate to release some of it, before D stayed my hand.

Chest heaving, I spun away and stalked to the car, slamming the door behind me. I wanted to break shit, to make everything look as damaged as I was feeling. My volatile emotions were like a rising tide intent on pulling me under. I needed to think, to process everything that had happened in the last few hours, but I was too emotionally twisted. D's eyes caught mine in the rearview mirror, and he looked at me like I was a petulant child before shoving an ice pack at me. "Put this on those knuckles. And next time you want to go all Chuck Norris on shit, let me know so I can at least tape you up before you start breaking them dainty-ass hands of yours."

Shaking his head, he picked up his cell phone and shot out a text, all while mumbling about "rock stars and their goddamn tantrums." Once he was done, we pulled out on the street and headed in the opposite direction of the hotel. Too tired to care much one way or the other, I leaned my head back and closed my eyes. What felt like hours but was likely only a few minutes later, the car stopped, and my door magically opened. "Well, boss, we're here. Now get yourself inside before a bunch of rabid fangirls show up and ruin my day."

Still completely baffled as to where we were and why we were there, I followed orders and stepped inside. The clang of the door echoed around an empty room, then a white interior door opened, and Trev's concerned face appeared. "What up, dude? You look like shit."

His cornflower blue eyes scanned me from head to toe, and he cocked his head to the side. "In fact, I wager shit even looks good compared to you right now."

Trev propped the door open with a sneaker-clad foot and asked, "You coming, bro? The rest of the guys are setting up. RJ said he got a weird text from D spouting off some poetic shit about music being a balm to the soul and ordering him to bring us to the studio. Now that I see you, I think D may have been on to something."

As we moved through the shadowy room, I noticed a beam of light seeping from underneath a closed heavy-duty door. The muffled sounds of the guys' voices as they joked around, along with the familiar thumps and twangs of instruments being tuned, met my ears, and I sagged with relief. Trev led me inside, and seeing the tools of our craft began to soothe my raw feelings.

Rhys and Zane paused and gave me a swift perusal, followed by a head nod in greeting. Dante glanced at my rapidly swelling bruised hand and held out his drumsticks. "Here." His gruff voice was kind. "You look like you need to hit some shit, preferably without breaking yourself in the process."

For the next six hours, I lost myself in music, the notes slicing my skin, allowing my feelings to bleed out, falling to the floor one beat at a time. We played until our fingers were numb and our voices were hoarse. We played until sweat rolled down our backs and matted our hair. Until exhaustion made our limbs heavy and our fingers clumsy. We played until, for the first time since Katie opened her door, I could breathe. Then, just to be sure, we played some more.

CHAPTER 20

CADE

> "Every experience, no matter how bad it seems, holds within it a blessing of some kind. The goal is to find it."
>
> — GAUTAMA BUDDHA

Groaning, I stretched and felt my overused muscles pull. I set my hand flat on the mattress, intending to push myself up, and gasped as pain shot up my right arm, causing my swollen hand to throb. I inhaled through my nose and held my breath until the pain subsided, then pulled off the bandage and assessed the damage. *Son of a bitch.*

The knuckles on my middle and ring fingers had been split wide open. Dried blood coated the rest of my fingers and tendons, disguising the deep bruising that spanned the back of my hand. I tried to make a fist and bit out a curse when fire traveled across my nerves.

Kelly was going to kill me. Bryce might be our manager, but Kelly handled all our PR, and she was not a fan of surprises. Though, all things considered, there was an excellent probability that Kelly wouldn't be working with us much longer, so it might not matter much anyway.

I slid on a pair of flannel pajama pants and headed for the French press in our kitchenette area. For the most part, we as a group were fairly chill when it came to our riders and room requirements, but the few things we specifically requested we considered absolute necessities. My sole condition was decent coffee.

I drank a minimum of three cups of caffienated happiness each morning and couldn't function without them, so it would be a cold day in hell before I used crappy coffee. Every place we traveled, I had a local roaster send beans over so I could grind them and brew a fresh pot every day. Something about the normalcy of it helped keep me grounded.

The smell of coffee drew the rest of the guys out—one by one they stumbled into the kitchen like zombies rising from the grave, blindly searching for a mug. Twenty minutes later, we were all more awake, and I was faced with four pairs of expectant eyes wanting to understand why I'd turned up pissed off and bloody the day before. In all the years we'd been friends, I'd never gotten so out of control that I'd started punching or breaking things. I snapped, I yelled, I stomped around, but I had never damaged anything before, so I knew they were all waiting for an explanation.

Hoping to break the tension, I waved my pulpy hand in the air. "Thanks for last night. I needed to get out of my head for a while. Dante, let me know if you need me to buy you new sticks to replace the ones I killed."

Dante waved a hand in dismissal. "Nah, man. You know me, I always have spares."

I smiled for a second then let it fall. "You guys might want to sit. We've got things to discuss."

This announcement got me a raised eyebrow from Trev, which was no surprise. For the most part, Trev was the one who called for "family meetings" to discuss whatever ridiculous mess Rhys had gotten himself into, whoever had managed to find themselves on the receiving end of Dante's temper, or whatever computer system Zane had illegally hacked into for "fun." While I always attended and participated, I was never the front-runner, so this was uncharted territory for us all.

I was trying to figure out where to start when Rhys began rambling. "It wasn't my fault! I blame the chick I banged last night. I mean, it's not like I could have helped myself...you would've understood if you were there. Her lips were all shiny and red, and they were just begging to latch onto Kong. How was I supposed to know a pap was in the hallway?"

What the hell is he talking about? I knew I shouldn't ask, but I couldn't help it. "Kong? Who the hell is Kong? And what about a pap?"

Rhys gave me an irritated huff and gestured to his crotch. "Dude! *Kong!*"

A chorus of groans sounded, and I cringed. Any explanation that centered around Rhys's junk this early in the morning could go nowhere good.

"Like King Kong? 'Cause he's king of the jungle, and when he takes chicks for a ride to the top of his Empire

State Building, he keeps them screaming the whole way. Why does no one ever get that?"

Trev rolled his eyes and let out an exasperated sigh. "No one wants to discuss your dick. For any reason. Ever. And we don't give a shit whose lips were on it last night. I highly doubt Cade would call a family meeting because yet another gossip rag has a picture of you getting Hoovered by a random in a grimy-ass hallway."

He shifted his focus to me and added, "Besides, judging by the confused look on his face, he knew nothing about it— and we don't want to. Cade, the floor is yours."

I nodded in appreciation and forced the mental image of some chick going down on Rhys from my brain, then braced for the shit storm I was about to brew. "So, I went to see Katie yesterday. Obviously, it did not go as planned."

Zane barked out a sarcastic laugh. "No shit."

Ignoring him, I went on. "Things were going along pretty damn well until the door opened, and a tiny whirl-wind who happened to look *exactly like me* came barreling inside."

The smirk dropped from Rhys's face and he gave me a blank stare for a beat before saying, "Holy shit!"

Dante leaned forward, bracing his elbows on his knees, looked me dead in the eye and asked, "Are you saying what I think you're saying?"

An image of Finn formed in my mind and made my chest ache in the very best way. I was terrified of the idea of being a father. I knew jack shit about taking care of other people, and had spent so long only focusing on myself that I wasn't sure I even remembered how to include others. But as pissed as I was about how things went down with Katie, as soon as Finn's ocean eyes hit mine, I was sunk. She was mine, and I wasn't giving her up. Period.

"Yeah, I am. Apparently, Katie found out she was knocked up after I left, which is the reason her crazy-ass uncle kicked her out. It's also why he was screaming at me about "not abiding whores" or some shit when we were at his house. Problem was, if you recall, I made sure there was no way for her or my family to reach me outside of the label, i.e., Kelly."

Trev let out a whistle and studied my face. "Okay, so first off, are we excited about baby-Cade?"

I didn't even bother trying to hide to giant grin that spread across my face at the mention of my daughter. *My daughter*. Hell. Smiling at my expression, Trev said, "Okay, so we are crazy stoked to have a pint-sized-Cade, which kicks ass, and also we want to meet her as soon as her sexy mama bear allows. That just leaves Kelly. She's a controlling bitch, and I wouldn't put it past her to pull some serious shit, but at the same time, I really don't think she'd go so far as to hide your kid from you."

I couldn't fault Trev for his train of thought, mainly because I had come to the same conclusion after I'd left Katie's yesterday. "I was thinking the same thing, but right before she kicked me out—and yes Rhys before you ask, she did indeed kick my ass out, and no, I am not giving you a play-by-play—she told me she'd contacted Kelly several times trying to reach me before she gave up. At this point, I'm not sure what the hell happened, but I am damn sure gonna find out. Since it involves one of the people responsible for our careers and a couple of additions to our family, I need you guys in on it."

Dante stood and made his way over to the minibar. He pulled out a bottle of Jack and dumped it into his coffee then added a dash of cream before he sat back down. Taking in our confused faces, he shrugged and said, "I'm guessing our next step is to call Kelly, and I cannot deal with her sober. Sorry, bro."

It took only a moment for us all to agree Dante was on the right track. We took a break to refill our beverages—some with a healthy dose of jack some without—before settling back into our previously occupied seats. Braced for what was going to be one hell of an unpleasant conversation, I pulled up Kelly's number on my phone, hit speakerphone, and waited. Far too soon, Kelly's nasally voice filled the room as she cawed, "Cadey Cade! You sexy thang! Whatcha calling me so early for? Is there something I can do for you?"

The blatant invitation in her voice made me wince, and I stared at my cup of coffee for a beat before deciding it was most definitely not strong enough for this shit. Wordlessly, I pulled Dante's mug from his hand and took a large gulp, then offered him a shrug of apology. Dante, being awesome, grabbed my plain coffee and pointed to his mug, which I was clinging to for dear life. "Keep it. We both know you're gonna need it."

He pulled the phone over toward him, and his gravelly voice boomed when he said, "We've got some questions."

Unconcerned by his serious tone, Kelly let loose an obnoxious giggle. "Oh! Is that my muscles talking? What a treat! Are all my boys there, or just you two handsome fellas? Trevy-poo! Are you there? I'm sitting here all lonely, just dying to see your pretty face. Do you miss me?"

The look of disgust on Trev's face made me shake with silent laughter. His gaze snapped to me and he flipped me off before saying, "Enough, Kelly. We didn't call you to get hit on. We have shit to discuss, so I suggest you sit down and shut your mouth for once."

Finally grasping that this would be a serious conversation, Kelly let out an annoyed huff and a petulant "Fine."

Not knowing how long we had until she either got bored and hung up or started being a creep-ass again, I dove into the topic at hand. "So, funny thing happened the other day, Kelly. We're all sitting in a VIP lounge, throwing back some drinks and chilling, when all of a sudden, the curtain opens and in walks Katerina Troyer. You remember Katie, don't you, Kelly?"

The sound of Kelly's claws tapping against her desk grated on my nerves, and the uncharacteristic silence made my gut clench. Intuition was telling me I was not going to like whatever she had to say, but I needed to stay in control if I was going to obtain the information I needed. I took another gulp of my boozed-up coffee and forced myself to wait her out. Finally, in a too-bright tone, she replied, "Katerina Troyer? Hmm...Oh! Wasn't she the girl you dated back in high school before you left to take the music world by storm?"

At the blatant dismissal in her tone, I had to reign in the urge to reach through the phone and throttle her. Not bothering to disguise my anger, I bit back, "Stop your shit, Kelly. You know exactly who she is, and I don't have patience for your games today. What I want to know is, did Katie ever leave messages for me with you?"

"Well, hon, *of course* she tried to get me to give her your information. You were becoming famous after all. If I gave your personal information to every girl who called me asking for it, you'd never sleep. I was just doing my duty to protect my client."

I was going to kill her. Protecting her clients, my ass. I reached for the phone so I could tell Kelly what a bitch she was, but Zane smacked me on the shoulder to get my attention and shook his head no. He pointed at my coffee, telling me to take a sip, and turned his focus to the phone still lying in the center of the coffee table. "Kels, quit beating around the bush. Did she contact you looking for Cade or not?"

Knowing we were at our limit with her shenanigans, she quietly replied, "Yes."

Zane's mouth turned down at the corners, and his green gaze held mine when he asked, "Once, or multiple times?"

"Well," she hedged, "I can't recall for sure, but it may have been more than once...like say, a handful."

Hearing her admission that she had intentionally kept Katie's messages from me made my blood boil—particularly because I'd made it very clear that if Katie ever reached out, Kelly was to notify me immediately, regardless of Bryce's opinion on the matter. I was seconds away from unleashing the full extent of my fury, when Dante gave me a sharp shake of his head and held up a finger, asking me to wait a moment. His tone was void of any sympathy or understanding when he demanded, "Explain in detail what every one of those messages said, Kelly. Every. Single. One. Now."

Kelly might like to play like she was brainless, but we had worked with her long enough that we knew she was anything but. Sneaky and underhanded? Yes. But clueless?

Absolutely not. And she had worked with us long enough to realize Dante's temper was legendary for a reason, and she had found herself dangling at the end of the little bit of patience he had. She sucked in a breath, and I could almost hear the wheels in her brain kick into high gear trying to find a way to keep herself on his good side.

She unsuccessfully tried to keep her tone indifferent when she replied, "Fine. She contacted me more than once. The first few times, she was trying to find out where you were, to make sure you were doing okay. Then the messages started getting more frequent, and more urgent. She kept telling me that she needed to speak to you and that she understood you might not want to be contacted by her, but that whatever she needed to talk to you about was really important and to please have you call her. I ignored her because keeping the crazies away is part of my job."

"Eventually, the messages slowed, and I got fewer and fewer of them and figured she was *finally* getting the message that you didn't want to be bothered. I got one or two more after that, then nothing, which is how it was supposed to be. You were busy becoming famous; you didn't need an old girlfriend dragging you down."

Unable to handle it, I had gotten up and started furiously pacing about two sentences into her "explanation." Checking my anger was a serious struggle, but we weren't done yet. Her crafty ass had left out all the crucial pieces, doing what she always did and only giving up enough information to be convincing without casting any blame her way.

I was tired of slowly prying answers out of her and wanted this damned conversation to be over. I set my hands on my hips, gritted my teeth, and bit out, "I do believe

Dante asked for what those messages said *in detail*, Kelly. No more bullshit. What did Katie say?"

Cornered, and fully grasping the precarious position she was in, Kelly gave up all pretenses and said, "She said she was pregnant, about six months along, and it was yours. She told me she wasn't asking for handouts and didn't expect you to put your life on hold for her, but thought you deserved to know there would be a little girl in the world who was half yours. She also said that if you wanted to be a part of her life, to give her a call."

"I got another email when she was about nine months along asking if you wanted to attend the birth, and the last contact I had from her was a voicemail notifying me after the fact, asking me to tell you there were a few complications but that they were both fine and that she'd sent a photo in the mail in case you wanted to see the baby. She also included her contact information, in case you ever wanted to reach out."

I couldn't comprehend how someone could keep that information to themselves. Katie hadn't been lying. She had tried to tell me, and now thanks to Kelly's deceit, I had a baby mama who thought I didn't care and a daughter who didn't know I existed. Betrayal burned deep, and I let loose a feral scream, before shouting, "WHAT THE FUCK, KELLY?"

Scrambling for a way to diffuse the situation—and more importantly save her ass—Kelly started talking at a rapid-fire clip. "I did it for you! Things had just started picking up for the band. Your album was coming along, and from the feedback Bryce had given me, we were aware it would probably be a hit. I had spent so much time and effort cultivating your online persona. I had interviews scheduled with all the big magazines, I had photo shoots planned, hell, I even coordinated strategic run-ins with the paps to make sure you were seen at all the right places"

"I was not going to sacrifice your potential success and the advancement of my own career because some nobody was claiming she was having your kid. She had zero proof it was yours aside from her word, which was useless to me. Plus, she waited to announce her pregnancy until you had been signed on as the openers for Night's Edge's international tour. If that doesn't scream gold digger, I don't know what does."

She snapped her gum a few times before adding, "Her kid wasn't something you needed to be concerned about at the time. Whether you like it or not, I was doing my job, and I did you all a favor, because look at where we are at now. If anything, you should be thanking me."

Thanking her? Her delusional ass thought I should be thanking her? I looked around and realized all the guys wore expressions that were somewhere between livid and baffled after her crazy explanation. I was debating how to handle the situation when Trev held up a piece of paper with "FIRE HER" scrawled across it in Sharpie. My gaze traveled around the room, and each of the guys gave me a thumbs-up. The vote was decided, and I picked up the phone with a sinister smile on my face.

There was not an ounce of forgiveness in my voice as I held the phone a few inches in front of my mouth and said, "Kelly, first off, you can go fuck right the hell off with that bullshit. You are a selfish and self-serving shrew, and I hope that at some point in your life someone steals something precious from you so you understand exactly how I feel right now. Secondly, you are fucking fired, and if you ever attempt to speak to me or the rest of the guys again, we will sue you for all you're goddamn worth."

I ignored her indignant sputtering, and hung up on her. My rage from before had disintegrated and been replaced by a keen sense of loss and shame. No matter who I pointed fingers at, I still held the majority of the blame for not knowing about Finn. It had been my decision, and mine alone, to cut-off contact with Katie. My need to separate myself from her, and from my feelings for her, had given Kelly the ability to sneak in and make life-altering decisions on my behalf. She might have been the one who fired the gun, but I was the one who loaded it.

"Quit beating yourself up."

I snapped my head up, trying to figure out who had spoken. Dante's towering frame stopped directly in front of me, and he repeated himself. "I said, stop beating yourself up. We all fuck up, Cade. There is not a single one of us who hasn't made at least one horrible decision in our lives. We all decided to let Kelly take the reins, even though we all were aware that she gave zero shits about us and only cared about what was piling into her bank account. Now, you can either sit there and play the martyr, or you can go fix your shit and be happy for once. I know which choice I want you to make, but ultimately the decision is yours."

Zane nodded. "I second that. No one is perfect. Just remember, we are a family, and we will always have your back. That being said, we are now out a PR rep, and since we are hitting the European leg of our tour soon, we definitely need to rectify that. I'm thinking Quinn Haliburton. What do you guys think?"

Trev's eyebrows shot up, and his eyes lit with excitement. "Do you think she'd take us? I heard she has a wait list a mile long."

Zane shrugged and gave us a sheepish grin, "We're kind of friends. We got to talking at one of those award banquets we're always forced to go to awhile back. She mentioned having some issues with people sneaking onto her network, and I got bored one night and built a program to beef up her system. I'm not sure if it'll be enough to move us to the front of the line, but we won't know until we ask. I'll touch base with her and see if we can pick her up. I also think once things are calmer, we should seriously discuss parting ways with Bryce and Soundscapes when our contract is up next year. I'm tired of being treated like a brainless puppet."

The idea of being free from Bryce and Soundscapes sounded like a dream come true, and given the enthusiastic applause Zane was getting from the other band members, I wasn't the only one who thought so. Once the claps died down, each of the guys lightly punched me on the shoulder in a show of solidarity before they each slipped back into their rooms.

I went into my room and pulled out the old worn photo of Katie and me that I kept tucked in my wallet. I ran my finger over her crinkled cheek and thought of Finn. Dante was right—the time for wallowing in self-pity was over, and it was time that I took control of my life.

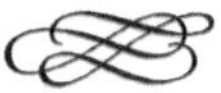

CHAPTER 21

KATIE

> "I don't want just words. If that's all you have for me, you'd better go."
>
> — THE BEAUTIFUL AND THE DAMNED F. SCOTT FITZGERALD

My phone chimed, and I dove for the coffee table, hoping it was Cade. Since The Incident, I hadn't heard a peep from Cade or anyone on his staff, and I'd turned into one of those girls who was continually checking her phone for a message that never came. I *hated* it. Part of me felt an intense amount of relief, knowing that the life I had so carefully cultivated for Finn and myself would remain the same.

The rest of me, however, was a mixture of disappointment and sadness. I had kicked him out—which he rightfully deserved after being such an unabashed jackass—but for some reason, the fact that he hadn't even bothered to try to reach out grated. I swiped my thumb across the screen, only to be disappointed to find a text from Ryan.

You would think after all the times Cade had let me down in the last few years that I would know better than to trust him, but apparently I was still a sucker. I had fallen for his "excited dad" routine hook, line, and sinker. If I were being honest, though, the only person to blame for my current mood was myself. In all the talking we had done, Cade had never actually told me he wanted to be part of Finn's life.

Days ago, when I opened my door to find Cade standing there, my mind and heart had been unable to separate the rock god he was now from the boy who I'd loved so fiercely years before. I understood they were no longer one and the same, but all I could picture when I looked into those aquamarine eyes were memories.

I saw every time he'd cooked me chicken noodle soup when I was sick, all the times he'd sung me to sleep, how he had shown up after every final with a cupcake 'just in case,' and the way he had pretended to hate the red Sour Patch Kids because they were my favorite.

Long-buried recollections had come flooding back in a rush, and I had been helpless to stop them. Ever since our encounter, memories kept popping up, unbidden, out of the blue. No matter how hard I tried to cram them back into the abyss, they kept coming back, unwarranted and unwanted, gouging me with their sharp edges and bruising me from the inside out.

It wasn't Cade, but at least texting Ryan would keep me preoccupied for a while.

Ryan: Hey, there, pretty lady! How is the slayer of rock star hearts doing today?

Me: Not funny, Ry. And I'm fine.

Ryan: I highly doubt that. Have you talked to him at all?

Me: No, and I don't really want to talk about it either.

Ryan: Give him time. His head can't stay crammed up his ass forever. Also, don't be mad, but I called in reinforcements.

Me: You what now?

Ryan: Just remember I love you! And please forgive me. She can be TERRIFYING.

Moments later, a light rapping on my door pulled my focus from Ryan's confusing text. Upon opening the door, I discovered a visibly annoyed Layla. Without waiting for me to invite her in, she shoved inside and demanded, "Why, pray tell, did I have to find out from Ryan that Finn's baby daddy made an appearance? I mean, seriously, Ryan? God love that boy, but a font of sympathy and advice he is not."

Her astute pale-blue eyes scanned me from head to toe, taking in my greasy ponytail, stained "I Don't Want to Taco Bout It" T-shirt, and baggy sweats with a disgusted curl of her lip.

She waved a manicured hand at the hot mess standing in front of her and gave me an arch stare. "Yeah, no. You, Miss Secret Keeper, are going to go shower and put on something that looks like it was washed sometime this century. Then, we are going to walk my fabulous mini over to hang with Mrs. J for an extended amount of time while you come with me."

Uncomfortable with her scrutiny, I mutinously planted my feet firmly on the floor and crossed my arms. After a silent stand-off, I gave in first, and asked, "What precisely are we going to be doing for 'an extended amount of time?'"

"Why, that's easy." A smile broke through her irritated expression. "We'll be having enough drinks that your lips will all of a sudden feel loosey-goosey so you can share all those juicy details you've been hiding for years with *moi*."

I couldn't help but grimace at the idea of reliving the awkward and depressing events of the last four years, but I owed it to Layla to come clean about the whole mess. Layla and I had run into each other at freshman orientation and bonded over our shared love of coffee and old musicals. In the two years I'd lived in Greenville, she had become my rock.

No matter what I needed, she was there, no questions asked. That she'd allowed me to keep the other half of Finn's parentage a secret up until now was astonishing. Layla might seem flighty to those who didn't know her, but the girl was sharp as a tack and had no qualms about using her intelligence to crack people like an egg. Since it seemed my borrowed time had expired, I let my shoulders drop in defeat and shuffled down the hall to shower and get ready.

Forty-five minutes later, our Uber dropped us off at my favorite pizza place. Seeing my questioning gaze, Layla grinned. "Girl, we are gonna have a conversation that will involve feelings. I have a sense that we will be needing some greasy pizza, cannoli, and unlimited amounts of wine."

She grabbed my hand and started to lead me inside. I gave a half-hearted tug, so she tightened her grip and said, "Trust me."

We paused just outside of the entrance, and Layla gave me an affectionate pat on the head, then shrugged and added, "Also, since you refuse to waste money on booze, and I plan to get you at least tipsy, my options were limited. At the moment, Nick is keeping my bed busy, and coincidentally he is tending bar at this fine establishment tonight—ergo, pizza, cannoli, and as much free wine as we can drink."

~

Nick all but melted every time Layla made eye contact, and watching his tripping all over himself and her pretending not to notice was proving to be the perfect distraction from the serious conversation looming in the distance. The poor boy was head over heels for Layla, which was a pity.

While Layla would go to the mattresses for anyone she considered a friend, romantically she was a hot mess. If there was even a hint of feelings, she fled like someone had lit her ass on fire. I'd never dug the why out of her. I figured that if I was entitled to my secrets, it was only fair I didn't pry into hers. My guess was that as soon as Layla noticed Nick mooning over her, she'd kick him out of her bed with a handshake and a wave, and that would be the end of Nick.

Layla laid her hands across her flat stomach, leaned back, and let out a contented sigh. Just then, Nick swung by and dropped off another glass of Merlot. Layla gave him a playful wink and picked up the glass, but rather than take a drink, she looked at me expectantly over the rim. My reprieve had come to an end, and I was still not ready to discuss my current situation.

Layla drummed her fingers against the tabletop, and I chugged the remainder of my wine, hoping it would give me some liquid courage. The best place to start was always the beginning, so I gave Layla a quick run down of how Cade and I met and became best friends. I made her laugh with stories of our shenanigans—like the time Cade locked himself in the principal's office my sophomore year and sang horrifyingly off-key renditions of terrible eighties love ballads until I forgave him after our first fight—watched her sigh when I told her how we fell in love when I was fifteen, and saw her soft expression turn hard when I told her about him leaving shortly before my eighteenth birthday.

The story came to an end when I finished with "And then I told him to get out, and I haven't seen or heard from him since."

At some point, Nick had magically refilled my Moscato, so I downed half of it and signaled for glass number three. Layla sat staring at me, mouth gaping slightly, for an uncomfortably long time. I started to become concerned when she silently began just nodding her head, and was nervous that my admission had unintentionally broken my friend.

A few nods later, Layla stilled her head and blinked a few times. "Sorry. It took me a minute to process the fact that Cadeon Cross is your baby daddy and that ya'll were gonna get married someday. I'm good now, though, and am fully prepared to ignore that that man is hotness personified and instead burn all my Devil's Cross posters and bash his flaky ass in solidarity. I vote we take him down."

A surprised laugh escaped before I could contain it. God, I loved Layla. "It's cool, Lay. I won't hate you for liking their music, and we don't need to go after Cade. If he doesn't think Finn is worth getting to know, that is his loss. Plus, ultimately, hurting Cade will only hurt Finn, and I can't have that. So, instead, let's finish this delicious wine and put this not-so-secret secret back in its box and go back to life as we know it."

Layla's long arms reached across the table and pulled me into an awkward hug. "You are one badass lady and one kick-ass mama. You are a strong, independent woman who don't need no man...though, if you decide you want one, I'll be your wing-gal in one hot second."

She gave me a wink and added, "Though, to be honest, girl, we should hop on that. I'm getting worried that it's been too long since that lady garden has had a proper plowing. But that is a discussion for another day."

She gave me one final squeeze, then mimed zipping her mouth shut and throwing away the key before giving me an affectionate grin. "Come on, girlfriend, time to head back home."

Cade

It had been three days since I'd seen or spoken to Katie, and I was hoping that I had given her enough time to cool off. I realized I had massively fucked up and still could not believe I'd accused her of keeping Finn from me.

Katie might not be the same girl as she was before, but she had always been honest to a fault, and I couldn't see that changing about her. I'd been antsy to talk to her ever since the band's eye-opening conversation with Kelly, but I was walking a fine line and didn't want to upset her any more than I already had by pushing things too hard.

The comforting presence of my bandmates flanking me allowed me to relax some. I was grateful that when I told the guys where I was heading, they all got ready in record time, no questions asked. They understood how much hinged on playing my cards right, and having them there for support was something I needed.

We'd been waiting only a minute when the back door opened and pervy Tom waved us inside. Tom quickly escorted us to the same VIP lounge we had been in the night I spotted Katie, then promised that our servers would be right up.

Anticipation and nerves burned in my gut. Looking around at the guys, I noted each one seemed to be as anxious as I was. I couldn't blame them. Aside from Rhys, none of the other guys had been given many opportunities to get to know Katie. To them, she had become a modern-day unicorn—one of those precious things people spouted fantastic tales about and occasionally caught a glimpse of, but never really saw in its entirety.

We'd held practices in Denver at Rhys's house two weekends a month and conferred via Skype the rest of the time. More often than not, Katie would sit off to the side and listen to our shows and practices, but she was much shyer back then and rarely interacted with the guys.

The rustle of the curtain drew our collective attention to the door. I perched myself on the edge of my seat, fully prepared to leap out of it and chase Katie down if necessary, only to be disappointed. The server who ambled our way was undeniably gorgeous. She was taller, maybe five-nine or so, and had curves for days. She reminded me of a modern-day Lottie Graves.

Her bright-pink waves tumbled past her shoulders and complimented miles of flawless tawny skin. I could hear a few of the guys suck in a breath, and one of them muttered a quiet "Holy shit." Had it been a week ago, I would have joined them and likely given her a flirtatious smile and a wink. However, today she was inconsequential, and I found myself looking past her, waiting for Katie to appear.

An unpleasantly intense gaze was boring into my forehead, so I let out an irritated huff and sought out the source. The waitress had stopped a few feet shy of our couches, and her striking arctic-blue gaze glowed with an unholy anger that was focused solely on me.

I racked my brain, trying to figure out what I had done wrong, and came up short. She crossed her arms and glared at me so hard I was convinced the only reason she had tucked her hands away was to prevent herself from doing me bodily harm. Too focused on the pretty package to notice her anger, the guys were talking over one another, trying to be the one to win her attention.

The nameless woman let loose one epic eye roll and whipped her head to the side so she could address the band. "Enough comments from the peanut gallery over there. Goddamn! I have zero intentions of taking any of y'all's asses to bed. None of y'all are the reason I'm in here anyway."

With that established, her icy gaze swung back to me and she pointed an accusatory finger in my face. "I'm here for your sorry ass, you son of a bitch."

Taken aback, I blinked and frantically scanned my memory, wondering what the hell I did to incur this gorgeous yet terrifying Amazonian warrior's wrath, and still came up blank. Whoever she was, she was as crazy as she was beautiful. I just hoped she wasn't a rabid fan. I'd had a few stalkers already, and that was never a pleasant experience for anybody. Unsure of what else to do, I gave the guys a panicked look. "I think maybe you're looking for someone else. We've never met before..."

Her vivid blue eyes chilled even further, sucking all the warmth from the room. "I'm aware," she bit out. "I'm not here on your behalf; I'm here on *hers*. So, listen closely, because I will not be repeating myself."

Understanding dawned on everyone's faces, and I sat, unable to move as she leaned over my chair and brought her face inches from my own. "Cadeon Cross, I don't know why you're here, and I don't care." The vehemence in her tone was both astonishing and intimidating, and made me feel about two feet tall.

"Hopefully it's because you've managed to pull your over-sized head out of your ass, in which case you better have some damn good knee pads for all the groveling you're going to be doing. Hopefully it is because—contrary to what I've seen so far—you have the ability to be more than a sperm donor and have the desire to be an actual parent. If not, you need to leave. They are doing just fine all on their own; they always have."

"If you aren't here to help, you and your god complex can get up and get out. She doesn't need you; she never did. So, if you're intentions aren't pure, you'd best be scooting along, because if you hurt either of my girls, I will hunt you down, rip your balls off, and make you choke on them. Understood?"

Eyes wide with fear, I nodded. She gave me one final death glare before she stood and slid a flirtatious grin on her face. "Now that that's out of the way, what can I bring y'all?"

The swift change in her demeanor all but gave me whiplash, and I was still recovering from the entire episode when she snapped her notebook shut and slid it into her back pocket. When she pivoted to leave the room, she looked at me one more time and gestured that she was watching me before exiting the room.

I released the breath I'd been holding and rested my head in my hands. I had a sinking feeling I'd somehow screwed up again, only for once I couldn't figure out how. Zane's smooth baritone broke the silence when he said,

"She is terrifying, but extremely hot. Like a rabid Easter Bunny. I think I might be in love."

His ridiculous statement made me snort, but the dash of humor was short-lived. I ran my hands through my hair a few times, impatient with my self-imposed inaction. A large hand clamped down on my shoulder, and Dante's gravelly voice carried over the pounding bass of whatever Top Forty remix they were playing. "It'll be cool, man. She's protective of Katie, which is a good thing. She's the gatekeeper, and while she is probably the scariest hot chick I've ever met, she basically gave you the okay to move in on her girl as long as you have good intentions. Just make sure not to fuck shit up. I'm thinking the whole threatening your balls thing was *not* a figure of speech."

Too amped-up from nerves to keep sitting, I hopped up and started pacing. Katie would be coming up soon, but the longer she took, the more rattled I became. At long last, I caught the flutter of the curtain. The neon lights danced across her raven hair as she turned to say something to the bouncer and threw her head back in laughter before continuing inside.

Her laughter abruptly died when she spotted us, and a look of irritation took up residence on her face. Swiftly, she strode over to our table and slammed down the tray of drinks we'd ordered. Judging by her reaction, The Bunny had been right. Mentally slapping on my knee pads, I stepped toward Katie, ready to grovel.

KATIE

> "A stiff apology is a second insult...The injured party does not want to be compensated because he has been wronged; he wants to be healed because he has been hurt."
>
> — G. K. CHESTERTON

It had been three days, six hours, and ten minutes since Cade had left my apartment, and the knowledge that I was aware down to the minute of the last time I set eyes on him made me want to punch myself in the face. I'd done a lot of growing up since Cade left, and I'd long ago lost my rose-colored glasses.

My experiences on my own, after my impromptu emancipation courtesy of my uncle, had fully extinguished whatever small amounts of innocence or naivete I had left. After a few weeks alone in the world, I'd shucked my cloak of optimism and replaced it with layers of realism and pragmatism out of necessity, and had never looked back.

Over time, I had discovered that feelings are like mud: thick, unpleasant, and able to keep you stuck in the mire. For some, being suspended in one place was fine, but when you were responsible for caring for an innocent human being, stagnancy was not an option. Thus, I'd cast aside the messiness evoked by feelings, and relied instead on cold logic.

Every path in Finn and my life had been meticulously mapped out after extensive research and a detailed pro-con list. Once I determined the correct route, I moved unerringly in that direction and never allowed myself to look back or wonder *what if*.

Yet now, I was sitting here at the bar, rubbing an ache I didn't understand in the vicinity of my heart, lost in a sea of *what-ifs*. It made me want to hunt Cade down and do him bodily harm for barging into my orderly life and turning it upside down.

The sound of a throat clearing interrupted my internal rant, and I jerked my gaze over to the new bartender. What was his name? Cody? Kevin? Feeling bad about being unable to recall who he was, but too distracted to care, I reached over, grabbed my tray, and offered him a small, apologetic smile before heading up to the VIP room.

Ty provided a momentary distraction from stewing over how to handle Cade, but when I stepped into the room and found myself face-to-face with the bringer of chaos himself —along with every other member of Devil's Cross—I felt an unyielding urge to chuck my tray of drinks straight at his frustratingly attractive face.

Not in the mood for another confrontation, I almost high-tailed it back downstairs to safety, but I was tired of riding the emotional rollercoaster that was Cadeon Cross. The moment he registered I was there, his face lit with anticipation, making my chest feel tight and my eyes burn.

His complete disregard for my feelings over the past few days upset me more than I'd wanted to admit to myself, and having him sit there acting like nothing was wrong *hurt*. Even though we had fought, I had been so sure that Cade would show up and make things right.

Instead, he chose to disrupt me at my workplace yet again, which just pissed me off. Three days of absolute silence, without so much as a hello, and now he's sitting there looking at me like I should be happy to see him. At this point, all I would be happy to do is shove this bottle of Jack where the sun don't shine. Screw this and screw him.

I stomped over to the table and slammed the tray down onto its shiny red surface, uncaring that my harsh movements were causing alcohol to slosh over the edge of the glasses. Channeling Vanna White, I waved my hand over the half-empty drinks and bit out, "Here. Y'all can serve your own asses." Then I whipped around and moved toward the door.

I barely made it a foot before a familiar hand grasped my upper arm. I jerked from Cade's grasp, spun around, and shoved him. Hard. He stumbled back, and I took pleasure in the fact that it took him a second to regain his balance. Usually, I would feel bad, but calm and collected Katie had taken a walk as soon as I saw him sitting there with a smile on his face. I crossed my arms protectively over my middle and snapped, "Unless you want to lose them, you will keep your damn hands to yourself, Cadeon Cross!"

I eyed Cade, watching him as he slowly held the two offending appendages up in surrender and lowered himself back onto the couch, giving me as much space as possible. The rest of the band sat wide-eyed, watching Cade and me with rapt attention. Finally, a raspy voice I would know anywhere broke the tension. "I don't know about you guys, but if a fight breaks out, my money is on Katie."

I rolled my eyes and glared into hazel eyes filled with mirth. "Oh, screw you, Rhys."

Moments later, a startlingly sexy beast covered in ink, whose muscles had muscles, argued, "Nah, I'd bet on Cade. He's got a good foot and a hundred pounds on her."

A man with messy blond hair and glasses tapped his chin in thought, and his familiar cornflower-blue gaze held mine. When he was sure he had my attention, his lips quirked up and he argued, "Dante, you are wrong, my friend. Katie would totally win. She has years of pent-up rage and frustration, plus she's hot as hell. There's a reason the Norse Valkyries were petite and beautiful—it made people underestimate their abilities and viciousness. I'm with Rhys on this one—my money is on Katie."

Recognition dawned, and I glared at Trev, annoyed that he had chimed in and kept this ridiculous conversation going. I looked at the only one who hadn't given his opinion and gave him an arch stare, waiting to see if he would toss in his two cents. Grass-green eyes surveyed me for a moment, before Zane shoved his unruly auburn waves off his fore-head, gave me a confident grin, and said, "Sorry, Dante, but I'm with Trev and Rhys. She's terrifying."

I scanned the lot of them and shook my head. "Y'all ain't right."

Cade's apologetic "Guys, not helping," carried above their voices. "I'm sorry about them, Katie."

I didn't want his half-assed apology though. I needed him to show regret for how things had gone down the other day and remorse over the accusations he'd carelessly hurled my way. I wished he would grow up and take responsibility for his actions and their consequences—to work on mending the fences he'd so easily broken. But ever the realist, I was also aware that there was no point in forcing my expectations on other people. I could not control their reactions, but I could control my own. It was time I drew the line.

I shook my head sadly and allowed all the emotional exhaustion from the last few days to bleed into my tone. "You know what, Cade? I don't give a shit why you're here. I really don't. You want to insult me—in my own home— then ignore me for three days, before popping up without even bothering to apologize for your shit behavior? Fine. You wanna sit here with your bandmates drinking and laughing while you watch me dodge grabby hands all night? Fine."

"Screw with me all you want, Cade. I have a thick skin now, I can take it. But leave Finn out of it. She's still full of softness, wonder, and innocence, and that is something with which *you will not fuck.* Do I make myself clear?"

Cade

Katie's barbs were well placed she flayed me wide open yet again. I had wrongly assumed Katie would need time to come to terms with my piss-poor reaction to learning about Finn. I figured giving her a few days to process all the old emotions and hurts that we had dug up while talking, and also to figure out how I would fit into the picture, seemed like an excellent plan.

Instead, I had once again decided that I knew what she needed and had been utterly wrong. The stink of failure clung to me as I took in the bags shadowing her eyes and the stress lines bracketing her mouth.

Unsure of how to proceed, but knowing my time was drawing to a close, I tentatively began, "Katie, I am so, so sorry."

I imbued all the sincerity I could muster into my words, hoping it would be enough. "I didn't come here to screw with you or Finn, I swear. I was trying to give you space. The way we left things, what I said, I figured you would be angry—rightfully so. I was trying to give you time to cool off. I was hoping we could talk about Finn and about us. I just... I messed up."

Her expression was unreadable, the neutral mask she wore like armor once again in place. The sound of the blood rushing in my ears seemed to get louder each second we sat in silence. Eventually, Katie dropped her arms and gave me a paltry "Whatever."

Frustrated, I gripped my hair and pulled. "Katie, I said I'm sorry, and I meant it. What else do you want me to do? Tell me what you want from me. Please."

"That's the problem, Cade!" she spat back. "You don't *do* anything. You're all words and no action. That may have worked for you before, but I've long since learned that when it comes to you, your words mean nothing. Your multitude of 'I'm sorry's' are lip service at best and insults at worst. Finn deserves more than empty promises, and so do I. As far as I'm concerned, we have nothing to discuss. Now, if you'll excuse me, I need to get back to work."

I could do nothing but stare at her retreating form, too numb to move. Feelings of inadequacy peppered me, knocking my confidence level down one peg at a time. I was at a loss as to where to go from here. All I wanted was Katie and Finn, yet every time I tried to bring us closer together, I ended up shoving us further apart.

I kicked the table leg in frustration and let loose a string of curses when pain vibrated up my foot from the contact. Defeated, I hung my head, ready to give up for the night and go home. Sensing the direction of my thoughts, Rhys topped off one of the shot glasses and slipped it into my hand.

I turned to look at him, and sincerity burned in his hazel gaze when he said, "Don't give up, man. The rest of the guys might not have seen you and Katie together much, but I did. She's your person, dude. You'll get there. Trust me. Also, I think it might be time to bust out the big guns. We're trying, bro, but none of us are good at this relationship crap."

~

I pinched the bridge of my nose and willed the pounding in my head to go away before tossing back a few aspirin and chasing them with water. My phone was clutched tightly in my hand, and I took a few deep breaths to gather courage before finding the contact I needed.

As much as it pained me to admit, Rhys was right, and no matter how much I loathed the conversation that was coming, it was high time I tagged in our resident relationship expert. I hit the green button, sat back, and listened to it ring twice before a voice that was far too perky for that early hour enthusiastically said, "Hey, baby! Whatcha doing up already?"

"Hi, Mom. Sorry to call so early, but I need your help."

There was rustling in the background, then she told me, "Okay, sweetie. I got my coffee and I closed the door to my office, so your dad and Casey should leave me alone for a bit. Start at the beginning, and we'll see if we can't figure this out."

I opened my mouth to start talking, but nothing came out. After a few more false starts, I decided to just dive right in. "So, it wasn't just Katie I found."

"Oh no, baby! Does she have a new man? If she does, that's okay! Don't worry! Whoever he is, while I'm sure he's a very nice young man, he's not for our Katie. We just need to show her how wrong he is for her. Hmm..."

I flopped down on my bed, stared at the ceiling, and waited a beat before telling her, "Mom, it isn't that. She's single."

" Oh, thank goodness! What's the problem, then, honey?"

"It's not necessarily a problem, Mom. It's...well...Finn."

"Cade, sweetie, I'm not following. Who is this Finn fellow, and why is this a problem, but also not?"

"Finn is short for Finnley. And she is Katie's ...or rather, mine...or, well..."

All levity had left her tone when she demanded, "Cadeon Jackson Cross, you better finish that sentence *right now*, young man."

I mentally girded my loins and said, "Finn is...ours."

The clacking of her heels across the hardwood floor of her office carried across the line, and she audibly sucked in a breath before she screeched, "Are you telling me I have a grandbaby?"

I winced and jerked the phone away from my ear. Once she finished yelling, I cautiously answered, "Yes?"

The screeching picked up again, and I kept my cell at arm's length, waiting for the noise to die down. The creak of a door opening let me know someone else was in the room, and my dad's concerned voice asked, "Carol, hon, why on earth are you screaming like a banshee at seven o'clock the morning?"

I didn't catch what my mother said, but it was apparent that she had broken the news when my dad's "WHAT?" overpowered over my mom's unintelligible ramblings.

Never one to miss out, Casey's inquiry of "What'd Cade do now?" carried across the line.

The whole gang was there. Awesome. Above the cacophony, I heard my dad shout, "Damn it, Cade! Did you forget the safe sex talk we had when you two started dating?"

Sighing in exasperation, I reminded him, "Dad, there was no safe sex talk. You dumped half a box of condoms on my bed and told me they were to protect the sheep, laughed at yourself for two minutes, then told me to, and I quote, 'wrap it before you tap it,' and left."

"Exactly! What part of 'wrap it before you tap it' did you miss?"

"Really, Paul? *That* was your safe sex talk? No wonder he got her pregnant. With advice like that, I'm surprised I only have *one* grandbaby! Oh, my goodness, I have a grand-baby. I'm a grandma!"

For the first time in ten minutes, the only sound was heavy breathing and a silence that was broken by my father's succinct exclamation. "Holy shit, Carol. We're grandparents."

Not wanting to miss out on the gap in conversation, and simultaneously hoping to bring them back on topic, I smiled and said, "Yes. You are. Her name is Finnley Cadence Troyer. She's three, and she is amazing."

"Finnley," my mom cooed. "You said she's three? Oh, no. That's the reason Katie's uncle kicked her out, isn't it?"

I nodded my head, then remembered I had intention-ally opted not to Face Time her so she couldn't see me. "Yeah, but that isn't what's important. Katie has done so well for herself, Mom. She's got a place, and she's going to school. You can see how much Katie adores Finn, and honestly, I don't think either of them would be as happy as they are had they stayed in that house."

I could hear the relief in my mom's voice when she said,

"Thank God. I'm glad she is safe and well. I was worried sick over her when I found out what had happened. Now, tell me more about my granddaughter."

I gulped, ashamed when I realized that my list only consisted of the few things Katie had mentioned. I had been so focused on doing what I thought was in Katie's best interest that I had overlooked the fact that I had a daughter I desperately wanted to know. No wonder Katie was so pissed.

Shamefully, I admitted, "I don't know a lot about her yet, Mom. I just found out about her a couple of days ago and haven't had the chance to learn much about her—and I'm not sure I'll get to if I can't fix things with Katie."

"Well, luckily for you, I give excellent advice. But first, you have to explain precisely what it is you did. In detail. After that, we can discuss when I get to meet my little Finn."

CHAPTER 23

CADE

I closed my eyes and reviewed the conversation I'd had with my mom—after she had finished reaming me out for my "colossally stupid choices thus far"—hoping her suggestions would put me back in Katie's good graces.

My knuckles rapped against her door, and I said a silent prayer that she would answer. When it jerked opened, I was greeted by a visibly pissed off Katie, but I swore in that moment she was the most beautiful thing I had ever seen.

Her raven locks were in a bun precariously perched on the top of her head. The wide-neck *Star Wars* shirt had slipped off one of her shoulders, showing tantalizing glimpses of creamy skin. Tiny pink shorts peeked out from the edges of her top, and fuzzy black socks encased her dainty feet. She was breathtaking.

The pitter-patter of tiny feet echoed, and I looked past Katie, searching for their owner. Seconds later, I caught a flash of purple in the periphery. Turquoise eyes regarded me, narrowing with suspicion, and their petite owner tugged on Katie's shirt and made grabbing motions with her hands before imperiously ordering, "Mama, pick me up!"

Not taking her eyes off me, Katie lifted Finn and positioned her on her hip with practiced ease. Katie reached up and tucked a few of Finn's more rebellious curls behind her ear then nuzzled her hair, making sure to keep her cool gaze locked on mine. Finn, still unsure about my presence, shyly curled her face into Katie's neck. I hated that she was so wary of me.

Wanting to put her at ease, I smiled and waved my fingers at her like I had seen my mom do when she saw little kids at the store. Finn eyed me for a moment before her face broke out in a beautiful grin. She lifted a finger and pointed at my cheek before excitedly announcing, "Look, Mama! He has dumples too!"

Relieved that I had successfully broken the ice, I laughed and replied, "Well, yeah! Didn't your mommy tell you all the best people have dimples?"

She giggled and started to reach out for me, but the moment was broken when Katie moved out of my reach. Katie held up a finger to let me know she'd be right back and carried Finn over to the couch. She leaned down and said something to Finn in a low tone too quiet for me to hear before she grabbed the remote, turned on *Sesame Street*, and handed Finn her sippy cup. Once she was satisfied that

Finn was comfortable, she crossed back over to me and waited.

"Katie," I started. "First off, this is for you."

I held out the steaming caramel macchiato I'd picked up on the way there. "I know how much you used to love coffee, and I'm hoping you still do. If not, tell me, and I will find another *I'm sorry I'm an insensitive ass* apology offering."

A ghost of a smile passed her lips, and she hesitated for a moment before holding out her hand and taking the cup. Relieved that she accepted it, I released the pent-up breath I had been holding.

"Second, I spoke to Kelly. She never told me you tried to contact me. Ever. She did it intentionally for her own selfish reasons, but as much as I would like to lay all the blame at her feet, she wouldn't have been able to interfere if I hadn't given her the opportunity. I need you to understand that had I gotten even one of those notes or calls or emails, before or after you found out about Finn, I would have been there in a hot minute."

"I realize I have failed you in more ways than I can even begin to understand. I was MIA when you needed me most. Because of my selfishness, I not only lost out on the life we should have had, but I also sacrificed the chance to know my daughter. Then, when you gave me the opportunity to right those wrongs, I was too lost in my own needs and desires to recognize that I was failing you once again. I've missed so much; I don't want to miss out anymore."

Her uncertain eyes studied me over the rim of her coffee cup, and she took a few sips, biding her time until she made her decision. I had never been someone to beg, but I would grovel at her feet if she would grant me one last chance to get things right. She'd said she needed actions, not words, but how could I show her I meant what I said if she wouldn't let me try?

Out of options, I did the only thing I could. Taking her other hand in mine and looking into her eyes, I pleaded, "Please, Katie. I am begging you. Let me show you I want to be here. That I can do this. I want to earn my right to be part of the family you and Finn have created. Please, let me give it one more shot. Don't give up on me. Not yet."

She tilted her head to the side and her observant green eyes traveled over my face in search of any deceit. I stood, unmoving, giving her all the time she needed. Waiting for her to tell me my fate was agonizing, but one thing my mom had stressed was that I needed to let Katie decide how things were going to go, rather than trying to force it. Finally, after what felt like eons, Katie pulled her hand from mine.

Defeat was a heavy burden weighing down on me and making it hard to breathe. My attempts to earn her forgiveness were too little, too late. Sick with loss, I held on to the door jamb, not trusting my legs to keep me upright.

The knowledge that I was about to shatter on her doorstep forced me to move. Turning away from the life that should have been mine was almost impossible, but I had done enough damage. Slowly, I put one foot in front of the other and started dragging myself toward the stairwell.

An exasperated "What is it with you? Jesus..." was all I heard before a delicate hand grabbed my shoulder with surprising force and jerked me to a stop.

Katie stepped in front of me and gave me a once-over.

Her eyes were still burning with suspicion, but I thought I could detect a hint of indecision there as well. That miniscule speck of something soft and tender reignited my small glimmer of hope. She bit her lip and scanned my face one final time before she gave me a small smile. "Cade, would you like to join Finn and me for breakfast?"

CHAPTER 24

KATIE

> "There is a space between man's imagination and man's attainment that may only be traversed by his longing."
>
> — KAHLIL GIBRAN

I rubbed the sleep from my eyes and sipped my coffee as I watched the sun slowly creep into the sky, letting thoughts of Cade slide into the forefront of my mind. Today marked two weeks since Cade had shown up on my doorstep, begging for one more chance. After a heart-to-heart over breakfast, I'd fully expected Cade to be a regular part of Finn's life, but I assumed that because of his lifestyle, it would mainly be via calls, presents, and occasional visits. I was unprepared for him to dive in with both feet and make himself at home.

In the beginning, I resisted having him be a part of our daily lives, but he wore me down with his thoughtfulness, consistency, and blatant adoration of Finn. He made it a point to take every opportunity available to make memories with her.

Now, my day didn't feel right without him in it. I should be more concerned than I was, but I couldn't muster up the energy to keep distancing myself from him. Having Cade back in my life was so easy. Plus, I had forgotten how wonderful it was not to be alone. Between Cade and his parents, I had been reminded—repeatedly—that Finn and I had a family outside of the small one we had created here.

Every single morning since I'd agreed to let him try, Cade had shown up at my doorstep before Finn woke up with a grin on his face and a delicious latte for me in his hand. Some days Finn slept in long enough for us to chat, giving us the opportunity to gradually become reacquainted.

Other days, Finn was up as soon as I opened the door, knowing her new friend "Tade" was here. The first few times she had called for Cade to get her out of bed instead of me, there was an unfamiliar pang of jealousy, but now I only grinned, knowing I had some extra time to enjoy my morning before I switched into mom mode.

Each time Cade was here, he would do little things for me. With each gesture, a chunk of the wall I had erected around my heart crumbled. Cleaning the kitchen every evening since he remembered how much I had always loathed doing dishes? There went a brick. Demanding I take a bubble bath because he didn't think I took enough time for myself? Another block down. Learning to make macaroni and cheese from scratch because Finn liked it so much? Yep, you guessed it, one more chink in the armor. Add in the fact that every single night I had dreams of licking the abs that lay hidden under his fitted T-shirts like an ice cream cone, and I was most definitely in trouble.

The quiet knock on the door pulled me out of my musings, and I had to fight the urge to sprint to the door. A grin split my face at the knowledge that he was on the other side. I wasn't sure what today would bring, but I could guarantee that it would be fantastic as long as it involved Cade. My hand grasped the knob, and I took a moment to remind my inner hussy to keep it in her pants. Just because I was having problems lusting after Cade did not mean he needed to be aware that every time I saw those dimples, I wanted to get naked and climb him like a tree.

When I felt in control of myself, I opened the door. Cade's enthusiastic smile greeted me, and I did my best to put the butterflies currently having a rave in my stomach back into their net. I inhaled the scent of chocolate and caramel and excitedly made *gimme* motions with my hands until he relented and passed me the steaming cup of coffee he'd been holding hostage. After I had taken the first glorious sip, he gave me an affectionate kiss on the forehead before walking inside. "Good morning, beautiful. Is our girl awake yet, or do I have some time with her sexy Mama first?"

"She's still sleeping. Wanna watch some TV while we wait for her to wake up?"

Cade grabbed my hand and led me to the couch, where we both flopped down in our respective spots. We flicked through a few options before settling on one of the new Netflix shows. A few minutes in, Cade surprised me by pulling my feet onto his lap and beginning to massage them.

I had never really been one who enjoyed having her

feet touched. In actuality, feet grossed me out, but at that moment, I was feeling anything but disgust. With each stroke of his hands, pleasant tingles began erupting all over my body. Though his actions were meant to be innocent and friendly, if Cade glanced in the vicinity of my chest, he would know exactly how much I was enjoying his touch and how non-friend-like my current thoughts were.

I cursed my traitorous nipples and crossed my arms over my chest to hide their overenthusiastic response to the brush of his hands over my feet, doing my best to tamp down my growing arousal. I silently cursed myself for my inability to control my libido and did my best to focus on the television. I mean, it had been a while, but this was bordering on ridiculous. Maybe Layla was right, and it was high time I went out on a date or two.

After weighing the pros and cons for a bit, I decided that was the perfect solution to my problem and added *'Find man I want to see naked who is not Cadeon Cross'* to my mental checklist. High five to me for my amazing problem-solving abilities.

Lost in thought, it took me a second to notice that Cade's hands had begun a slow progression north. Still watching the program he'd selected, his focus was away from me, but those magical hands were working their way up my legs inch by agonizingly slow inch. Every brush sent a jolt of arousal straight to my core, and I had to fight the urge to rub my thighs together to ease the growing ache. Finally, when he passed my knee, I couldn't take it anymore and pulled my feet from his lap.

Cade's brow scrunched in confusion, and his blue eyes

filled with concern. "Was that okay? Did I do something wrong?"

Not wanting him to get the wrong impression, I shook my head and quickly said, "Nope! Just needed to shift."

Cade studied me suspiciously before offering me a lopsided smile and pulling me into the crook of his arm. Absentmindedly, he began tracing patterns on the exposed skin of my shoulders. I willed myself to relax, but I couldn't. Even though his touches were innocent, I was achy and needy all over. I needed some space between us, and fast. Abruptly, I stood and started to move toward the bathroom figuring a cold shower was in order, but I was stopped short by Cade.

In one fluid motion, he grabbed my hand and pulled me into his lap. He released his grip and moved his hands to cradle my face. His thumb slowly traced my lower lip, and desire simmered in his azure gaze. He paused, allowing me time to stop things if I so chose, but I had no intention of stopping this. Instead, I leaned in.

His luscious lips kicked up at the corner, then he closed the short distance that remained, and his lips met my own. Whisper soft, they brushed across mine, each pass sending a new wave of heat straight to my center. I arched my neck, purring as he began nipping and licking the column of my throat. Dissatisfied with how much space there still was between us, I widened my legs, settling me deeper into his lap, eliciting mutual gasps of pleasure as my core slid against his hard erection.

Abandoning his gentle approach, Cade's hands cupped my ass, and his mouth hungrily crashed into my own. Our tongues tangled together, and Cade's hands worked my body back and forth over his length. I moaned in approval and slid my hands under his shirt, reveling in the way his hard muscles shifted underneath my fingertips. Lost in a sea of lust, I wantonly rubbed myself against him, and was just about to suggest we move this to the bedroom when a tiny voice called out, "Tade? Tade, is yous here? I get up now!"

Hearing Finn's voice was like being doused by a bucket of ice water. My lust instantly dissipated, and all that I was left with was disheveled clothing and uncomfortably wet panties. I sighed at my misfortune, climbed off Cade, and went about readjusting my pajamas. Once I was presentable, I held out a hand and pulled Cade up. He patted down a few wayward hairs on his head before leaning in and nibbling on my earlobe. When I let out an involuntary shiver, he whispered, "Just so you know, we *will* be picking up where we left off. Soon."

After one last long, drugging kiss, he released me. Cade playfully smacked my behind and gave me a cheeky grin before saying, "Now, go take a shower while Miss Finn and I work on whipping up some breakfast. I've got some hungry girls to feed."

CHAPTER 25

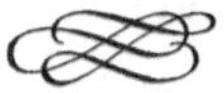

KATIE

"You cannot swim for new horizons until you have the courage to lose sight of the shore."

— WILLIAM FAULKNER

I turned the shower on and adjusted the water temperature until it was a few degrees shy of boiling and stepped into the spray. Resting my chin on my chest, I let the water stream down my back and kneaded the tense muscles at the base of my neck.

My mind was going a million miles an hour, and I was distinctly unsettled. A large part of me wanted to storm into the living room, toss Cade over my shoulder cavewoman-style, and have my merry way with him. At the same time, my more logical side was screaming at me the myriad of reasons that was an absolutely horrid idea.

On the one hand, it had been an embarrassingly long time since I'd had an orgasm compliments of someone other than myself and my handy-dandy vibrating friends. On the flip side, blurring the boundaries of Cade's and my burgeoning friendship would be the equivalent of holding a lit match to a piece of paper and hoping it didn't catch fire.

My heart wanted Cade, but I was terrified the cost would be too high. I was drowning in a sea of questions, and I *hated* it. *What happens if it blows up in my face? What about Finn? What about our plan? What happens when he leaves?*

The last thought stopped me short. I was such an idiot. I had been so wrapped up in our perfect bubble that I had completely ignored the fact that Cade wouldn't be sticking around. He couldn't—according to the official Devil's Cross website, he was scheduled to perform in London in three weeks, before spending the subsequent four months traipsing all over Europe.

No matter how hard I pretended otherwise, I was still nothing more than a naive child. Finn and I didn't fit into Cade's world, and Cade had proven to me once that when faced with a choice between me or his career, he would choose the latter. The only thing I could do was prepare for the inevitable and do my best to mitigate the fallout.

Obviously, we had a lot of things we needed to settle before he took off for parts unknown. We had yet to explain to Finn who he was, mainly because I hadn't been ready. Cade had wanted to tell her on day one, but I'd wanted to let Finn get used to having him around and get to know him first, so I had drug my feet. Now, Finn worshipped the ground he walked on, just like the rest of the world.

The only difference was Cade worshipped her back. She'd had him wrapped around her dainty pinky two hours into his first visit, and he seemed perfectly happy to remain there. Continuing to keep Cade's parental status a secret from Finn would be unfair to them both, so I needed to put on my big girl panties and tell her about the other person who helped bring her into the world.

As painful as telling her would be, I knew the harder part would be forcing myself to trust that he wouldn't fail Finn the way he'd failed me. I could handle being abandoned. It would hurt like hell—especially since whether I wanted to admit it or not, I still had some epic lingering feelings where Cade was concerned, but I had already done it once, and I would do it again if I had to.

Finn was another matter entirely. She was going to have a hard-enough time once she realized he wouldn't be here every day, so infrequent contact was not going to be an option. We needed to discuss how he would keep in touch with her while he was away, so she didn't think she had been forgotten.

Realizing I had been washing my hair for the last ten minutes, I decided my thought-filled shower session needed to come to a close. Once I had rinsed away the suds and given myself a quick scrub, I hopped out and dried off just in time to hear Cade holler, "Katie, you all done, love? I made omelets!"

I threw on some clothes and headed down the hall to find Cade staring intently at Finn. "So, you're telling me"—Cade scooped some eggs on Finns plate—"that you think Minnie is cooler than Mickey? No way, Mickey is the coolest! He has Pluto and super-awesome red pants."

Finn's chocolate curls bounced as she forcefully shook her head then she stubbornly crossed her tiny arms. "No.

Minnie's better. She's pwetty and hab pokey-dots on her dwess and her dwess is pink! Me hab more juice, pweas."

Cade refilled her cup and considered her viewpoint before answering, "Okay, fine. I'll let you have this one. Polka-dots are kind of cool, and I know how much chicks dig hair accessories. I'm not gonna say I'm a convert from Camp Mickey, but I can admit Minnie is kind of cool too."

After Finn clapped in approval, Cade grabbed her fork and fed her the last bite of eggs, complete with train noises. Smiling at his antics, I let my presence be known when I asked, "Train noises? I thought the standard was airplanes, and why are you feeding her anyway? She can do it herself."

Cade arched an eyebrow and replied, "Airplane noises are strictly reserved for the unoriginal. I'll have you know we've also done car honks, semitruck horns, tugboats, motorcycles, a guitar riff, and a funky retro seventies beat. We were simply starting over at the beginning. And I'm feeding her because she asked me to 'gib her bites, pwease.' How am I supposed to say no to that?"

I couldn't help but smile. Those two really were two peas in a pod. Seeing how much Cade enjoyed spending time with Finn gave me hope that we would be able to work everything out. Taking a seat next to Cade, I dug in, watching as he cleaned Finn up and set her down so she could go play.

Once she was out of earshot, Cade turned to me and asked, "You're looking far too serious for this early in the morning, sunshine. What's on your mind?"

Unsure of how to begin, I nervously twisted my napkin a few times, then decided on a soft approach. I focused on keeping my voice light when I spoke, wanting to feel him out a bit before determining the best way to approach the discussion. "Nothing much. I just realized this morning that you leave in a few weeks. It took me by surprise is all."

Understanding dawned on Cade's face. "You're afraid I'm going to leave to finish the tour and not come back."

I was taken aback by how quickly he'd drawn my most profound worry into the light, which made me wonder if he had been aware of it all along. Not interested in beating around the bush, I replied, "Yes, that is one of my concerns. My biggest one, if I'm being honest. However, right now, I'm more focused on what you'd like to do about Finn. She already adores you and isn't going to understand why you're not here."

He grabbed my chair and turned it so we were facing one another. His blue eyes were troubled and looked a touch sad at my admission. "Katie, I need you to understand something. These last few weeks with you and Finn have been amazing. Being able to come here every day, to experience this beautiful life you've built for you and Finn blows my mind."

His foot hooked the leg of my chair, pulling me closer so our knees brushed. Gently, his hands pulled my face in so he could give me a soft kiss. "When I was younger, I mistakenly thought fame and fortune were what I needed to have a successful, happy life, but I was wrong. The music made me happy, but the rest of it? The exhaustive touring, the booze, the drugs, the girls? Nah."

"Seeing you all soft and sleepy in the morning? Making a mess of your kitchen while Finn and I bake? Hearing little giggles all day as I watch some princess movie for the thousandth time? Spending an hour trying to unsuccessfully wash glitter out of my hair after Finn and I do crafts all afternoon? I have felt more alive and more fulfilled these last two weeks with you two than I have in all the years I've been performing combined."

Happiness flooded my body, and hope flared in my chest at his words. The possibility of having Cade around full-time called to me and filled me with bone-deep longing. Yet, as much as I wanted that, my main focus was making sure he would be there for Finn. I reached out, grasping his hands, beginning to trace patterns across the back while I gathered my thoughts.

"Cade." My voice wavered with uncertainty. "That is all well and good, but you can be content and satisfied in one place and still choose to be somewhere else. I understand you have obligations. Your band and your fans are all relying on you, and neither Finn nor I are asking you to ignore those duties. I just want to know you're not going to let Finn fall through the cracks."

Cade stood, pulling me up with him and into his arms. Leather and pine filled my nostrils, calming me, letting me relax into his hold. Cade ran his nose along my hairline, and a contented hum rumbled in his chest. His lips touched my forehead before he kissed the tip of my nose.

His smile was affectionate as he teased, "Oh, my Kit-Kat. I am shit at explaining things properly, aren't I? I'm not going anywhere, love. I may have to leave now and then for tours or press events, but at the end of the day, the only place I want to be is here. I've been tap-dancing around my feelings for you, not wanting to come on too strong or scare you away, but there's something you need to understand. You and Finn? You two are my home. Wherever you are is where I want to be. At the end of the day, that is what matters, and you and I can figure out all the rest."

Happiness infused my entire being, and when his lips claimed my own, the last of my walls crumbled. My heart hovered on the precipice—all it needed was a tiny nudge and it would tumble over the edge. I could only hope Cade would be there to catch me when I fell and that he would take more care with my heart this time around.

CHAPTER 26

CADE

I thrust my hands in the soapy water, pulled out the dirty plate, and made absent-minded swipes across the surface with the sponge. I could have used the dishwasher, but I needed a distraction after my talk with Katie this morning, and found the repetitive motions soothing. I'd meant every word I said to Katie. She and Finn were mine, and I would fight anyone and anything that stood between my girls and me.

Katie might not realize it yet, but she'd captured my heart before I even fully understood what love was, and she still held it in the palm of her hand. I'd known when I gave it to her that no one else would ever deserve it, and I had been right. All the women between then and now had been nothing more than bed-warmers, unworthy of extra time or attention, so I had never worried about the fact that I'd lacked a heart. They didn't need to know that it lived outside of my chest, sitting with its other half, waiting for me to find my way home.

I was all-in, but as hard as Katie was trying, she wasn't there yet. I had three weeks to convince Katie that I was worthy of her love and to show her that she, Finn, and I would be amazing as a family. I also wanted to try my hardest to convince her and Finn to come on tour with me.

I remembered how often Katie had talked about wanting to backpack across Europe when we were younger, and while a tour would be a little different, I knew she would love it. I was also reluctant to leave them both for so long. I was barely able to handle being away from them long enough to sleep, so I wasn't sure how I would be able to function being on an entirely different continent than them. The question was how to go about showing Katie that coming with me wasn't a terrible plan.

Out of nowhere, a thought slammed into my brain, and I wanted to bang my head against the wall for being such an idiot. Here I was planning to ask Katie to disrupt her entire life for me, to leave everything familiar behind so that we could be a unit, and I hadn't even bothered to think about showing her what she would gain. I was hoping she would make a decision in my favor without giving her all the variables. That was a situation I needed to remedy. Drying my hands, I quickly shot off a text, praying I was making the right choice.

Me: Hey, what are you guys up to?

Trev: Not much. Just watching *Lord of the Rings* and debating whether if you saw a female hobbit naked, would it have more of a seventies bush or an untamed jungle forest? So far, the votes are divided.

Me: Wha...why...what in the actual fuck, dude?

Trev: In my defense, Rhys was the one who started the debate. I just chose to participate. Dante and I are firmly thinking untamed jungle due to the natural hairiness of hobbits in general. Zane says seventies bush because he's assuming lady-hobbits prune the garden. What do you think?

Me: Fair enough, and honestly, I have zero desire to picture a female hobbit naked, so I'm pleading the Fifth. Do you and the guys feel like coming over to Katie's later and chilling out with some pizza?

Trev: Hells yes! Do we finally get to meet baby Cade? Do we, do we, do we?!?!

Me: LMAO. Yes. Finn and Katie will both be here.

Trev: No shit? We get to hang with the badass baby mama too? Hot damn!

Me: You're a jackass. See you all in two hours.

I slid my cell into my front pocket and crept down the hall. I snuck a peek into Finn's room to find her sitting on Katie's lap, laughing hysterically, while Katie read *Bear's Book of Feelings* by Jenny H. Lyman in silly voices. Silently, I gazed at Katie, in awe of how stunning she was in that moment.

The sun peeking through the curtains made her glossy black hair shimmer, her green eyes sparkle with laughter and love, and her smile so bright it was almost blinding. I knew that fifty years from now, when I was old and gray, I would still be able to close my eyes and picture every detail of this moment in my mind.

Tentatively, I stepped into the room. Katie caught my eye and gave me a wink, never pausing her dramatic retelling of the myriad of feelings Bear experienced in the short book. When she finished, she picked Finn up and blew a raspberry on her tummy before setting out crayons and a coloring book. She held out a hand, and I pulled her to her feet. Studying me for a moment, she squinted her eyes and shook a finger at me. "You're looking awfully suspicious, mister. What did you do?"

I casually threw my arm over her shoulder as we strolled out of the room, and replied, "Your masterful skills at deduction are unparalleled. You are correct—I did do a thing, and I'm *really* hoping you won't be mad at me for it."

Her teasing gaze turned suspicious, and she waved an imperious hand at, me telling me to go on. I thought about holding out on sheer principle, but ultimately gave in. "Katie, my Katie, I hope this doesn't make you angry, but I invited the guys over for some pizza. They'll be here in two hours."

Panic overtook her features, and her eyes began to rapidly scan her small apartment, as if doing their best to decide if it was tidy enough for company. Before she got any more riled up, I held up a finger, asking her to wait just a moment. This had seemed like such a fantastic plan just a few minutes ago, but now I wasn't so sure. She looked freaked out—the question was if it was because the guys specifically or the idea of company in general. "Katie, calm down, babe. I realize I probably should have run it by you first, but hear me out, okay?"

I took her silence as assent, and went on, "I was thinking, and I realized that I've been asking you and Finn to make a place for me in your lives, but I've failed to bring you into mine. My parents and Casey adore you and call me daily asking when they will be able to meet Miss Finn. I know for a fact that when you are ready, they are going to spoil the shit out of her. Yet, as fantastic as they are, they are the family I was born with. Trev, Zane, Rhys, and Dante are the family that I chose. They are my bandmates, sure, but they are also my brothers. I cannot go on tour and have you wondering who I'm with or what I'm doing. I want you to be comfortable texting any one of the guys at any time, for any reason, no matter how small. I never again want you to feel like I am unreachable."

Then I paused, taking a deep breath. This was it.

"Besides, I'm also hoping they charm you enough that you and Finn will agree to come on tour with me, so I don't have to suffer the agony of loneliness without you for the next couple of months. I've been spoiled the last few weeks having two gorgeous gals light up my mornings, and I'm not keen on going without."

Katie grasped my shirt and pulled me in for a quick kiss. She gave me a sexy smirk before she said, "That, Mr. Cross, is a conversation for another day."

Patting my chest, she added, "Now, do be a dear and grab the broom from the closet. You're the one who invited over the guys. Therefore, you can also be the one to make the apartment company-ready. Luckily for you, your butt looks good enough in those jeans that I shall kindly offer to help you so I can enjoy the view."

Doing as instructed, I grabbed the broom and couldn't keep the goofy smile off my face. Damn if I didn't love this girl.

CHAPTER 27

CADE

The rapping of knuckles echoed across the quiet apartment. I gave Katie a reassuring grin and a thumbs-up before opening the door. In an instant, the peace was replaced by the best kind of chaos. All the guys were tripping over one another, each one trying to be the first to enter "the sacred castle" and see firsthand grown-up Katie and "baby Cade."

Laughing at the ridiculous scene, I snagged the pizza from Trev to prevent it from being dropped in the melee. After I set it on the counter, I took a seat, content just to observe for the time being.

Katie was standing off to the side, shuffling her feet and worrying her bottom lip. Her nervousness made me smile. She didn't realize it yet, but as soon as I claimed her as mine, she had also become theirs. As far as the guys were concerned, she and Finn were family. She had nothing to be worried about. Rhys shoved his way to Katie first, scooping her into a giant bear hug. "Kit-Kat! My long-lost love! I'm so glad we found each other once again!"

Katie giggled and returned his hug. "I missed you too, you big oaf."

Rhys set Katie back on her feet then backed away so each of the guys could greet Katie. After she'd been enveloped in her fourth hug, her shoulders visibly relaxed, and a grin had taken up residence on her face. At some point, the noise had drawn Finn out of her room, and she'd sidled over to my chair, eyeing the strangers hugging her mom.

Once their attention turned our way, Finn tugged on my pant leg and held her arms up. Warmth flooded my chest, knowing she felt safe enough with me to seek me out for comfort when she was unsure. I picked her up and sat her on my lap. After she was settled, I kissed the top of her soft curls and waited to see how she would react to meeting everyone.

Each of the guys made an effort to talk to Finn, but she wasn't having it. Rhys tried to lure her into conversation with pictures of his oldest brother's new puppy. Zane whipped out his phone and offered to let her play a game. Trev made every funny face he could think of, but Finn wouldn't even crack a smile. I wasn't shocked. In the last few weeks, the only people I'd heard her mention with any consistency were Layla, Mrs. J, and Ryan. She wasn't used to having her space invaded by overgrown man-children, so it made sense that she was a bit nervous.

I waited a few more minutes and was getting ready to

jump in and break the ice, when Dante's deep bass carried over the din. His black eyes zeroed in on the character filling the front of Finn's T-shirt. "You like Ariel?"

Finn warily nodded her head, not taking her eyes off Dante. Dante gave her a soft smile and shocked the rest of us when he began belting out "Kiss the Girl." Finn perked up and leaned forward, excited to hear more. The guys watched Finn with rapt attention and once it was established that this was the way to her heart, each of the guys started chiming in with a different song, creating one hell of a Disney medley. When they were finished, all of Finn's apprehension had faded away. She offered an enthusiastic round of applause before demanding, "Down! Down!"

As soon as her feet hit the ground, she ran over to the guys, happily crying, "Yay, singing fwends!"

As Katie and Finn allowed themselves to be fully enveloped into the fold, the last of my missing pieces clicked into place. Now, if I could only convince Katie to come with me, so they stay that way, things would be perfect.

Two hours later, Katie tied the last trash bag closed and handed it to me. With a mischievous grin, she said, "Okay, rock star, let's see if you remember how to do things normal people do—like take out the trash. The dumpsters are down the stairs and around back. Oh, and mind any screaming girls you encounter along the way!"

Confident I would obey, she sashayed into the living room, reaching down and starting to put the toys away. I bit my knuckle, staring at her heart-shaped ass. In short order, images of her naked and bent over the couch flooded my mind. I shook my head to clear the drool-worthy mental image I had conjured up. *Down, boy.* I picked up the bag, pulled the door open, and almost ran over a tiny older woman standing in the hall. "Hey, babe?" I called back to her. "There's someone at the door. I think it's for you?"

Katie leaned around me and released an excited "Eek!" And I found myself being shoved aside as she pulled the older woman in for a hug. "Mrs. J! I'm so happy to see you! Finn has missed you so much. How was visiting your son? How are your grandbabies?"

The older woman affectionately patted Katie's back, and replied, "Oh, the visit was lovely, dear! Kevin and his wife are doing fabulous. He just got a promotion, and his wife Lisa told me that in a few months, they'll be adopting. I'm terribly excited to have another small one to spoil. My little Tommy is getting so big, and his brother, Chad, is turning into quite the charmer. Those two will make excellent big brothers when their new sibling arrives."

Both women maneuvered around me into the apartment. Katie looked down at the bag as they passed, then back at me, and made a shooing motion with her hand. I rolled my eyes in mock irritation, but did as ordered and headed to the dumpster.

When I stepped back inside, I found Mrs. J watching at Finn with rapt attention, patiently listening as Finn told her about everything that had happened in the last few weeks. Katie carefully carried a cup of hot tea over to her and motioned for me to join them. I knew about Mrs. J from all the stories Katie and Finn had told, and it was evident that both of my girls adored her, and that the feeling was mutual.

Not wanting to intrude on their visit, I quietly slipped onto the couch, watching the girls chatter with amusement.

Not long after my return, Mrs. J's astute chocolate gaze scanned my features, before sliding down to Finn then shifting over to Katie. Her eyes hovered on Katie, catching the slight softening of Katie's features whenever she looked my way. After a beat, Mrs. J's intense brown eyes once again landed on me, and I resisted the urge to squirm. The woman studied me intently for a moment, then her heart-shaped face split into a knowing smile. She rose from her chair with a surprising amount of grace and made her way over to me. "Hello, dear. I'm Mrs. Jenkins, but everyone calls me Mrs. J."

I took her wrinkled hand in mine and gave it a firm shake. "It is nice to meet you, ma'am. I've heard lots of great things from Katie and Finn, and I'm glad to be able to pair a face with the name. I'm Cadeon Cross, but my friends call me Cade."

She eyed me for a moment, then nudged Finn in Katie's direction. "Katie, do be a dear and start Finn's bath for me? I'll be in to take over in just a moment."

Katie slid her hand around Finn's, gave me a look I could only interpret as *good luck,* shrugged, and moved down the hall. As soon as they were out of sight, the atmosphere became frosty, and Mrs. J pointed an accusing finger in my face. "Young man, I know very well who you are. I believe the more pertinent question is, where have you been? I know it hasn't been here, because I have lived next door to that young woman for over two years and haven't seen hide nor hair of you."

Taken aback, I nervously tugged on my collar. I didn't

owe this woman an explanation, yet felt compelled to give her one. I tried to stay strong, to be stoic, and had every intention of waiting her out, but I was withering under her chastising glare. The fight was lost when she crossed her arms and started tapping her foot, taking me back to when I used to get scolded by my grandma. In a rush I blurted out, "I didn't know. About Finn, I mean. I, um, well, Katie and I have a...history."

The foot-tapping frequency increased, and her gaze narrowed. Intimidated by this pint-sized fury, I kept going. "I came looking for her. I knew I had messed up by letting her go, and wanted her back. I didn't find out about Finn until later. I missed a lot, but I'm trying to make up for it. Truly, I am. Finn and Katie, they are what dreams are made of, and I'm working on being worthy of them. I'm not there yet, but I will be."

She leaned forward and held her face inches from my own, scrutinizing my face in search of even a hint of deceit. Appeased when she found none, her eyes filled with warmth, and a wrinkled hand patted my cheek. "Yes, you'll do. You will do just fine for my Katie and little Finn."

Mrs. J then cocked her head to the side, listening, before making her way back to the armchair she'd abandoned, moments before Katie re-entered the living room. Katie took in the woman's sly smile and the confused expression plastered on my face, and turned to Mrs. J. "What did I miss?"

"Oh, nothing, dear. Just getting to know your Cade is all."

With that, she rose and began to walk down the hallway to monitor Finn's bath. Halfway there she paused, and casually said, "Oh, and Katie dear? Tell me when your next day off is. I do believe you and that young man are overdue for some special time together. Also, if you happen to snap a few photos of him without a shirt on and decide to share, I wouldn't be opposed. I'm old, but I am most certainly not dead, and that is one handsome fellow."

Aghast, I looked over at Katie to find her doubled over, laughing so hard tears were streaming down her face. "Should I tell her that if she googles you, she can do one better and see a picture of you in your underwear? Bet you're regretting doing those ads for Calvin Klein now!"

Picking up a pillow, I tossed it at her. "Very funny Kit-Kat! If you show her those, I get to show her that photo I took when you were twelve and accidentally singed your eyebrows off at Mrs. Litterbaum's barbecue!"

Katie's jaw dropped, and she pegged me in the face with the pillow I'd thrown her way. Her lower lip jutted out. She pouted for a beat before releasing a dramatic sigh. "Okay, fine. I promise not to inform her that she can find pictures of your half-naked body all over the internet if the pictures of me sans brows never see the light of day. Deal?"

"Deal. Now, on to the next major question: do you have to go into work?"

Katie's green gaze narrowed in warning. "Don't push this, Cade."

Gently, I ran my hand down her arm to reassure her that I wasn't trying to start an argument. "I'm not trying to push it, Katie, honest. I just really don't like seeing you go to work somewhere you hate when there is no need. Every time you mention work, your whole demeanor changes. It's written all over your face how much you despise being there, and it kills me. I don't want to take away your independence."

I twined my fingers with he's and gently squeezed. "I want to give you the freedom to do whatever it is you love. If there's anything you want to do or something that you're passionate about, I will support you one hundred and ten percent in whatever way you need. I have money, Katie, more than I could ever hope to spend. Let me share it with you and Finn. You don't have to go it alone anymore. I'm here, and I'm not going anywhere."

Katie's eyes were wise, yet touched with sadness when she said, "You are so sweet, Cade. Sometimes too sweet, because it makes it so hard to say no to you. I get what you're saying, and I am so grateful that you want to support my hopes and dreams, but I don't want you to show your support by throwing money at me. Be there for me. That is all I ask and all I need. As for Finn, you are welcome to spoil her within reason, but there will be no puppies, kittens, or ponies without prior discussion."

The soft kiss to my cheek lessened the sting of her words, but I knew my unhappiness at her response was written all over my face. Katie smiled playfully, shaking her head at my disapproval. "Quit being a baby about it. Besides, if we try to do this, to be a family, your fans are not going to be happy. They will want blood as payment for any ways in which they think I wronged you. That will be enough to deal by itself. We don't need to give them the opportunity to add the label of "gold digger" to the list. Now scooch, I've got to finish getting ready."

CHAPTER 28

KATIE

> "You pierce my soul. I am half agony, half hope."
>
> — PERSUASION JANE AUSTEN

It was the first time in weeks that my morning wouldn't begin with a latte from Cade, but he and the band had a conference call with their manager and their new PR rep, Quinn, to get her up to speed. I missed him, but he wasn't the only person who would be having an overdue conversation today. I tilted Finn's face back and forth, wiping the last traces of syrup off her chin. Satisfied that I got it all, I placed kisses on her chubby cheeks before lifting her out her highchair and carrying her to the couch.

Once we were settled, I tucked a curl behind her ear. Finn's wide, innocent eyes looked at me expectantly, and my whole body filled with love for this wonderful tiny being. I gave her a big smile and excitedly said, "Hey, baby girl, guess what? Mama has a surprise for you!"

"A s'prise? For me? Yay! I lub s'prises!"

"Yeppers! A surprise! You know, Cade?"

At the mention of Cade, Finn gave me a gigantic, toothy smile. "Yes! Tade is Finn's fwend. I lub Tade."

Her obvious adoration for Cade eased any misgivings I might have had, reassuring me that my choice to explain who Cade was to her was the right one. "I'm so glad you love Cade, 'cause guess what, bug? Cade loves you too. Great big bunches. In fact, Cade is extra special because he isn't just Finn's friend, he's something much cooler. Do you understand what a daddy is?"

Finn placed her finger on her lip and scrunched her brow, thinking about what I'd asked. After a long moment, she wiggled until I put her down and ran over to her bookshelf. Her ocean eyes scanned the covers for a moment before she grabbed one. Proudly, she held up a book displaying a cartoon bear family having a picnic on the cover in one hand, then pointed at the biggest bear wearing a hat and bow tie with the other. "Daddy! See? Daddy bear, mama bear, baby bear!"

I kneeled before her so that we were face-to-face, then confirmed, "Yes, that is a daddy! That is the little bear's daddy. Do you know what a daddy does?"

She was quiet, pondering hard about my question before she said, "Yes! Daddies gib hugs, and pway, and tiss boo-boos, and sing night-night songs."

I pulled the book from Finn's fingers and slid it back onto the shelf so I could wrap my arms around her narrow shoulders. Emotion clogged my throat, and I found myself blinking back tears. She was getting so big, and there were so many changes ahead of us. I wasn't sure what the future held, but I did know that hers would be filled with love.

When Finn pulled back, I held her hands and said, "Yes, ma'am, that is what daddies do! And you know what, kiddo? Cade is your daddy. He will love you, and help take care of you, and snuggle you for always."

A sharp knock, followed by the opening of my front door, drew my attention, making me forget what I had planned to say next. I was well on my way to irritation, when the man in question stepped inside. As soon as she saw him, Finn flew out of my lap and raced toward him, yelling, "Daddy!"

Cade scooped her up and pulled her in for a tight hug. A look of amazement crossed his face just before his teary gaze caught mine and he mouthed, 'Thank you.' Cade's arms tightened around Finn once more, then held her out in front of him. With a wobbly smile, he asked, "Hey Finn, could you call me Daddy again? I really, really liked it."

Finn giggled and smooshed his cheeks. "Daddy, I lub you."

"I love you too, bug."

Cade kissed her on the head, set her down and watched, misty-eyed, as she toddled over to her coloring books. With a goofy grin on his face, Cade pulled me up and into his embrace.

"Thank you, Katie. Hearing her call me 'Daddy' is by far my favorite sound ever."

My head rested on his chest, and as I stood there in his arms while Finn happily played in the background, a spark of yearning lit in my chest. The desire to have unlimited moments like this was overwhelming, but fear of the unknown still stood in my way. Not ready to examine those feelings further, I focused on Cade's wonderment. "You're welcome. She deserved to know, and over the last few weeks, you've earned the title. Now don't screw it up."

"I won't. Promise. I won't screw it up with you either, Katie. Not this time. We're at the edge of something amazing, but I can't go over it alone. I need you, Katie-mine. Fall with me?"

His azure gaze was full of adoration and hope, making my heart kick against my ribs. I understood what he was saying, and what he was asking. I'd found myself peering over the cliff's edge when it came to Cade more than once over the last few weeks, wondering if I could summon up the courage to jump and hoping that Cade would be there to catch me.

I wanted to lay claim to him, to shout to the world at the top of my lungs that this man was as much mine as I was his, but I couldn't quite make myself take the leap. Not yet. Needing to distance myself from the truth shining in his gaze, I quipped, "Katie-mine, huh? So, does that mean you're claiming me?"

Cade's smile dimmed when I dodged the question, but after a beat, his defeat morphed into determination when he said, "Well, duh! You've always been mine—I just let you forget it for a while. I'm thinking that I might have to jog that memory of yours. Good thing I ran into Mrs. J in the hallway, and she agreed that tonight would be perfect for Finn's very first sleepover. Don't worry though. I get that it may take some time and patience to remind you why we belong together. Luckily, I'm fully prepared to do whatever is necessary, even if it takes *all* night."

Immediately, every fantasy I'd had over the last few weeks flitted across my brain. Images of Cade naked and panting, sweat dripping down his corrugated abs as he moved over me, came to mind, making my nipples hard and my panties wet. Standing on tiptoe, I bit his ear and brushed the front of his jeans with my fingertips before informing him, "Oh, trust me, it will most definitely take all night."

I gave him a smirk, promising all kinds of naughty things, before sauntering down the hallway and into Finn's room. Once inside, I placed her small suitcase on the floor, closed the door, and sat down. I was so turned on I was sure I was going to spontaneously combust. The clock showed it was barely past noon, and I cursed Cade's sneaky ass for getting me all hot and bothered, knowing full well we still had hours before it would be time to drop Finn off.

If he thought I was going to walk around all day as horny as a thirteen-year-old boy who just discovered dad's porn stash, he was sadly mistaken. As far as I was concerned, if I had to suffer, so did he. Speaking of suffering, he'd damn well better be able to deliver on his promise, because after weeks of dancing around each other, I was due some orgasms.

Abandoning Finn's empty suitcase, I slipped into the bathroom across the hall for a very necessary personal grooming session. Once I was smooth and silky, I stepped out of the shower and slathered myself in lotion before putting on a short black silk robe. Tonight called for a Victoria's Secret level of hotness, so I grabbed a round brush and the hair dryer to give myself a quick blowout.

Once I finished my hair, I applied light makeup, then stepped back. Satisfied that I had achieved a perfect balance between just enough and too much, I adjusted my robe to ensure it just barely covered my ass and showed enough of my cleavage to be a tantalizing distraction.

Ready to cause some mischief, I peeked out the door, waited until I spotted Cade at the end of the hall, then casually crossed the short distance from the bathroom to my bedroom. Just outside my door, I paused, flipped my hair over my shoulder, and called out, "Cade? Can you do me a favor and grab Finn's backpack? I'd like to pack some toys for her to take over."

His blue eyes widened, and he ran a shaking hand down his face as he took me in. *Score one for Team Katie.* Ready to enact part two of my plan, I bit back a smile and let myself into my bedroom. Cade wasn't going to know what hit him.

~

Cade

She was trying to kill me. That was the only conclusion that made any sense. Since this morning, I'd had to witness Katie traipsing across the hall in the world's smallest bathrobe, followed by her parading around the apartment in a crop top and the tiniest shorts I'd ever seen. Now, she was torturing me as she went around the living room, picking up toys.

First, I'd had to watch those teeny shorts creep up ever so slightly every time she bent at the waist to grab stuffed animals. Then, I'd gotten teasing glimpses of the swell of her breasts every time she leaned forward to fluff a pillow or place a folded blanket in the basket. Now, I was biting my knuckle to prevent myself from groaning as she knelt in front of the couch, fishing toys out from underneath it with her ass in the air. Every time she stretched, the material of her shorts pulled taut, perfectly framing those luscious globes.

The sound of Finn singing carried down the hall, and I reminded myself that even though I had the worst case of blue balls I'd ever experienced in my life, I needed to keep myself in check for a little while longer. Unable to tamp down my obvious erection by sheer will alone, I shook my head in shame and went to my go-to destroyer of hard-ons from high school, forcing myself to picture the Golden Girls naked. Thank goodness for old tricks, because moments later I heard a soft knock at the front door.

Tiny feet raced past me, and Finn flew toward the door, only to stop short when Katie grabbed her arm. "No, ma'am." Her tone brooked no argument. "You do not open the front door, do you understand? Only grown-ups can open that door."

Finn stubbornly glared at Katie and shoved her lower lip out. There was a momentary standoff, but Finn crumbled when Katie busted out the "mom look." Satisfied with her victory, Katie pulled open the door and was greeted by Mrs. J. There was a flurry of activity as the two women bustled around gathering Finn's things, followed by a misty-eyed Katie giving Finn no less than eight goodbye hugs and kisses. After reminding Finn to be a good girl four times, and three "I love yous," Finn was on her way.

The snick of the lock echoed around the quiet apartment, and the sexual tension that had been plaguing us both all day was back in full force. We stared at each other for a moment, desire swirling between us, before we crashed into each other in a tangle of lips and teeth. My greedy hands ran down the body that had haunted my dreams, memorizing every contour. Needing more contact, I pulled her flush against my body. Katie's pants filled the air, and I groaned when she hooked her knee around my waist and began to roll her hips, stroking her center against my hard length.

Typically, I was damn good at controlling myself, but after weeks of wet dreams and pent-up sexual frustration, I needed a bedroom—and fast. I cupped her ass and lifted her. Instinctively, her long, sexy legs wrapped around my waist, and I ground myself against her, reveling in the low moan that came from her perfect lips. Annoyed at the clothes in my way, I impatiently tugged Katie's shirt over her head and peeled off my own before claiming her mouth once again.

Desire rode me hard, and the need to be inside Katie was swiftly overpowering my ability to take things slow. Katie broke our kiss, ran seeking hands down my abs, and cupped me through my jeans. Her voice turned husky with arousal as she said, "Take me to bed, Cade," and it almost brought me to my knees.

Not waiting for a second invitation, I strode with purpose toward her bedroom, growling in approval as she nipped and licked along the column of my throat. When my knees met the mattress, I laid her down, softly biting the tender skin on her hip before I stood, taking her shorts with me.

I hungrily took her in. Katie's eyes had darkened to a deep forest green that sparked with desire. Her full breasts spilled over the top of her bra, and her dusky pink nipples peeked through the sheer black lace. Each time she shifted, the matching lacy boy shorts gave me tantalizing glimpses of heaven, and damned if I didn't want to enter those gates.

~

Katie

Cade stood at the edge of my bed, looking like a modern-day virility god. His eyes traveled down my body, desire shimmering in their blue depths. He looked at me like a starving man sitting down to a feast, and I couldn't wait for him to take a taste. The longer his gaze ate me up, the more impatient and needy I became. I wanted his hands on me. Now. Taking the initiative, I unhooked my bra and let it dangle from my finger for a moment before dropping it to the floor.

Cade sucked in a breath, and his eyes darkened at my boldness. When he began to work his jeans down his muscular thighs, I sat up on my elbows, not wanting to miss the way his tattoos danced across his rippling muscles. Cade caught my stare and held my gaze as he stepped out of his boxer-briefs. At the sight of his naked body, heat rushed to my core, and I reached for him, craving the slide of his skin against mine.

With a sensual grin on his lips, Cade leaned forward and began licking and teasing his way up my body, making me writhe in anticipation. Once he reached my lips, he kissed me deeply. One hand cupped my breast, strumming my nipple with his thumb, while the other made its way south. Cade chuckled, running his fingertips across the damp lace of my panties. "So soft, so pretty, and I bet you're so wet. Let's see, shall we?"

His white teeth flashed as he nipped the sensitive skin on my hip, then he hooked his fingers in the waistband of my lacy panties and dragged them down my legs with aching slowness. When I was completely bare, he sat back on his haunches, intently studying every dip and curve with awe. Even though it was apparent he was enjoying the view, self-doubt started to rear its ugly head. My body was not the same as it had been at seventeen. My hips were wider, and the faint stretch marks spanning my lower abs that I usually concealed were on full display.

Unsure, I began to cover myself, but Cade caught my hands. "Never hide from me, Katie. You are by far the most beautiful woman I've ever seen. I just needed a minute to absorb that the most perfect being in all the world is here, in bed, with me."

I melted at his sweet words and let him guide my arms above my head. After a drugging kiss, Cade's large hands wrapped around my knees, pulling my legs wider. Anticipation lit his gaze as he dragged one long finger back and forth across my center in maddening circles. Frustrated, I twisted my hips, chasing his touch. Cade laid a palm on my stomach, stilling my movements. "Eyes, Katie-mine."

His intense gaze locked on mine, and when he was sure he had my full attention, he plunged two fingers into my waiting heat. Screaming in pleasure, I rode his fingers, intent on reaching the finish line that was so close. Suddenly, his fingers were gone, and I was left writhing on the brink of an orgasm. The protest on my lips died when his tongue took their place. My mewling cries and uninhibited moans filled the room. Sensing I was close, Cade thrust two fingers back inside me, causing me to topple over the edge in bliss.

Cade's body settled between my thighs, and he

captured the last of my moans with his lips. Ready for more, I reached down, wrapping my hand around his hard length. The feel of him in my palm, so hot and hard, made me purr in anticipation. Unable to wait any longer, I blindly rummaged in my bedside table and grabbed a condom. Cade slipped on the condom, then his lips touched mine softly. I slid just a touch closer to the cliff's edge when he paused and asked, "You ready?"

Since my brain was too scrambled to speak, I gave him a sweet smile and a nod before guiding him into my waiting heat. There was a momentary twinge of pain as my body adjusted to his size. Cade, always the gentleman, held himself still and peppered my face with kisses until I moved my hips, signaling I wanted more. "So perfect. It's like coming home. With you, like this, I'm home."

Adoration and love burned in his gaze, and I couldn't help but admit, "I feel it too."

Tentatively, Cade gave a small thrust, sending pleasure zinging through my nerve endings. Rolling my hips, I took him deeper and sighed at the wonderful feeling of fullness. Eyes blazing, he thrust harder, causing me to scream in pleasure. Within seconds, all thoughts of gentleness were thrown out the window, replaced with need and impatience.

Our hips slammed into each other, as we moved with abandon, lost in the friction of our bodies coming together. All too soon, a second orgasm began building, and I arched into Cade. Knowing intuitively what I wanted, he leaned down and pulled my nipple into his mouth as he pounded into me, rapidly sending me flying over the edge. "Cade!"

I'd hardly finished crying out his name, when he followed me into bliss.

CHAPTER 29

KATIE

"We cannot turn the clock back, nor can we undo the harm caused, but we have the power to determine the future and to ensure what happened never happens again."

— PAUL KAGAME

The bed dipped as Cade slipped back between the sheets, and a smile lit my face as he pulled my back to his chest. Tender kisses danced across my shoulder blades, and contentment suffused my being. "Morning, beautiful. How are we today?"

I rolled so we were facing one another and gave each of his dimples a kiss. "We are a little tired and a little sore, but happy."

Cade's large hands cradled my face, and his lazy smile made my heart smile. "Happy is a good look on you. I think if I got to wake up to you naked every morning wearing nothing but happy, I would consider my life well-lived."

Warmth spread through my chest at how sweet he was being, and I rewarded him with a kiss. "Well, considering how much I like naked on you, I feel like an arrangement can be made. Seems all those years bouncing around on stages did your body good."

Barking out a laugh, Cade shook his head at me and asked, "Oh, yeah?"

I swung my leg over his hips and let my eyes travel down his chest, considering each of the rippling muscles before confidently replying, "Yep."

From my perch I had the perfect angle to view the tattoos across his body. Curious, I let my fingers roam over his skin, familiarizing myself with the beautiful artwork covering him. We had been in such a rush before, I hadn't had time to see everything he'd had done. Yet looking at the tattoos now, it was obvious Cade had taken great care when choosing his artists and his designs.

From the vibrant oak tree curving around his ribs on his right side to the ravens looking at me from his twin sleeves, each needle prick had been delivered with skill. Of all the pieces, though, the one stretching from the center of his chest up over his left shoulder was the most striking. My finger traced the curves and edges of the intricate filigree pattern, slowly making my way to the center, where a carefully crafted clockface sat directly over his heart. The longer I looked at it, the more details I noticed. Intrigued, I leaned in, wondering what else I would see. "I like all of them, but I think this one is my favorite."

I tapped the clock hands and asked, "But why is the time set at 10:43?"

Cade's calloused hand gently tucked my hair behind my

ear before he grabbed my shoulders and pulled me up so we were face-to-face. Tenderly, Cade covered my forehead and cheeks with kisses before replying, "Because sometimes there are moments that will forever change you. Tiny specks in time engraved on your soul, reminding you of how important every decision is, and how quickly even the most important things can be lost."

Scrunching up my face in confusion, I blew an errant hair out of my eyes before asking, "What happened at 10:43 that was so important you wanted a permanent reminder?"

Cade gave me a deep kiss, then rested his forehead against mine. Sadness clouded his features when he said, "The night I left, I lay with you for as long as I could. When I knew my time was up, I kissed your forehead and climbed out the window onto the branches of that tree. I tried so hard not to glance back, but I couldn't help it. I needed one last memory of you to take with me. When I did, your clock was lit up, showing the time 10:43 p.m. Some moments change you and deserved to be remembered. This tattoo is for you. My heart is like a clock—it only works when it has all the parts. When I left, the most important piece was gone, and it couldn't keep time anymore—it just stopped."

Cade had always been sweet and considerate, but he'd never been someone I would've labeled as sentimental, so knowing he had willingly put a permanent reminder of us on his skin made my heart swell. I had spent so much time being angry with him. I had always assumed that once he left, he'd never given me a second thought, sure the years that had always meant so much to me had meant nothing to him.

That clock made me realize that I had always been

there with him, both in his heart and on his mind, soothing an ache in my soul I'd been carrying for far too long. Emotion clogged my throat, and I didn't trust myself to speak. Instead, I leaned down and laid a kiss on the center of my rock star's clockwork heart, before placing another on his lips.

Cade brushed away a stray tear before giving me a sly smile. "Now that you're here, and all my parts are back together, you know you're stuck with me, right? 'Cause I'm an old-school clock—I need to be wound regularly so I keep on ticking."

I only had a second to be confused before Cade rolled me onto my back and began nibbling down the column of my neck. He passed my collarbone, and I squeaked when he pulled one nipple into his greedy mouth. Electric tingles traveled straight to my center when he gave it a gentle tug. On a gasp, I asked, "What are you doing?"

Cade cocked a brow and released my nipple with a *pop*. "Why, we're winding the clock, of course. Tick-tock, Katie-mine."

I threw my head back, laughing at his ridiculousness. "Well, in that case, my left nipple is feeling ignored. Since you pointed out how important all the parts are, I wouldn't want any of them to be overlooked, so you might want to hop on that."

A devilish smirk was my only warning before his dark head descended underneath the sheets and he began meticulously licking and caressing every inch of skin he found. Whether I wanted to admit it or not, I had once again fallen in love with Cade. I could continue to pretend that I hadn't, but to what end? Fate had thrown us back together, giving us a second chance to get it right.

There were so many ways Cade and I could go wrong, and judging by our history, heartbreak was almost inevitable, but whatever time we had together would be so worth the pain later. With that thought in mind, I let myself fall, crossing my fingers that I would be caught this time.

CHAPTER 30

CADE

"Experience is the teacher of all things."

— JULIUS CAESAR

As I watched the morning sun kiss Katie's face for the seventh day in a row, I sent up a silent prayer, thanking whoever or whatever had put me in her path that first night. Since Katie had begun letting me stay over, my previously lonely life had been filled with contentment and love. I knew soul deep that I would never tire of waking up to Katie's beautiful face every day or grow bored witnessing Finn's eyes light up with excitement or curiosity. Things between Katie and me were better than I could have ever hoped for, and our future together beckoned me, coaxing me to renew the promises we had once made to one another under a bright summer sky.

Ever since our night together, the doubts that had always seemed to be lingering on the edge of Katie's gaze had disappeared. Every day I fell a little bit more in love with her and the family we had created. The only cloud looming over my head was the fact that I was going to have to leave soon, and we had yet to discuss how we wanted to handle my tour. My phone chimed, letting me know Finn would be up soon. Carefully, I slid out from in between the sheets and placed a kiss on Katie's forehead, before quietly closing the door so I wouldn't wake her and going across the hall to check on Finn.

Finn's chest rhythmically rose and fell with each of her breaths, and I gingerly tiptoed to the kitchen. She would wake soon enough, but in the meantime, I desperately needed a cup of coffee. Once the coffee pot was turned on, I busied myself whipping up a smoothie for Finn. A few minutes later, the pitter-patter of her feet reached my ears just as the pot finished percolating. Her eyes lit up when she saw me, and a dimple-filled grin spanned her face. She raced across the kitchen into my open arms and gave me a smacking hello kiss. "Morning, sunshine! How did we sleep? You want a smoothie?"

"Mo'ning Daddy! I sleeped good and hab good dreams. Yay, a smoothie! Is it st'awberry?"

I kissed the tip of her nose, making her giggle, and sat her in her highchair. Once I set the smoothie down in front of her, I poured a cup of coffee for myself and replied, "Yep! It's strawberry banana. We'll have this for now, and I'll make pancakes when mama wakes up, okay?"

Nodding, Finn answered back, "Tay!" before digging in.

By the time she had finished her smoothie, Katie still wasn't awake yet, so I set Finn up with some cartoons, snagged a cup of coffee for Katie, and headed down the hall to wake her. When I pushed open the door, I found Katie sitting up in bed, staring with a sad expression on her face at the Fender Strat that had made its home in the corner of her bedroom.

Concerned, I made my way to the bed and passed her the coffee before I sat down. "Why so glum, Katie-mine?"

Katie leaned over to greet me with a morning kiss before replying, "We're almost out of time, aren't we?"

I settled back against the headboard, putting an arm around Katie. This conversation would be a turning point for me because I had been dead serious when I told Katie that she and Finn were my home. Whether she realized it or not, the future of my career rested in her hands. I had made the mistake of putting my aspirations first once, and while I loved the music and performing, I loved Katie and Finn more. All I could do was cross my fingers and hope to hell that I was lucky enough to keep both.

My fingers twined with hers, and I rested my cheek on her hair, needing to feel our connection while we talked. "We are running short on days before I have to leave, but you and me? Nah, we've got all the time in the world."

A ghost of a smile flitted across her face, and I figured that would have to do for now. Needing things to be settled, I went on. "So, speaking of the tour, I had something I wanted to ask you. Will you and Finn come with me? Please?"

Katie tensed up, set her coffee on the nightstand, and shifted so we were facing one another. "Cade," she began, "I would love to, but we can't."

Taken aback at how quickly she shot me down, I ran my hand through my hair before demanding, "Why?"

Katie sighed and restlessly tugged at her tank top. After a short pause, she threw her hands up in frustration. "Because we can't, Cade! I'm in my last year of school. I don't have time to find a place to store my things or sublet my apartment. I wouldn't be able to put in my two-weeks' notice or anything! I understand that you're used to being able to drop and run whenever you're told to, but Finn and I have a life here. We can't just up and leave and have nothing to come back to!"

I bit back my retort and forced myself to let what she'd said roll around in my mind. Once I was past the initial wave of disappointment, I could see where she was coming from. But if there was one thing Katie had forgotten, it was how awesome I was at planning.

My brain always worked a mile a minute, and since I couldn't focus without a set plan, my brain's default was to come up with multiple solutions for any problem so I never felt like I was drifting. For the first time in a while, I was extremely grateful for the weird-ass way my brain worked. I caught her hand so she'd stop fidgeting, and patiently waited for Katie's eyes to meet mine before I began. "Katie, we can totally do this."

She started to reply, and I placed my finger over her lips to silence her and went on. "We can. You're so used to being the only one who handles everything that you forget that I'm here now, too. Take this year off school. You've already paid for this semester, so just ask them to apply that payment to enrollment for your next semester when we're back. As for the apartment, leave it."

"Like you said, you, Finn, and I have a home here. It's important that it is still here, waiting for us when we come back. We can stay here while you finish up school, then discuss where we want to settle permanently after you graduate. Let's keep paying the rent while we're gone, and we can ask Mrs. J to check in on the place for us and collect mail once a week or so. I can't do anything about your job, but you've told me before how much you hate it, so let's find you another one after the tour. What do you think?"

I crossed my fingers and hoped that she would at least consider my proposition before shooting me down, then waited for her response. Katie considered me for a long moment before she steepled her fingers under her chin and said, "Okay, taking all of that out of the equation, how do we travel with Finn? She's too little to be cooped up for long periods of time, and she has a schedule she needs to stick to that may not work on a tour bus."

Excitement coursed through my veins at the realization that she was seriously thinking about coming along, but I held it at bay. She still hadn't said yes yet, so I needed to keep my head in the game.

"We usually have the band together on one bus, and everyone else travels separately. If you and Finn come, I'll set us up on our own bus so you will have a quiet place to take Finn for naps and for bedtime, and so we can have some privacy. The rest of the time she can either stay with you on our bus or stay on the main bus with the band so she'll have lots of people to play with. I'll tell our PA, Sam, that you two are coming. He'll set up anything you need, plus a room for us at each stadium separate from the greenroom—that way, the guys can do what they want, and we can hang out together before I go onstage. We can make it work, Katie, I swear we can. Please come."

She eyed me for another moment before her face split into a wide grin. Her arms circled my neck, and she kissed the tip of my nose before saying, "Well, I guess you and your PA better get cooking. It seems like you two have lots of plans to make before we all head out of the country."

Katie

It was my second to last shift at The Field House, and while I loved my coworkers, I could not wait to be finished working here. Tom hadn't taken my leaving well and had made damn sure to be as big of a dick as possible to ensure my last few days were absolutely miserable. He'd tried to corner me in the hallway twice, and the only reason I was currently working the floor rather than hanging out on a cot in a jail cell was because Layla had decided she was "sticking to my ass like glue" until I left.

Unsurprisingly, while Ryan was stoked about my trip and how things were going with Cade, Layla had been less enthusiastic—until I told her that I had bought her a plane ticket so she could spend her Christmas break on tour with us. Now, she was almost as excited as I was. Yet nothing Tom did was going to put a damper on my mood, because in three days, I would be on a plane with my little girl and my love. Life was perfect.

The buzz in my back pocket startled me, and I anxiously scanned the room, relaxing only when I noted that Tom was nowhere in sight. Slyly, I pulled out my phone and couldn't help the goofy grin that spread across my face when **Sexypants** flashed across the screen. I motioned to Layla that I would be back in a second, ducked out a side door, and slipped into the alley, before answering the call.

"Hey there, Katie-mine." Cade's voice had a quiet seriousness to it that immediately put me on edge. "Do you have a minute?"

I bit my nail, bracing myself for bad news, but tried to keep my voice light in case I was wrong. "I always have a minute for you. What's up?"

His loud exhalation echoed from the speaker, and the tension radiating through the line put me on edge. Antsy, I began to pace, and after a small eternity, Cade simply said, "I'm sorry, Katie. I'm so sorry."

Giving up all pretenses, I let the stress bouncing around my insides rise to the fore. "I'm gonna need more than that, Cade. How about we start with what you're sorry for and go from there? We need to make it quick, though, because I'm still on the clock."

Regret filled his voice when he said, "They found out, Katie. I'm not sure if they were told, or if someone spotted me going to and from your place and put two and two together. Quinn called to tell me she's been fielding calls from entertainment rags wanting to know more about you and our relationship for the last two hours. I know you aren't off yet, and that you promised you'd work a few more shifts, but I think you should come home before they figure out where you are. I'm so sorry, Katie."

I couldn't help but chuckle at him. "Cade," I chided, "I was fully aware when I agreed to be with you that I would be allowing my privacy to be invaded. I don't care. We knew they would find us out sooner or later—it just happened to be sooner. What does Quinn think we should do?"

"Quinn thinks we should get ahead of them by snapping a few pictures ourselves and posting them on our social media. She said if we did it that way, we control which pictures they see first and set the tone of the narrative, making it harder for them to put a spin on it. It won't stop them, and chances are you'll read some horrible crap about us both in the next few weeks, but if you're up for the chaos, I'll gladly tell the whole world who owns my heart."

I rolled my eyes at his ridiculousness and started to answer, but was distracted by the sound of feet shuffling. My eyes swung toward the mouth of the alley, searching out the source of the noise. My jaw dropped when I spotted a cluster of people with cameras who had thankfully not noticed me yet. "Of course I'm up for it. You might want to get a move-on with those pictures, though. From the look of things, I've already got some friends here, and I'm not sure what their turnaround time is."

A flurry of curse words was my response, followed rapidly by "How about the one Rhys took of us at dinner the other night? Also, you're coming home. I'll have D send someone over to pick you up—I'd rather you not drive with them out there. They can be ruthless, and I don't want you getting into an accident."

Bristling at the demand, I snapped back, "I certainly will not. I have shit to do and will do it whether they are here or not. And while I respect your intentions, you do not get to make decisions for me. I am not a child, and don't appreciate being treated like one. If you ever take it upon yourself to decide for me what I will or will not do without discussion again, you will find yourself without balls. As for D, I will text him and politely ask him to have someone pick me up after my shift as a compromise and see if he has someone free to pick up my car tomorrow."

The sound of teeth grinding echoed in my ear for a few seconds before Cade answered, "Sorry. I didn't mean to be pushy. I just know how they are, and I'm worried. I don't want you to get hurt. If you want to stay, okay, but please let me have D send someone to keep an eye on you until you get home?"

My first instinct was to give in and let one of D's guys come by for the remainder of my shift, but my happiness was just as important as Cade's and I was not going to allow myself to be coddled. "I know, Cade, and I get it. I'm okay with D sending someone to pick me up, but I don't need someone here all night. I'll tell Ty that they are here, and he'll make sure none of them come inside. I get off at one thirty, so make sure whoever's is picking me up is here then. I promise I will not go outside without an escort, okay?"

Resigned to my decision, Cade sighed and said, "Okay, Katie-mine. Please be careful. I don't think I could handle anything happening to you."

I wasn't sure if I would ever get used to the warm feelings that flooded my chest whenever he said something sweet, but I hoped not. Relieved that I wasn't going to have to argue with him more, and anxious to slip inside before I was spotted, I added, "I'll be extra careful. Scout's honor. Also, use the photo Rhys took. I think it is the perfect one to announce us." Then I gave the phone a loud, dramatic kiss and hang up, heading inside to find Ty.

CHAPTER 31

KATIE

> "Jealousy is never satisfied with anything short of an omniscience that would detect the subtlest fold of the heart."
>
> — GEORGE ELIOT

The sound of my phone vibrating made me cringe, and I was seconds away from chucking it into the wall out of frustration. Cade hadn't been lying when he warned me the journalists and paparazzi would be relentless. Last night, what started as a small group of paps had rapidly grown, and by the time I got off work, there was a solid wall of cameras flashing as D promptly tucked me into the town car and sped off. We lost most of them, thanks to his abrupt departure, but a few of the more seasoned ones had managed to catch up. It took us over an hour of D taking random turns and backtracking before we finally lost them and he decided we were safe to go home.

Once I was inside my apartment, I was so exhausted I

passed out as soon as my head hit the pillow, only to be rudely awakened at six a.m. by my phone blowing up. Apparently, every person I had ever met had felt the need to call me and rekindle our friendship now that Cade had announced our relationship online. Whoever had leaked my name to the press in the first place was also kind enough to give them my cell number as well. If I ever found out who that person was, I was going to light them on fire in my mind. I could only hope the frenzy would die down soon, but since #Cadtie had been trending on Twitter for the last two days, I doubted it.

Aside from the annoying buzz of my phone, the apartment was silent. Cade and I may have let the world know there was an "us," but we had mutually decided to keep Finn under wraps until we got to Europe, in the hopes that the excitement about her would fizzle out by the time we got stateside again. After talking it over, Cade, Quinn, and I decided our best bet of keeping Finn out of the spotlight was to have her stay with Mrs. J at Cade's hotel until we left.

Cade's PA, Sam, turned out to be some sort of miracle worker. He not only got everything sorted out with both my place here and our accommodations in Europe, but he also snagged Finn and Mrs. J a room that had a connecting door to an "empty" room at the hotel. Now, any time I wanted to spend time with Finn I could sneak in through my "empty" room without getting caught.

If I wasn't so big on keeping my word, I would be in that room snuggling Finn and watching movies on HBO. Instead, I was sitting here, tossing back a few Tylenol and getting ready to go to my final shift at The Field House—not because I felt indebted to Tom, but because Friday nights were always brutal. I owed it to the other girls I worked with not to make it worse by having to cover my absence as well.

I checked the time once again and wondered where my bodyguard du jour was. D ran a pretty tight ship, so it was odd that whoever he assigned to guard me for the evening wasn't here yet, but I was tired of waiting and didn't want to risk being late.

After giving myself a final once-over to double check that my winged liner was even, I grabbed my backpack and peeked out the window. There were several men and women with cameras carelessly flung around their necks milling about near the main entrance, so I opted to take a detour.

Focused on being stealthy, I cautiously slipped out my front door and made my way to the stairwell that lead to the dumpsters at the back of the building. Once I hit the ground floor, I opened the door and let out a sigh of relief when I didn't see anyone. I knew time was not on my side, so I hustled to my car and weaved through a few alleys before hitting the main strip and making my way to work.

I pulled into the parking lot, feeling like a badass for having made it to work without a single photographer following me. My feet touched the pavement, and I paused, taking in the sunshine and slight breeze, feeling like I could breathe for the first time in days. I grabbed my phone to check the time and saw a notification from Sam on the screen. My brow wrinkled in confusion because one, Sam was the band's personal assistant, so I had no clue why he would need to speak to me, and two, I didn't even realize

Cade had put his number in my phone. Shrugging, I opened the message to see what he needed.

Sam: Hi, Katie! This is Sam, Devil's Cross's PA. Could you give me a call or shoot me a text when you have a second? It's really important. Thanks!

I hit reply and was poised to type back, when a camera flashed in my periphery. *Son of a.* Not in the mood to have to wade through a sea of paparazzi to get inside, I snatched my bag and made a dash for the back door before more of them arrived. When I stepped inside the locker room, I rechecked the time and realized I had somehow gone from a few minutes early to just shy of late. Cursing a blue streak at my bad luck, I threw my stuff into my locker, made sure my uniform covered all the essentials, and all but ran to clock in.

I was almost to the doors leading to the bar when Tom's hand wrapped around my arm and stopped me. My brow kicked up in irritation, and he quickly removed it. I supposed that was the silver lining to the shit-storm the paps had created. As far as Tom was concerned, I was "famous by association" so he'd been somewhat tolerable since Cade had announced that we were an item. Tom was sweating profusely, which was both odd and disgusting. After tugging on his collar a few times, he cleared his throat and informed me, "You're not on the floor tonight. You've been requested for VIP service in the Penalty Box."

A kernel of hope flared that maybe it was Cade and the boys coming to make sure my last night was easy, but then I recalled the laundry list Sam had emailed over this morning of meeting and conference calls they had to do today to make sure everything was finalized for the tour. There was only one other person who would specifically request me for VIP, and I didn't want to deal with him.

Making sure it was blatantly obvious how annoyed I was, I told Tom, "But it isn't Saturday night! He has never been here except on Saturday nights, Tom. I smell some bullshit, and I don't like it. Find someone else."

He narrowed his eyes at me, and old Tom came out to play when he bit out, "You may think your shit don't stink now that you're banging a rock star, but you're nothing but a distraction. When he tosses your ass out, you'll be looking for a job, and I would hate to give you a shit recommendation after such a good history because you pissed off one of my best customers. It's one goddamn night, and you will serve him with a smile on your face, or so help me I will make Layla's life a living hell while you're off pretending to be something you're not."

It took every ounce of self-control I possessed not to punch him in the face. I knew that Cade and I were solid, and that there was zero chance I'd ever come back to work here, but Layla needed this job. I couldn't risk my actions negatively impacting her, which he knew, the bastard. I looked Tom dead in the eye when I told him, "I'll do it, you jackass, but if you think I'm going to forget this, you are sadly mistaken. I will make sure you will regret being such an insufferable dick."

$\sim$

I had just got done checking that all the food Vicari had asked for would reach the VIP lounge on time and was on my way to the bar to grab a few bottles of Dom in preparation for his arrival, when my phone buzzed for the sixth time in thirty minutes. At first, I figured it wasn't anyone important, but then Sam's text came to mind. My cell was halfway out of my pocket when Tom barked, "Troyer! Get your shit together. Antonio's driver called,—they'll be here in less than five!"

My eyes scanned the area, looking around to make sure no customers were watching. Not seeing anyone, I held up my middle finger in Tom's general direction. Still annoyed, I slipped my phone back in my pocket and made my way to the bar to load up the order. I'd have to text Sam back later.

One of the few things I had always appreciated about Antonio Vicari was his predictability. He always came in on a Saturday night at the same time, ordered the same food on the menu, and started with the same beverages. The only thing that changed was the number of people in his entourage. More people meant larger orders, but no matter how many friends and acquaintances tagged along, he always—and I mean *always*—started the night off with five bottles of Dom Pérignon and one bottle of Don Julio. Therefore, it was one hell of a surprise to me when I reached the bar, ready for a full tray, only to have Zack slide a single bottle of Dom and a single bottle of 2005 Chateau Latour Merlot across the bar to me. My confusion must have been obvious because Zack shrugged and said, "Boss said this is what he asked for."

I took my time arranging the drinks, making sure to balance them. Nothing about this evening was going as planned, and it was making me feel off-kilter. It didn't make sense that I had only been met by a single pap on my way here after having them up my ass all week. I also couldn't understand why Vicari was here on a Friday night. In fact, I had intentionally made sure I didn't work Saturdays since I had rekindled my relationship with Cade so that I didn't have to deal with Antonio or his unwanted advances.

The more I thought about it, the more uncomfortable I became. I was just about to say "Screw it," hand off my tray, and leave, when the green light for the Penalty Box lit up, announcing Antonio had arrived. I shook my head at my ridiculousness, picked up my tray, and made my way up to the VIP area. Once I reached the top of the platform, I paused to observe the sea of people laughing and drinking down in the Central Zone of The Field House. I smiled wistfully, wishing I were down there, relaxing and having fun, instead of up here getting ready to deal with this mess. At least this would be the last time.

With that thought in mind, I made my way over to the ropes separating the VIP lounges from the rest of the club. There was no bouncer guarding the divider, and I didn't spot a single one on this floor. Something was not right, but the idea of pissing off Vicari—and in turn, Tom— made my stomach turn. I didn't care one way or the other if either of them was upset, but Tom would have no problem taking it out on Layla after I left, and she didn't deserve that.

My teeth worried my lip while I weighed my growing unease with my desire to avoid making waves. After a beat, I settled on greeting Antonio to keep him happy, then excusing myself for one reason or another so I could go find Ty and figure out where my bouncer was. I wasn't sure how many people Vicari had brought along today, but I was positive I was not navigating that chaos without some backup. Decision made, I unhooked the clip and made my way down the hall.

The red curtains loomed in front of me, and for some reason, I couldn't seem to force myself to part them and go inside. Annoyed with myself, I inhaled through my nose and exhaled through my mouth in an attempt to get some zen when my phone began vibrating again. *Shit.* I still hadn't texted Sam, and he had said it was important. Once I made my escape, I was going to slip into the locker room and call him. We had a no-phones policy, but what would Tom do, fire me?

Grinning at my own joke, I ignored my discomfort, opened the curtain, and walked inside to find Antonio alone, sitting on the arm of the couch. His black hair was slicked back and gleamed underneath the dim lighting. The expensive black suit jacket he wore was folded in half and laid over the back of a chair, and the sleeves of his violet shirt were rolled up to his elbows, exposing muscular forearms. His black trousers had a lean cut and were tailored to perfection. All in all, he looked every inch the spoiled rich heir I knew him to be.

Not in the mood for his shenanigans, I made a beeline for the table and set down the champagne and wine. While Antonio had never been my favorite customer, I had never felt uncomfortable in his presence—annoyed, yes, but not uncomfortable. Yet right now, all my warning bells were going off. I needed out of this room. Now.

I plastered a pleasant smile on my face that I prayed masked my rising nerves, and gestured that I would be right back. My internal alarms were blaring, but I forced myself to walk casually toward the door so I wouldn't arouse his suspicions. Ten feet...eight feet ...four feet...Freedom was almost within my grasp when a broad chest appeared between me and the exit.

Hoping it was just Antonio being his usual overly familiar self, I gave him a placating smile and said, "Silly me! I completely forgot the bottle opener. Be right back."

My heart was galloping in my chest, and my inner voice was screaming at me to get away. Fake smile still in place, I moved to edge around Antonio, only to have him block my way once more.

Realizing he had no intention of letting me leave the room, I moved back a step, making sure to keep my movements relaxed even though I was anything but. My first thought was to scream, but we were alone up here, and the chance of anyone hearing me over the music was slim. The anxiety that had been simmering below the surface boiled over into full-fledged panic.

I scanned the room, spotting the emergency exit in the back corner. My feet shuffled backward while I kept my eyes on Antonio. The farther away I moved, the more agitated he became. Needing to defuse the situation, I held my hands out in a nonthreatening manner and adopted the same tone I used when Finn was having a tantrum.

"Antonio, I know we've known each other for a while now—heck, one might even call us friends—but I've gotta be honest, you're making me a little nervous right now. I know it is probably my fault, since I know what a nice guy you are, but Ty had to kick out a few guys who got a little rowdy with me earlier, so I'm a little on edge. How about we have a seat and relax for a little while?"

Antonio stilled, and I almost released a sigh of relief, but then I registered what he was saying. "Ah, *cara mia.*" He shook his finger as he continued to scold me, his voice rising like an angry tide trying to pull me under. "You think you can play tricks, no? You think you can make the Antonio fall in love with you and suffer your games, then instead of giving him his prize, you run off with some *cazzo* who can sing? No, no, no. I am a Vicari!"

With this announcement he pounded his chest with a fist. "Vicari's get what they want, and they do not have their *tesoro* stolen away from them! You belong to me, *mia amore,* and I will have you!"

I looked into his eyes, searching for any hint of the Antonio I had come to know, only to come up empty. Rather than finding a cocky playboy who meant well, I was faced with a whole lot of crazy. His pupils were blown and had overtaken his iris, making his ordinarily friendly brown eyes a threatening wall of black. Fury and possessiveness colored his features as he began to advance on me slowly. *Danger Will Robinson!* With each step he took in my direction, I took one back.

Wait, my phone! My fingers slid into my back pocket, fumbling around until my thumb and pointer finger pinched the hard case. I gave it a tug, but my bottoms were so snug it wouldn't budge. Weighing my choices, I stopped for a split second, allowing the material of my shorts to relax enough so I could tug it free. Antonio's eyes snapped to my hand, and he released a string of unflattering Italian before lunging at me. I managed to dodge him and sprinted for the emergency exit, only to find it locked. Cursing fate, I spun around and found myself face-to-face with a whole boatload of insanity. Running out of options, I decided to stop working offense and throw in some defense.

My mind latched onto the only escape plan I could think of. I stopped fleeing and turned to face Antonio. Even though it pained me, I gave him the sultriest smile I could muster, stepping forward and running my hands across his well-defined pecks. My top teeth sunk into my lower lip in what I hoped was a sexy manner, and I batted my eyelashes, doing my damnedest to recall every tip I had ever read about seductive mannerisms. All I could do was pray Antonio was buying my pathetic attempts at flirting.

I set my palms on his shoulders, gently massaging the frighteningly large muscles, and gave him a sexy wink. As soon as his posture relaxed, I jammed my knee full force into his groin and screamed like a banshee, hoping by some miracle someone would hear me over the pounding bass of the music. A spike of pride shot through me when he groaned, cupped himself, and fell to the floor.

Not wanting to lose my window of opportunity, I leapt over his body, doing my best to channel an all-star hurdler, but his hand shot out and latched on to my ankle. I flung out my hands to catch myself and watched in horror as my cell phone flew across the room and crashed into the wall, shattering the screen. A heartbeat later, I yelped at the jolt of pain that traveled up my arms when my palms slammed into the floor.

Bracing myself as best as I could, I raised my legs, and threw all my weight into a mule kick. The sole of my wedges smashed into Antonio's face with a satisfying crunch. He released my ankle and clamped down on his nose to stop the bleeding. I sprinted to the VIP entrance, screaming for help as I fled.

When I finally reached the curtain, I jerked it open, racing full speed for the steps, frantically scanning for anyone who could help me. I passed empty lounge after empty lounge, shouting for help every step the way, but finding no help in sight. The terror of knowing we were completely alone up here was almost debilitating, but I couldn't stop now. Focused on getting away, I maintained my pace, slowing down only when I reached the landing of the stairs. Looking down, I noted the mass of people swaying on the dance floor and spotted the flash of Layla's hot-pink ponytail swishing as she moved. But now they were no longer just people—they were my salvation.

Had I not been so intent on finding help, I might have heard it. I may have registered the rapid tap, tap, tap of Italian leather shoes on the metal floor. Might have noted how much louder and closer the footsteps were getting. But I didn't. Rather than hear him, I felt him, like an ominous fog coming to swallow me up. The rage and jealousy emanating from him tasted bitter on my tongue.

My grip on the railing tightened, and I began my rapid descent to the main floor—and more importantly, to help. My heeled wedges slammed into the steps, sending sparks of pain up my shins. I hoped that the metallic clang of my wedges beating against the corrugated stairs would draw someone's attention, but not a single head turned our way. I was almost to the halfway point when large hands slammed into my back.

One minute my heel was firmly planted on a stair, and the next I was airborne. All the air whooshed out of my lungs as soon as my body made contact with the first step, and after that, there was only pain—searing, blinding pain as my body bounced off the sharp corners of each metal ledge. Once I eventually came to a stop, I tried to take stock of my injuries, but couldn't. My body had ceased to be and instead had been replaced with sheer agony.

Every breath I took felt like hundreds of knives were driving into my lungs. I forced myself to open my eyes, grateful to see that my saviors had arrived in the form of terrified, screaming faces. Seconds later, Ty's cornflower-blue eyes widened in horror, and he rushed over, barking orders as he kneeled in front of my prone form. Finally safe, I closed my eyes and let myself sink into oblivion.

CHAPTER 32

CADE

> "Surrounded by the flames of jealousy, the jealous one winds up, like the scorpion, turning the poisoned sting against himself."
>
> — FRIEDRICH NIETZSCHE

The guys shifted restlessly and looked between Sam and me, silently asking what the hell we were supposed to do, and I honestly had no idea. Frankly, though Sam had already filled us in, I still didn't understand what the hell was happening.

All I knew was that an hour ago, Sam had unexpectedly come barreling into our meeting with Bryce and Quinn, ranting about "fucking Kelly" and delivering a shit ton of information in between pants. Whatever he said had Quinn bolting out of the room, cell phone glued to her ear, barking commands to whoever was on the other line.

The only thing I registered after hearing *fucking Kelly* was the part where Katie needed to come home as soon as possible. After that, nothing else he had to say mattered. I had been blowing up her phone ever since and still hadn't gotten an answer. The knot of worry in my stomach grew each time I called or texted and got no response. Katie had told me she wasn't supposed to have her phone with her on the floor, but she always kept it on her anyways and had never failed to text me back as soon as she could.

Zane's worried gaze swung to mine. "Any answer yet?"

When I shook my head, he announced, "Fuck this, I'm calling D. That man keeps such close tabs on us that I'm pretty sure he can even tell you when I take my daily shit."

Before Zane had even reached for his phone, D's imposing frame blocked the doorway, and his voice boomed in the small room. "I can, and the answer to that is 11:05 a.m. in case any of y'all were wondering."

The guys chuckled at Zane's shocked expression, but I was too concerned to crack a smile. Sam rubbed his blood-shot eyes, and though he was exhausted, he studied me for a moment before shoving a Red Bull in my hand. He waited for me to take a drink before telling D, "We have a situation."

D's posture went from semi-relaxed to battle-ready in a matter of seconds. Pointing a finger at Sam, he ordered, "Explain."

Sam took a deep breath and recounted the situation yet again. "As you are aware, the last few days before a tour, I route most of the guys' calls to my cell, so I can screen them to minimize interruptions," he began.

"Well, late last night, my phone started blowing up. At first, I ignored it and let it roll over to voicemail, because when I say 'late,' I mean *late*, but after getting woken up a few more times, I decided to see who the hell it was. The number was unknown, so I was planning on continuing to ignore it and most likely deleting the voicemails, but I got a weird feeling, so I gave them a listen. Every single one was from Kelly. She started off apologizing and begging for her job back, but by the time I got to the last message, she had gone completely off the rails. She was screeching about how she "was going to make that bitch pay for ruining her life."

"The only person I could think of that she would blame for her firing was Katie, so I threw a bunch of stuff in a bag and hopped on the first flight out. I tried to call you guys to tell you what was going on, but no one picked up. So I hauled ass here. The problem is that none of us can seem to reach Katie, and while I wouldn't usually think Kelly would legitimately set out to harm someone, she was not in her right mind in those messages."

D sat for a moment, likely thinking of and discarding plans and scenarios until he had a set idea in his mind of how he wanted to handle the situation, before cracking his knuckles and pulling out his phone. He pressed a number on speed dial, then waited a beat.

When there was no answer, he hung up and punched a second number, then barked, "Why isn't Donovan answering his phone? We have a code orange, and I need The Robin's whereabouts stat. And once you reach Donovan, tell him I will be tearing his ass a new one for failing to answer his phone. When I assign a detail, I expect all calls and texts to be answered immediately, not whenever y'all damn well please. Get the info and coordinate with Donovan. Tell him to prep for a possible early extraction." With that, he hung up and waited.

Ten minutes later, I had called Katie two more times with no success, and D was so furious his head was about to pop off when phone call to Donovan went unanswered yet again. I couldn't blame him though—D ran his entire operation with an iron fist. His security company was the best in the business for a reason. D thoroughly screened and vetted every applicant, and the guys performed with the same precision that D's elite unit had when he was a SEAL. Mistakes were not taken lightly, nor were they usually forgiven.

The only reason Donovan might get a reprieve when he did finally answer D's call was because he had been with D for going on five years and up until today had a flawless performance record. The buzz of D's phone drew our attention, and I noticed that we were all sitting on the edge of our seats, hoping for good news. D's furious "Fuck!" followed by "Send Novak to check on Donovan. I want a full report as soon as possible. As for The Robin, send one of the guys over to The House. Now. Too many coincidences make me uneasy. Get there, get her out, and get her here," snuffed out whatever hope we had.

The knot of worry was now a full-blown monster shredding my insides. The thought of something happening to Katie made me want to vomit, and I tried to ignore it, but I knew that something was terribly wrong. Unable to keep the trepidation from my voice, I asked, "D?"

D ran a hand down his face and pinched the bridge of his nose before dropping his hands to his hips and releasing a long, frustrated breath.

"Okay, guys, here's the deal. Donovan never made it to Katie's. He got into a car accident on the way to her place and is in surgery now. He asked one of the nurses to call us and tell us what happened and that he hadn't reached Katie's place, but he passed out before the nurse got the last digit of my phone number. She said that while he's injured, it isn't life-threatening, which is good news."

"However, that means Miss Katie, a.k.a. our little Robin, has been flying solo all night, and the car accident paired with our inability to reach her ain't giving me warm fuzzies. Novak is going to check on Donovan, and I've got RJ heading to The Field House. Keyes is working on hacking the GPS on Kelly's phone, so we can keep tabs on her location. Cade, I know you want to get your girl—I can see your ass is already halfway out of your chair—but I can't let you do it, man. You gotta stay here. I can't do right by your lady if I'm chasing you all over town. Stay put and let us do what you hired us to do."

Frustrated beyond belief, I shouted, "Son of a bitch!" before throwing my bottle of water across the room.

My desire to go to Katie warred with the logic of D's argument. The more time that went by, the more difficult it was not to just say "Fuck it" and leave. Needing to do something, I pulled out my cell and dialed Katie's number again, praying she would answer.

When it rolled over to voicemail yet again, I listened to her recorded voice and waited for the beep. "Katie, love, it's me again. I know this is, like, the sixth message I've left, but I really need you to call me back. I'm getting worried. Please, please call...or text...or hell send smoke signals or some shit. Just let me know you're okay. I love you."

I waited a few more minutes on the off chance she'd call back. I had just gotten up, intent on getting the hell out of there, when D's cell rang. I couldn't hear what was being said, but as soon as I saw all the color drain from D's face, my stomach dropped. Without saying a word, D hung up the phone, and with one statement, my whole world stopped.

"Katie's had an accident. We need to go to the hospital. Now."

CHAPTER 33

KATIE

> "When I stand before thee at the days end, thou shalt see my scars and know that I had my wounds and also my healing."
>
> — RABINDRANATH TAGORE

My body was buoyant, rocking gently as it floated in a sea of black. Occasionally, the sound of beeping or indistinct voices penetrated the quiet, but they were easy to ignore and faded away as quickly as they came, leaving me peacefully floating on inky waves. Sometimes I heard someone singing a haunting melody full of sadness and despair.

I both loved and dreaded when the velvety tone would penetrate my dark sanctuary. The mysterious voice filled me with longing, making me feel as if I had somewhere I should be, or that there was something important I had forgotten. Every time the notes reached my ears, my heart would beat faster, and my limbs would begin to strain, as if they were trying to grasp some intangible thing. The song would eventually disappear, and once the pied piper's song was over, echoes of pain would bounce around inside me until it was almost unbearable.

At first, the melodies were few and far between, but now more and more they penetrated my dark walls, making it increasingly difficult to ignore the siren's song. Fighting its pull was becoming exhausting, and I was starting to become bitter that this haunting melody was invading my previously peaceful sanctuary.

The lilting tones came once again, and I forced myself to remain still, ignoring the way they beckoned me to follow. Eventually, the music stopped, and I allowed myself to become one with the dark yet again.

The sound of low voices caught my attention, followed by an incessant *beep...beep...beep*. A sharp spike of pain bounced around in my skull in time with every one of those damned beeps. As soon as I figured out whose alarm was going off, I was going to stab them.

I wanted to open my eyes, find the source of the repetitive noise, and turn it off, but no matter how hard I tried, my eyelids wouldn't budge. *Why can't I open my eyes?* Panic bloomed in my chest, but I tamped down my rising fear and forced myself to remain calm. I needed my wits about me as I assessed the situation.

Low voices carried over the beeping, and now that I was more awake, I felt something covering my mouth and nose that instantly made me feel claustrophobic. Desperate to pull it off, I tried to raise my hand to remove it, but none of my limbs wanted to obey my commands. The more I tried and failed to move my appendages, the quicker the beeps sounded.

Panic shifted to terror, and soon the cadence had changed to a clanging alarm. The low voices rushed closer, barking orders I didn't understand at a rapid clip. Someone placed a small hand on my chest, and something cool traveled up the veins in my arm, then seconds later, my body relaxed, and I succumbed to sleep.

The blackness slowly dissipated, yet my world was still dark. No matter how hard I tried, I could not open my eyelids, so I gave up and took stock of my surroundings. The repetitive beeping was still bouncing around in my head, but thankfully whatever had been covering my mouth and nose was gone.

My lungs burned with each breath I took, but I forced myself to inhale deeply, and the sting of antiseptic burned my nostrils. I turned my focus to my fingertips and managed to move one just enough to feel the scratch of coarse sheets against my skin. I wasn't positive where I was, but based on how badly my body throbbed, coupled with the sounds and smells, I figured I was in a hospital. What I didn't understand was why.

The sound of footfalls grabbed my attention, and a wonderfully familiar voice said, "She just moved."

A throat cleared, and a high-pitched voice with a touch of Staten Island in it said, "Ms. Mulroney, I know how you're feeling honey. I get that you want ya friend to wake up, especially seein' as how her heart rate spiked earlier today, but I'm telling ya that sedative they gave her ain't no joke, sweetie. She ain't gonna be up for a while, and I don't wanna get ya hopes up that the spike means she's comin' outta her coma. It might, don't get me wrong, but I don't wanna make promises until the doc has a chance to run some tests, ya know?"

If I thought I could have laughed, I definitely would have when Layla snapped back, "Look, Lexi, I'm gonna be straight with you. Of all the nurses, you are my fav girl-friend. I get what you're saying, but I am telling you, my girl just moved her finger. As much as I love you, I will lose my ever-loving shit if you don't find Cade and a doc right the hell now."

There was a moment of silence followed by a resigned "Okay, you got it, sweets. I'll snag the doc and Mr. Pretty and get 'em in here in two shakes."

Layla's comforting presence enveloped me as she approached my bed, and I almost cried when her hand brushed the hair off my forehead.

Her voice wobbled when she said, "Listen here, girl-friend. You done scared the shit out of all of us with your epic nap, but I think it's about time to wake up, kay? Your man's been doing his best with our little lady, but I gotta tell you, sister, at this point he's not even riding the struggle bus, he *is* the struggle bus. You know he tried to feed our girl foie gras? Seriously. I'm an adult, and I gave that shit a hard pass. Now, if I'm not mistaken, that obnoxiously loud slap-ping sound is a whole lotta sexy hauling ass your way, so let's go ahead and move them digits again, kay?"

~

Cade

I rubbed my gritty, bloodshot eyes and punched my selection into the vending machine, leaning my forehead against the cool glass while I waited for the granola bar to drop down. Exhaustion tugged at my limbs, and I was weary down to my very soul.

It had been just over three weeks since Katie's accident, and each day that passed without a change drew me deeper into the depression that kept threatening to pull me under. The only reason I hadn't fully succumbed was Finn. She had been my bright spot, hauling me back from the brink with a smile or a laugh, reminding me that I had a purpose.

I brought Finn by every morning and every evening to visit Katie and tell her all about our day. Katie had pounded into my brain very early on how important routine was to children, and she always made sure to tell Finn good morning and serenade her at bedtime every single day at home, so I had been doing the reverse, and Finn and I sang her good-morning and good-night songs every day without fail here. Finn didn't quite understand what was going on— all she realized was that her mommy had had a bad fall and was taking a long nap until her headache went away.

After that, we sometimes read to Katie for a bit, or Finn would draw a picture to put in her room before Mrs. J came and whisked her away for the day. Once Finn left, I would sit by Katie's bedside and tell her about all of my hopes and dreams.

I reminded her how important she was to Finn and me and told her how much I needed her to wake up. I made up stories about what our lives together would look like and how amazing we were going to be together. Then I would sing. Each day I sang until my voice was hoarse and my fingers cramped from strumming my guitar, hoping that somehow she would sense the depth of my love in each note and that it would bring her back to me.

I jumped, startled when cotton-candy-pink scrubs slid into my periphery. Forgetting my snack, I turned to face the nurse, wondering why she was down here. "Hey, Lex, what's up?"

She paused for a moment, indecision on her face, before she took a breath and said, "I'mma be straight with ya good-lookin'. It may be something, or it may be nothin', but Miss Layla swears Miss Katie moved one of her fingers and asked me to get you and the doc up to her room ASAP. Her heart rate spiked earlier, right after ya took the lil' cutie for some breakfast, and doc had to give her a pretty potent sedative to calm her back down. Doc said if she were wakin' up, it'd be a good coupla hours before she would be comin' to, since that sedative ain't no joke, but Miss Layla seemed pretty convinced. So, it's lookin' like you got someplace to be, and I got a doc to find." With that, she winked and walked off.

It took a few seconds for her words to sink in, and then I was sprinting down the hall. Layla wouldn't have asked her to find me without reason. I hadn't gotten to know Layla well before, but after three weeks of keeping vigil next at Katie's bedside, we had become friends.

I now understood exactly what Katie saw in Layla. She was smart as a whip with a wicked sense of humor, and though she seemed stuck-up or prickly to outsiders, once she let you in, you found out she was fiercely loyal and loved those she surrounded herself with deeply.

And Layla was not someone who gave into whimsy. She was blunt—almost to a fault—and was not prone to imagining things, so if she said Katie moved, then Katie moved. I skidded to a halt by Katie's bedside just as Lexi and Dr. Pierce came into the room. All my focus was on the hospital bed and the beautiful woman occupying it, so I ignored their presence. Gingerly, I grabbed Katie's hand and placed a soft kiss on the center of her palm. Unable to stop shaking, I was both exhilarated and terrified by the kernel of hope that was beginning to bloom in my chest. I clasped Katie's hand, held it over my heart, and began to talk, hoping she could hear me.

"Katie-mine, you're probably a little scared and a lot confused, but you've been sleeping for a while now, and I need you to wake up, okay? So, focus on my voice, and let me see those pretty green eyes I love so much. Can you feel my heartbeat? It's a little off, right? That's because it needs you. A clock needs all its parts to tick and mine is missing its biggest one right now. My heart doesn't work right when I don't see your smile every day—heck, none of me works right without you—so I need you to wake up and tell me good morning, okay?"

I closed my eyes, whispering, "Come on, Katie-mine," over and over, and waited.

I was just about to give up, when there was the slightest pressure on my hand. My eyes popped open, and I couldn't contain my excitement when I said, "She squeezed my hand! That's it, Katie. That's great, but I want you to open your eyes, okay? It's been too long since I had a chance to get lost in them, and I'm struggling here, so you need to throw me a bone."

I zeroed in on her face and watched as the side of her mouth hitched up ever so slightly. The kernel of hope was blossoming into a full-on bloom at that point, but I was still holding my breath. None of this would seem real if I couldn't look in her eyes.

Moments later, her lashes fluttered, and her brow creased with effort before her eyelids lifted. She scrunched her face in pain before slamming her eyes closed, and Lexi, bless her heart, leaned over and dimmed the lights. When this was all said and done, I was definitely going to have to give Lexi a gift for being awesome.

Once the lights were lowered, Katie opened her eyes again and blinked a few times before slowly turning her face toward me. She released my hand and raised her fingertips to brush away the moisture trailing down my cheek. I gave Katie a watery smile before leaning over and kissing her forehead. "Good morning, sunshine."

The sound of someone loudly clearing their throat reminded me that I was not the only person in the room. Making sure to keep Katie's hand in mine, I grudgingly slid over and made room for Layla. Sniffling, she reached down and gently pulled Katie into a hug, then slowly released her.

Tears were streaming down her face, but in true Layla fashion, she sassily said, "Girlfriend, you ever, and I do mean *ever*, do that to me again, there will be hell to pay. So help me God, I will find a legit Miss Cleo and have her séance my sexy self into your dreams, where I will sing obnoxious pop songs off-key into your ear until you wake up, and once you wake up, I will kick your ass. Are we clear?"

The confusion was written all over Katie's face as she looked from me to Layla. When she noticed Lexi and Dr. Pierce, her frightened eyes swung to me, seeking answers. Unsure of how to proceed, I gave her hand a reassuring pat and looked to Lexi for help.

Lexi's smile was kind, and her voice was sweet when she said, "Hey there, girlfriend. I'm glad to finally meet ya. My name's Lexi. I been helpin' Handsome, and Miss Sassy Pants over here, keep an eye on ya. Doc Pierce here will tell ya more about why you're here, but I don't want ya worryin' about nothin'. Your little lady is doin' just fine, and I ain't gonna lie, all of us nurses have loved the parade of hotness makin' the rounds in and out of your room—plus listening to this guy singing all day hasn't hurt my feelings none either. Maybe now that you're awake, ya can have him switch to somethin' more upbeat? 'Cause Lord knows he gots some pipes, but melancholy love songs can only go so far, ya know?"

Katie regarded Lexi for a moment before a small grin broke out on her face, and she replied, "I'm a little confused as to how I got here and why I'm here, but I think I can help out with the song choices."

Her voice was scratchy from weeks of disuse, and her words were stilted, like she had to force out each one, but I was positive that there had never been a more perfect sound. Lexi gave me a wink and Katie a wave before snagging Layla's arm and guiding her out of the room.

Dr. Pierce stepped forward and introduced himself. "Hi there, Miss Troyer. I'm so glad to officially meet you. You're probably a bit disoriented, which can be a bit scary, but trust me when I say it's perfectly normal. Do you know where you are?"

Katie arched her brow and sarcastically gestured to the room, causing him to chuckle. Nodding his head, he said, "Fair enough. Do you remember what happened?"

Katie's brow wrinkled in concentration, followed swiftly by a pain-filled grimace, as she grabbed her head and groaned. Hating to see her hurting, I began to rub her back soothingly while the doctor advised, "Easy, now. If you can't recall anything right away, don't worry. We don't want to try to force anything. You had a nasty tumble, Katie, and your brain and body needed a little time to rest and heal. I'm going to check your vitals, then Lexi will be back a little later to take you downstairs for a few scans so that we can make sure your noggin is doing a-okay. In the meantime, I need you to rest and relax as much as possible."

The more he spoke, the harder she clasped my hand. By the time he finished checking her out, her grip was border-line excruciating, but she could break it for all I cared—she was awake, and that was all that mattered. Dr. Pierce jotted a few things down on his clipboard before addressing Katie once again. "Your vitals are excellent, my dear. Lexi will be back in a few hours for you."

Dr. Pierce turned to address me. "Miss Troyer is likely going to have quite a few guests popping in and out, but I'm assigning you the responsibility of keeping an eye on her to make sure she doesn't over-do it. She needs to rest. Often. I also don't want any of you pushing her in any way. The fact that she can talk, albeit with some difficulty, after being awake such a short time is excellent, but we don't want to force anything. For now, keep the visits short and scattered throughout visiting hours."

I enthusiastically nodded and couldn't contain my smile. Mindful of her injuries, I carefully brushed Katie's hair out of her eyes so I could stare into the green depths I had missed so much. Not bothering to fight the temptation, I placed a tender kiss on her lips then carefully sat on the bed next to her, taking care not to jostle her too much.

Once I was settled, I wrapped my arms around her, being mindful of the sling covering her left arm. Her body had mended quite a bit while she was in the coma—most of the cuts and bruising were no longer visible, save for a few red streaks here and there, indicating fresh scar tissue—but she was far from completely healed.

Katie gingerly rested her head in the crook of my neck, and I played with the ends of her hair, content to sit there with her and just be. Our peaceful bubble popped, though, when her raspy voice asked, "Cade, why am I here? What happened?"

I knew that question was going to come up, but I was hoping I could put it off for a little while. I should have known better though—Katie wasn't someone who tolerated being out of the loop. Not ready for this conversation, but aware that it needed to happen, I took a deep breath, inhaling her familiar scent of peaches and honey, and centered myself. "I can't tell you everything, because I don't know it all. There's a lot of blanks to fill in once you've had some time to recuperate and remember, but I can tell you what I do know."

Just recalling the dread I'd felt when D said Katie had been hurt stopped me short. I had never been that terrified in my life, and every time I dug up the memory, those feelings swamped me and clung to me for days. This time would be different, though, because Katie would come along with me. I took a deep breath, twined my fingers with hers, and began filling in the gaps.

"I was sitting in meetings going over all the details for the European leg of our tour, and making sure everything was all set for you and Finn to come along. I wanted you to call in sick on your last shift so you could be there, but you've never been one to leave others in the lurch. You agreed to let D assign one of his guys to drive you to and from work, and keep a casual eye on you during your last shifts since the paparazzi had been so aggressive the last few days."

"I kissed you goodbye and told you I'd be waiting for you after work, and you went to your place to get ready. After that, I didn't hear anything for a couple of hours. Then, out of nowhere, Sam came barging into the conference room and was freaking out about some voicemails he'd gotten and panicking because he couldn't get ahold of you."

I kissed her forehead, needing to ground myself, and continued, "I'd never seen Sam like that, and I immediately had a horrible feeling. We all started calling and texting you, but you never answered. Finally, I brought D in, and after he touched base with a few of his guys, he found out the person assigned to you had gotten into a wreck and never even made it to your apartment. D was in the middle of sending someone new to the club to check on you when his phone rang, and he was told you'd had an accident."

"No one knows precisely what happened. All we've been told is that people heard a scream, and seconds later you came flying down the stairs. Once you hit the bottom, it was all chaos. Apparently, shortly after the paramedics came, Antonio Vicari made his way down the stairs, looking like someone had beat the shit out of him, and made a swift exit out the back before the cops could stop him. We all came straight to the hospital as soon as D got the call."

Katie's emerald-green eyes regarded me for a moment, before she quietly asked, "When was my accident, Cade?"

I opened and closed my mouth a few times, trying to decide the best way to proceed, when Katie's eyes narrowed, and she demanded, "When, Cadeon?"

Defeated, I broke down and admitted, "Your accident was three weeks ago yesterday.

CHAPTER 34

KATIE

> "Life is the flower for which love is the honey."
>
> — VICTOR HUGO

I kept waiting for Cade to break into a smile, or tell me he was just kidding, but judging by the bags under his beautiful aqua eyes and his solemn expression, I could only conclude that I really had been in a coma for three weeks. *Three freaking weeks.*

My pulse began to race, and a cloud of anxiety threatened to descend on me, but I beat it back. Enough time had been stolen from me while I'd lain unmoving in this damned bed. I would allow myself to fall apart later, but right now I had some things to figure out.

Obviously, something had happened to me, and while I appreciated Cade's attempt to fill me in, there were too many blank spots. I was positive there was more, but Cade seemed too concerned about stressing me out to tell me everything. I tried to remember what happened, but the pounding in my head drowned out any thoughts or memories I might have had. Hoping to ease the dull throbbing radiating throughout my body, I shifted restlessly, irritated I couldn't seem to get comfortable.

My arm itched, and when I absentmindedly went to scratch, my fingers touched hard plaster instead of skin. Alarmed, I looked down and found that my right arm was not only in a sling, but was also encased in a well-decorated purple cast that was peeking out past the edge of the material.

"Cade?" I paused until he was looking at me. "What's up with my arm?"

He grimaced and said, "You were in pretty rough shape when they brought you in, Katie. I'm pretty sure you hit every one of those damned steps on the way down, and you landed on your right side at the bottom of the stairs. When we got here, you were in surgery, and everyone was too busy to talk to us. Once you were out and stable, they didn't want to give me any information, because I wasn't family. I'm not sure what strings Sam pulled so I was allowed to visit you in the ICU and receive updates on your progress, and honestly I'm afraid to ask, though we probably should at some point."

Cade slid his arm around me, lifting me up enough to settle the majority of his large frame on the hospital bed. His presence soothed me, and I was incredibly grateful that he had been here to not only look after me, but also to take care of Finn.

I gave him a quick kiss and let him continue. "Once I got clearance, they told me you had a subdural hematoma and that there was a distinct possibility you could be in a coma once the anesthesia wore off. They told me your wrist was broken, as well as several ribs and your collar bone. If you peek inside the cast, you'll see some sweet pins sticking out—it's very Bride of Frankenstein, and I'm not gonna lie, it's kind of hot. You've also got some stitches around the back of your head and a few other places, but those will come out soon enough."

I took a minute to digest how badly I had been hurt, but decided not to dwell on the severity of my injuries, focusing instead on the patterns Cade was tracing on the skin on the back of my neck. Though I had only been up for a little while, my eyelids were beginning to droop as exhaustion took over. I rested my head right above Cade's heart and listened to the steady beats before sleepily asking, "Stay with me while I sleep for a little while? Then when I wake up, I want to see Finn."

Cade positioned me so I was partially laying across his body, and then he began to sing. The vibrations in his chest as he began the opening chorus of the Foo Fighters' "Everlong" carried through me, and I smiled before drifting off.

~

Cade

For the first time in weeks, my heart was light, and I was brimming with hope and joy. I couldn't wipe the grin off my face, and it grew even wider when the door of the hospital room opened and I spotted Finn's wild curls. I held a finger to my lips, letting them know to be quiet, and waved Finn and Mrs. J over to the bed. When she was close enough to reach, I pulled Finn into my lap. Together she and I quietly sang songs to Katie as she rested.

Before long, Katie's green gaze met mine then slid to Finn. A beatific smile spread across her face at the sight of Finn. Once we finished singing the final bars of 'Twinkle, Twinkle, Little Star," I helped Katie sit up. She held out her good arm, and Finn immediately abandoned my lap to snuggle up against her mother.

After a long hug, Katie asked Finn to tell her all the fun things she'd done while Mommy was napping. Seeing my girls together made my heart swell. I knew without a doubt that I was looking at my future, and it was going to be amazing. I couldn't wait to spend the rest of my life experiencing it.

Knowing they needed some time together, I hooked Mrs. J's arm with my own and asked, "So, wanna be my lunch date? The guys are gonna be here soon, and if we time it right, you can 'accidentally' brush Dante's ass on our way back up."

At that Mrs. J let out a cackle, and with a bit of mischief in her eyes, she replied, "Get me close enough to bump into Dante *and* Trev, and you've got yourself a deal."

~

Katie

The stars winked outside of the hospital window, and I let my mind wander as I stared at them. I had been feeling nothing but out of control since the moment I'd opened my eyes and found myself sitting in this hospital. The constant stream of what-ifs and unanswered questions plagued me. It was like memories were prodding at the edge of my subconscious, but every time I tried to grasp them, they disappeared into a fog. My body still ached, and I was tired but couldn't sleep. It was as if I were stuck in a never-ending episode of *The Twilight Zone*—and I hated it.

Yet within all the chaos, I had one constant— Cade. I had asked him to show me that he would be here for Finn and me, and he had in spades. When he'd stepped out to grab Finn a snack, the boys had told me that as soon as he got to the hospital and learned how severe my injuries were, he had demanded the European tour dates be postponed indefinitely until I was healed. Thankfully, they had all agreed. Bryce was pissed, but after realizing the band members would not bend, he gave in and made the arrangements.

There had been a deep-seated fear I carried within myself that if Cade legitimately had to make a choice between us or his career again, he would choose the latter once more. Yet hearing that his first thoughts had been of Finn and me, and that he hadn't hesitated to put his tour on hold, told me all I would ever need to know.

Even when I'd pretended otherwise and fought my feelings, I had been aware that Cade and I were meant for one another. From the first time his lips touched mine and we became more than friends, I had known soul-deep that he was my One. I had been on the fence about my feelings for Cade, too wrapped up in all the possible ways it could go wrong, but it turned out that almost dying tended to put things in perspective.

Life was short, and I was done waffling between what I wanted and what was safe. I longed for Cade with every fiber of my being, and there was no point in pretending otherwise. I wanted to wake up every morning to his face. I wanted to grumble about "kids these days" while sipping tea on the porch when we were old and gray. I wanted my forever.

The chime of an incoming text jerked me out of my thoughts. Hoping that it wasn't Cade checking on me, I awkwardly leaned over and grabbed my cell. When I suggested Cade go home and sleep in an actual bed for the night instead of on what appeared to be a slab of granite disguised as a bed in the corner of my room, you would have thought I committed blasphemy.

Once I realized Cade would not be leaving of his own accord, I gave Dante my "mom glare," and he'd wrapped the pythons he called arms around Cade's middle and physically dragged him out of my room and into the car. Up until now, I had completely forgotten that Sam had dropped my cell off when he came by, complete with a new screen, since my old one was sacrificed in The Great Fall. I swore whatever Cade paid the man, it wasn't enough.

I pulled up my messages, smiling at the picture Mrs. J

had sent of Finn sleeping perpendicularly in her bed with her foot dangling off the edge and chuckled. All the chaos of the day had turned to background noise when she curled up next to me and we read stories before she left for bed. There was no doubt that Finn and Cade were my happy place.

I was just setting my phone down, when I paused. When Cade was explaining earlier what happened, he mentioned that both he and Sam had been calling and texting me about something important the night of my accident. The longer I stared at the black screen, the stronger the push from my mind was, but I still couldn't drag the memories into the light. I bit my lip in indecision, before saying *screw it* and opening my texts, scrolling down until I reached "Sexypants."

Sexypants: Katie-mine, I need you to call or text me, love. Something is going on. I'm not sure exactly what, but Sam flew all the way out here from Cali and is freaking out. He said something about Kelly and that he thinks you aren't safe. Call me ASAP, please. Love you. XOXO

As soon as my eyes read the text, debilitating terror encompassed me, and memories slammed into my head like a freight train. With a shaking hand, I opened my contacts list and pulled up Sam's number, struggling to connect the call. With each ring, my body shook harder, and it felt like eons before he picked up. I didn't even bother with pleasantries, instead just spitting out, "Sam, I remember. I remember everything."

~

Detective Strohm closed his notebook before looking at me and asking one more time, "Are you sure that is all, Mrs. Cross?"

I pinched the bridge of my nose, biting back a retort, and resisted the urge to scream. Detective Strohm had been here for hours, asking me to repeat what had happened over and over. The only reason he was going now was because Cade had seen me flinch when the detective's cell went off and demanded he leave so I could rest. My brain felt like a colony of imps in stilettos was performing river dance choreography on my frontal lobe, and I was in desperate need of some ibuprofen.

Having had enough, I yelled, "Yes! For the last damn time, that is all. That was the same thing I told y'all when you first got here, and the same information I gave you when you asked again, and if you come back tomorrow, I will still say the same goddamn thing! *Jesus!* If you don't believe me, pull the video footage from the VIP lounge. Christ."

At this, the detective's shrewd black eyes snapped to mine. "What video footage?"

I rolled my eyes and answered, "The video footage from the cameras. Ya know, the ones Tommy-the-douche has planted in every single corner of every accessible area of the club except for the women's locker room?"

Arching an inquisitive brow, Cade piped in, "None in the women's locker room, huh? Funny, considering how pervy Tom is, I would've thought that would be the first place he'd put them."

"Oh, he did. But we're not stupid. We all have a rotation

schedule where one girl comes in a half hour early every night and scours the locker room and women's restrooms for cameras. After the seventh time Tommy Boy found his cameras in the trash and we threatened to Lorena Bobbit his ass, he stopped trying. We still check on the daily anyway, just in case."

The detective's unsmiling mouth turned down just a hint at the corners, which was the only indication he was not pleased with either piece of information. He was handing me a card just as Sam slipped into the room with some water for me.

The detective waited until his card was firmly planted in my hand before he said, "Mrs. Cross, I want you to keep that handy, and if you think of anything else, please give me a call. I'll be in touch."

Detective Strohm strode from the room without a good-bye. I waited a beat to make sure he was really gone, before saying a heartfelt, "Thank *God*."

No longer able to contain my frustration, I threw my good arm out and moaned, "Why does everyone keep calling me Mrs. Cross? Seriously! Doc Pierce and Lexi call me Katie or Miss Troyer, but literally everyone else is calling me Mrs. Cross. What in the actual hell?"

Cade shrugged, and we both turned to Sam. Without a word, Sam began to casually amble toward the exit, his face radiating innocence. Not buying it, I pointed a finger at him and demanded, "Samuel! You stop right where you are, mister! You know something. Spill."

He paused, and judging by the pained expression on his face, he was trying to decide how to say whatever it was he needed to tell us. He sighed dramatically and dropped his chin to his chest.

Avoiding eye contact with either of us, he said, "Well, first, they wanted contact information for your family. I kept explaining we *are* your family, for all intents and purposes, but they kept demanding a blood relative or a spouse. I tried bribing them but failed miserably. Cade was a hot mess. The rest of the guys were no better. No one knew how bad your injuries were or what was going on. I had to do *something*...so I did."

Doing my best to be intimidating, I narrowed my eyes and crossed my good arm over my cast, figuring it would have to suffice. "And what precisely did you do, Samuel? Hmm?"

Sam blanched, but didn't respond, so I narrowed my eyes and in a tone that brooked no argument said, "Samuel..."

He picked at his fingernails as his gaze traveled around the room, then admitted, "Well, I couldn't pull a blood relative out of thin air...but I could pull a spouse out of it. So, I made a few calls, and I may have *possibly* had someone potentially do something like make a fake wedding license that is close enough to the real thing to fool just about anyone. Then I *might* have told Dr. Pierce that you hadn't had time to change your name yet, so calling you Mrs. Cross would probably be confusing. Unfortunately, no one else paid attention to the note on your chart that you prefer to go by either Katie or Miss Troyer, so the cat's out of the bag."

Sam shrugged, gave us an impish grin, then said, "So, ya know, you might as well just make it official and all that. I'd hate to be in trouble when this is all said and done. If the media finds out what I did and that you guys aren't actually married, it would not go well for me."

We didn't even have time to pick our collective jaws up off the floor before he shot out of the room. Once we heard the soft *click* of the door latching, Cade and I looked at each other and burst into laughter at this strange turn of events.

"Well," Cade told me as he wiped a tear from his eye, "I can't pretend that it doesn't make me fucking ecstatic to hear people call you Mrs. Cross. Plus, I'd really hate for Sam to get shit on for helping us out. So, what do you say, you want to make it official?"

I looked in his azure gaze, overcome by the sheer amount of love reflected there. Without hesitation, I cupped his cheek with my hand and said, "Absolutely. I love you, Cadeon Cross. Now and forever."

Cade cradled my face and gave me a tender kiss. "I love you always, Katie-mine. You are my other half, and I would be lost without you and Finn. You two are my world. I swear I will spend the rest of my life showing you how much I love you both every single day."

With that declaration, he pulled me in for a searing kiss that left us both panting. It had been far too long since I'd felt the slide of his skin against my own, and even as banged up as I was, I wanted him. Cade grinned at my flushed face and kissed the tip of my nose. "Soon, my love. Your body isn't quite healed enough to play—yet—but trust me, when you're in the clear, I plan to worship every single inch of you. Repeatedly."

Keeping his eyes on mine, he shouted, "Sam, I know you're hovering outside the door. Get in here."

Sam poked his head in the door and nervously stuttered, "Y-yes?"

Cade kissed my palm, and a goofy smile split his face before he asked, "How quick can you get a justice of the peace in here? I got me a woman to marry before she changes her mind."

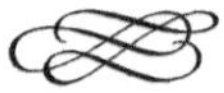

KATIE

> "Being deeply loved by someone gives you strength, while loving someone deeply gives you courage."
> Lao Tzu

Nine months later

I watched Cade's throat work as he chugged the water I had tossed him when he stepped off the stage. He finished the first bottle, grabbed a second, and took a few more gulps before dumping the rest over his head.

My eyes greedily followed the droplets as they tracked down the bare skin of his rippling abs, and my mind immediately went to the gutter, imagining how much I would enjoy kissing and nipping every square inch of my sexy man as soon as we reached the tour bus.

Cade always had energy to burn after a show, and I decided early on that I would much rather spend a few hours riding Cade like a prized bronco than running on a treadmill, so having some fantastic naked fun time after each show had become our norm.

Dante tossed Cade a towel, and he wiped his face before making his way over to me. Cade scooped up Finn, spinning her in a circle before blowing a raspberry on her stomach and passing her to D. D swung Finn up and onto his shoulders, causing her to squeal in delight. Once she was settled, Cade grabbed my waist and pulled me into a sweaty hug before bending me backward and giving me a smacking kiss that made me laugh out loud.

The chanting of "Encore, encore!" echoed around the stadium, and the dim lights pulsed brighter twice in a row, indicating the time had come for the guys to go back out. Cade gave Finn a fist-bump and leaned in for one more quick kiss from me. I gave him a playful smack on the ass, followed by "Go get 'em, tiger!" and admired the play of muscles as he strut onto the stage.

Moments later, the rest of the guys assembled in a line next to D and me. Rhys stepped up first, announcing, "Alright, Finnster, time for some knucks!"

Then, as they did every night, each member of the band waited patiently for their "good luck charm" to give them a fist-bump before heading back on stage to close out the show.

Once the guys began to sing, I held my arms out so D could pass Finn to me and headed to our tour bus, where I tucked her into bed for the night. When I came out, Sam was sitting on our sofa, and I gave him a small wave before ducking out of the bus and heading back to the wings off stage. On the way, I paused, taking in the beauty that surrounded me while contemplating the whirlwind this last year had been. The last nine months could have easily derailed my life, but Cade had been my rock.

After Detective Strohm left my hospital room, he'd gone straight to The Field House. He mentioned once how odd it had seemed that D was leaving Tom's office just as he arrived, but Detective Strohm dubbed it a sheer coincidence that once he slid into the seat D had recently vacated in Tom's office, Tom willingly handed over all the previously nonexistent surveillance videos.

Unsurprisingly, the footage showed Antonio Vicari assaulting me and intentionally shoving me down the stairs —which is why Tom had tried to pretend it didn't exist. Once Antonio was arrested, and he realized he was facing more than a mere slap on the wrist, he had no problem throwing both Kelly and Tom under the bus as well.

Turned out the night I was assaulted, Kelly visited Antonio, and over several glasses of vodka and an ample supply of bath salts, Kelly made sure Antonio saw every snapshot she could find of Cade and me. She also showed him the post we'd put on the Devil's Cross Instagram that confirmed our relationship, and pointed out, in great detail, how unfair the situation was to Antonio.

She went on to remind Antonio how Vicari's get what Vicari's want, and how disappointed his family would be if they found out that he had been chasing a waitress—*a wait-ress*—for months with no success.

Kelly convinced Antonio that he owed it to himself to put me in my place and teach me a lesson about what happened to those who disrespected a Vicari. She then oh-so-kindly offered to drop Antonio off at The Field House just before the drug-and-alcohol-induced paranoia and aggression she'd sparked morphed into a full-blown fire.

En route, Kelly called the paparazzi and made up a story about how Cade and I were at dinner across town, thus minimizing the possibility of being caught by an errant camera snap. Kelly made sure to slip Tom some extra cash upon her and Antonio's arrival as a bribe for him to ignore company policy—and all logical safety measures—and give us total privacy upstairs so we wouldn't be "interrupted." After all three were arrested, and the media got ahold of the story, things went from bad to worse.

When the story first broke, the media painted me as nothing more than a money-grubbing whore who had manipulated my way into not one, but two rich men's beds, pitting them against each other for my own gain. #Kancel-Katie had trended on Twitter for weeks, and I was public enemy number one for every Devil's Cross fan page that existed on the internet. Sam, bless the man, saw what was coming before I even realized all that was going on and confiscated my phone and computer with a stern warning that I was to avoid Google at all costs.

Once the trials started and previously ignored facts were dragged into the light, I abruptly went from the most hated person on the internet to a beloved treasure the world rallied around. Throughout the entire ordeal, Cade never left my side, and I was convinced that he was the only reason I made it through with my sanity intact. He was there for every meeting with my lawyers. His hand had clasped mine as I was forced to hear every testimony and sit through every trial.

Cade had wrapped a protective arm around me, lending me his strength both times that Quinn asked me to speak to the press. At night, when the monsters and memories became too much and I couldn't cage them any longer, he held me while I cried and sang to me until I fell asleep.

No matter what I needed, whether it was a hand to hold or space to myself, Cade gave it, no questions asked. Once I felt ready, Cade even helped me find an excellent therapist who I met with via Skype while we toured so I could process the trauma and stress the attack and subsequent media circus had caused.

Devil's Cross's badass PR gal, Quinn, used the distraction of the trials as the perfect way to sneak in an announcement about our nuptials as well as mention of Finn knowing full well it would be buried in the middle of all the trial coverage. I still got photographed now and then, but since Cade and I were no longer front-page news, I was mostly ignored. For the most part, my life had returned to normal—or at least what had become my new version of it.

The deafening applause let me know that the boys had finished their final set, and I couldn't hold back my smile as they playfully teased and pushed each other on their way backstage.

As the guys approached, I heard Rhys shout, "We kicked ass! Now it's time to get some pu—" The sound of me clearing my throat made him look up, and he took in my arched brow and hesitated a moment before continuing, "I mean, pleasant female company who we will enjoy in a respectful manner."

Dante shook his head back and forth and clapped Rhys

on the shoulder in commiseration while Trev cackled in the corner. Zane gave my ponytail a playful tug before saying, "Night, Mom. Don't worry, we'll be home by curfew."

I gave him a wide grin and flipped him off. Seconds later, I found myself upside down, staring at a flawless backside. Giggling, I whined, "Cade, put me down!"

Cade delivered an answering smack to my rear, and his smooth voice replied, "Listen here, wife, I've got plans for us, and you were taking too long. Let the boys do their thing. We both know none of them would ever take a girl to their bed who didn't ask to be there."

I jostled and bounced on his shoulder as his long legs ate up the distance between the green room and our tour bus. As soon as we reached the bus, Sam quietly slipped past us, heading to his own bunk for the night.

Once he was out of sight, Cade set me on the steps and claimed my mouth in a searing kiss. He smirked at my dazed expression before holding up a finger and looking in on Finn's bunk, making sure she was still fast asleep. Once he was sure she was safe and warm, he held out a hand and pulled me into our bedroom at the back of the bus.

As soon as the door clicked shut, Cade had me pinned against the wall as his hungry mouth plundered my own. In a lust-filled haze, I shoved my hands in his hair before wrapping my legs around his waist as our tongues tangled together. The sensation of his hardness rubbing against my core made me moan as electric tingles shot through my body. Frantic with need, I began tearing at Cade's clothes, anxious for the slide of his skin against my own.

Sensing my desperation, Cade leaned back, giving him enough space to pull my top off. One hand tugged at my bra, tugging down one of the cups, freeing my breast. Within seconds his hot mouth closed over my nipple, giving it a delicious tug while his other hand undid the clasp and tossed my bra away.

Cade set me on my feet long enough for us both to tug off our jeans. Desire swirled around us as he ran his eyes over my naked body and licked his lips. Anticipation burned in his gaze, and we came crashing back together in a tangle of limbs and moans.

My hand reached down, guiding Cade to my entrance. I gasped in pleasure when he slammed home, reveling in the feeling of fullness. Zings of pleasure filled my body with each thrust, and Cade began pounding harder until I was on the brink. Releasing my lips, he stared into my eyes.

Love and adoration filled his gaze, and I treasured the way his heart beat in time with mine. I rolled my hips, pulling a rumble of appreciation from Cade before he leaned forward and whispered in my ear, "Now, Katie-mine."

He gave me one last sexy smile before he slammed into me once again, toppling me over the edge into bliss and following my orgasm with one of his own. Tenderly planting small kisses across my shoulder, Cade waited until my breathing returned to normal before turning and carrying me to the bed. Gently, he laid me down, leaning in to give me one more long kiss before heading into the bathroom to clean himself up. Once Cade finished, he climbed into bed and tucked me into his side. "I love you, Katie-mine."

I inhaled the unique leather-and-pine scent that was all Cade and couldn't wipe the grin off my face at the knowledge that this wonderful man belonged to me. Kissing the center of his clockwork tattoo, I asked, "For always?"

"For always. Now, how about we discuss all those babies I was promised?"

The End

Dear reader,

Thank you so much for reading Lost Notes. I hope you had as much fun reading Cade and Katie's story as I had writing it. If you enjoyed Lost Notes, please leave me a review to let me know! I read every one, and your feedback helps me continue to create stories that you will love. Also, making new friends is the best, so make sure to follow me on Facebook and Instagram (@EmmaRaeBooks)!

Wondering how Cade and Katie met? Then head on over to www.EmmaRaeSullivan.com and sign up and join Emma Rae's Rockstars for a FREE copy of Love Notes, a Devil's Cross novella, to see how their story began. My Rockstars will also be the first to know about any upcoming books, giveaways, contests, and get exclusive content—so come join the party!

Sincerely,
Emma Rae Sullivan

Want more Devil's Cross? Continue reading for an excerpt of Trev and Rachael's story.

Releasing spring 2021

CHAPTER 1

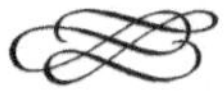

RACHAEL

I tucked my elbows in and slowly worked my way through
the mass of writhing bodies towards the bar. Honestly, I had
no clue why on earth I was even here. One minute I was
slipping into my super cozy and very adult Captain
America onesie geared up for a night full of Netflix and
cuddles from Bob Barker. The next minute I was being
crammed into jeans so tight I was afraid the seams would
split if I bent over and a top that felt two sizes too small—
which considering how lacking I was in the chest depart-
ment was saying something—and being forcefully crammed
in a car by Sabrina with her cawing, "Girls night!" in
my ear.

I appreciated her enthusiasm and her desire to "make
me an LA-er," but I was pretty sure at this point I was

lacking some key gene in my makeup that would allow me to enjoy the club scene. I finally managed to push my way to the bar and had an internal battle between my desire to be as inconspicuous as possible and my desperate need for a drink to help me power through this disaster of an evening. I hated drawing attention to myself. Hated. It. But I had a sneaking suspicion that the only way I would ever achieve the buzz necessary to drown out this truly atrocious music was to force myself to be noticed. Ugh.

I gingerly held up my hand, but swiftly dropped it when a muscular arm trying to get the bartender's attention shot out and almost clipped the side of my head. I grumbled to myself, and mentally prepared to try again when a large body collided into mine, knocking me over. Luckily, since we were crammed together like sardines, my descent towards the floor was stalled when my face crashed into a well muscled arm encased in a red T-shirt. I Stood up, rubbing my now sore nose, "Well, at least I had a nice landing spot? Though muscles are definitely not the softest. My poor nose. Now, I really need that drink. Ok, Hart, you got this."

"Excuse me," a velvety voice spoke near my ear that I realized belonged to red T-shirt guy, "Just out of curiosity, were you just giving yourself a pep talk? Out loud?"

Biting back a groan, I smacked my forehead on my palm a few times and mumbled, "Stupid, stupid," before sighing and turning and answering T-shirt guy. "Yes. I was talking to myself. I don't do crowds, and I don't do people, and I don't want to be here. But what I *do* want is a drink."

Turning more fully towards him, I took in his black ball cap with wisps of messy dirty-blond strands peeking out around the edges. Mirrored aviators masked his eyes, but judging by the smirk on his face I was relatively sure the question had been insulting rather than inquisitive. I hated social situations, especially here. I was not someone who dealt in subtleties, and I felt like trying to navigate the social scene in LA was like trying to find firm footing on a sand dune—impossible.

Tired of feeling judged, I momentarily lost my cool and snapped, "Like I said, what I want is a drink, and yes, I did need to give myself a pep talk to get that drink. However, since you're the douche wearing sunglasses inside at night I really don't think you have much room to judge."

An extremely tall guy with beautiful bronzed skin and intricate tattoos that covered a terrifying amount of muscles standing next to him I hadn't paid any mind to before threw his head back laughing, and clapped red shirt guy on the shoulder with one giant paw. "She called you a douche. This is by far the best part of the night. Wait till I tell Rhys about this shit. He'll never let you live it down."

T-shirt guy shoved scary muscle guy in the shoulder and bit out, "Fuck you Dante! You've got on shades too, so her comment applies to us both. Douche."

Grimacing, I immediately felt awful for being so rude. Twisting my fingers together, I hastily apologized, "I'm sorry, that wasn't a very nice thing to say. I'm sure you're both very nice—slightly terrifying—but nice. I'm just not having the best night, and while I may be ready to leave, the girls I came with seem to be having a really good time and I don't want to ruin it by making them leave. I'll just grab my drink and get out of your way..."

Scary muscle guy ignored my apology altogether

instead choosing to run a hand over his closely cropped dark hair and readjust his sunglasses before turning to scan the dance floor. Red shirt guy, however, gave me what appeared to be a genuine smile before saying, "I get that. Here, let me give you a hand."

I don't know what magic he weaved, but as soon as he put his hand up, the bartender hustled over to us. Red shirt guy pointed in my direction and I gave him a grateful smile then watched him saunter off with scary muscle guy, appreciating the view until they were out of sight. Remembering where I was and why I was here, I focused on the bartender and had to stifle a grimace as his eyes scanned me from head to toe. After looking his fill, he gave me a predatory smile that made me extremely uncomfortable before asking, "What can I do for you, sugar?"

Grinding my teeth at the unwelcome endearment, I waffled between saying never mind and walking away, or ordering a drink. Option A was starting to gain favor when a slew of girls to my right stopped and one of them shouted, "OMG, look how pretty this Cosmo is! I totally need to take a pic for my Insta Story. Oh, wait! We should Snap this too," and then watched as they each proceeded to make duck faces and pose dramatically for several takes.

At this point, I didn't even want a drink. I just really wanted to go home. I started to pull back from the bar when I caught sight of Sabrina and the other girls dancing and having a blast. Though this was a far cry from my idea of a good time, Sabrina had been trying to do a nice thing by inviting me out, and I didn't want to pay her back by ruining her fun. Decision made, I leaned over the bar so the bartender could hear me over the aggressive bass of the music and loudly asked, "May I have a whiskey sour, please?"

The bartender— who from here on out I was dubbing The Creep—spent a good thirty seconds staring at my unimpressive cleavage before winking and replying, "You got it, pretty lady."

While he set about making my drink he inquired, "So, you here with anyone? That guy earlier seemed to know you."

I nervously began picking at my cuticles, wanting nothing more than to get my drink and get far away from the bar. No matter how painful the rest of this experience was, I could say with absolute certainty I was not going to be setting foot anywhere near the bar again. Hoping if I answered his question he would hurry up, I distractedly answered, "Me? I'm just here with some friends."

I could have sworn he hadn't taken this long with any of the other orders I'd watched him make while I waited, but then again things always seem to take longer when you wanted to be somewhere else. I scanned the crowd and caught a flash of red out of the corner of my eye. I swung my gaze back and saw red shirt guy and scary muscles guy occupying a corner and sipping on their drinks while they watched the crowd. I toyed with the idea of trying to get his attention. I wasn't sure why, but I had a gut feeling that if he thought I felt uncomfortable he would be over here no questions asked.

Finally, the bartender slid my drink across the bar top and I gave him a small smile and a mumbled thanks before slipping him some cash and moving away from the bar and into the crowd. Grateful that I had some liquid courage to make this entire night more palatable, I took a few large sips before working my way back over to the last place I had spotted Sabrina and the other girls. Looking around, I realized I didn't see anyone I knew and I let out a frustrated sigh then pulled my phone out and sent her a text.

Me: Hey! My drink order took forever (sorry). I just swung by the dance floor and can't find you. Marco?

Sabrina: Hey Rachey-rach! We found us some hawt guys with a capital H. Invited us 2 party @ their place. Tried waiting 4 U, but didn't want to miss out. Srry, but a girls got needs, U kno? See U @ work Mon!

Once I deciphered her text, I went from resigned to pissed, but that feeling quickly passed when I realized it meant I could go home. Picturing myself snuggled in my big comfy bed with Bob Barker curled up at my feet, I hastily downed the rest of my drink and ordered my Uber. Ten minutes until I would be home free.

ACKNOWLEDGMENTS

It takes a village to write a book, and my village just so happens to kick ass.

Thank you to my mom for enthusiastically reading iteration and revision this story went through from start to finish. Dad, this never would have gotten finished if it weren't for your enthusiastic offers to take the minions to play so I could write and cheering me on. Brian, brotherest of brothers, don't feel bad. You loved me enough to attempt to read a romance, that still counts. Promise.

Julie, you are the best cousin ever, and I would be lost without you. Hannah, J.W. Wright, Empress Chang, and Laura Schoonover this book would not have come together without you guys. Thanks for talking me off the ledge a few times and making sure my boys were ready to make their debut!

Tiffany Tyer, editor extraordinaire, and Tugboat Designs, thank you for making the inside of my book as well as the outside shine. You ladies rock!

Emma Rae Sullivan is an animal keeper- gone-freelance writer and author of the Devil's Cross series. When not writing, she is most certainly at home, curled up on the sofa with her nose stuck in a book. She may also be drinking her twelfth cup of coffee—no judging. Emma Rae holds a B.S. in Zoology from Colorado State University, and currently resides in Cheyenne, Wyoming with her husband and two children.